TROMBONE

TROMBONE

CRAIG NOVA

GROVE WEIDENFELD

New York

Published by Grove Weidenfeld
A division of Grove Press, Inc.
841 Broadway
New York, NY 10003-4793

Published in Canada by General Publishing Company, Ltd.

Library of Congress Cataloging-in-Publication Data

Nova, Craig.
Trombone / by Craig Nova.—1st ed.
p.   cm.
ISBN 0-8021-1359-1 (acid-free paper)
I. Title.
PS3564.086T7   1992
813'.54—dc20   91-37689
                                      CIP

Manufactured in the United States of America

Printed on acid-free paper

Designed by Irving Perkins Associates

First Edition 1992

1   3   5   7   9   10   8   6   4   2

This book is dedicated to
Mary West Barnes and William Sprague Barnes

Where shall I see rise
The star of my deliverance?

—AESCHYLUS,
   Prometheus Bound

BOOK I

THE MAN IN
CHINATOWN

The first time Ray Gollancz and his father, Dean, burned down a building, they drove from Bakersfield, California, to Chinatown in Los Angeles. They went through the San Gabriel Mountains, and as they came down toward Los Angeles, Ray thought about the mornings, years before, when he and his father got up before dawn to watch the light from the atomic bombs that were set off at Yucca Flats in Nevada.

The man they went to see in Chinatown was Mei Yaochen. He had been paying Dean to get rid of buildings for some years now, although this was the first time Ray had come along.

"Listen," said Ray. "I don't want to make any mistakes when we meet him."

"Who?" said Dean.

"Mei Yaochen."

"Well," said Dean. "Just be careful what you say."

"Okay," said Ray. "Is there anything in particular I shouldn't say?"

Dean shrugged.

"Just be polite," said Dean. "Mind your manners. If I thought you were going to make a mistake I would have left you at home."

Dean drove a gray, four-door Chevrolet, which he had bought because it was the most anonymous car he could find. They went through the valley on the Hollywood Freeway, and after they had gone through the Cahuenga Pass they saw the city. When seen in the evening, Los Angeles has the appearance of an enormous web. The avenues, along which there are infinities of lights, run toward the ocean, and they are crossed by boulevards that are equally filled with lights. Here and there a red or green one is mixed with the yellow ones, and these give the web the impression of being decorated with rubies and emeralds. Ray turned to his right and looked through the window of the car at the city, which left him with a chill. The conglomeration of lights seemed at once warm and cold, like a bulb in a block of ice, and Ray felt uncomfortable looking at them because they implied contradictory things, hope and brutality, dreams and reality. It took a moment for Ray to remember exactly what it was that the feeling of the lights reminded him of: his skin when it crawled with fever.

Dean looked across the seat and said, "You can't see beauty, Raymond, you really can't, until you've got some regrets."

Ray looked away from the lights and thought about the bombs that had been set off at Yucca Flats. The flash from the explosions could be seen as far away as Los Angeles, but it was even brighter in Bakersfield, which was a little closer to Yucca Flats. When Ray and Dean watched the bombs, they waited by the fence in their backyard in the peaceful air of a California morning, the smog not bad yet and even having a smoky beauty.

Usually, Ray and Dean watched the light from the explosions when Dean was involved with a woman who wasn't his wife. Ray knew his father had a girlfriend when Dean and Ray's mother, Marge, sat on opposite sides of the kitchen table and debated, with a growing fury, about money or food or whether or not a woman would make a good president. Dean would stand up in the middle of these arguments and go out to the back porch, where he'd sit with his forearms on his knees, looking east.

On the morning of one particular test, Ray lay awake seeing the dark, humped shapes in his room, and as he looked at the ceiling there appeared before him, in the dim light, an image of the eastern sky as it was when the bombs were set off, the pulse from them suggesting to Ray the beauty and the power too, both malicious and benign, there are behind the appearance of almost all things. And even as he lay in the warmth of the sheets and blankets, whatever it was behind the light, whether benign or otherwise, held for Ray an almost unbearable attraction, as though he were standing at the edge of a cliff, where the space below beckons in a way that is never quite fully understood.

Downstairs, in the kitchen, Dean made himself a cup of instant coffee, mixing in hot water from the tap, and when Ray came in, Dean said, "I've been thinking, Raymond. Some morning we should set up a record player. A Gregorian chant. Or maybe even Benny Goodman. Something to go along with the light."

"It would wake up the neighbors," said Ray.

"Neighbors," said Dean. "They're always sticking their nose into my business. They see me someplace with . . . well, Raymond, with a friend, and the next thing I know your mother is suspicious."

They went out through the back door to the porch, where the boards were soft with dry rot. The backyard ran down to a fence, which was about waist high and beyond which was the horizon, where the sky was the color of a mourning dove.

Dean's house was a two-story building, covered with clapboards and with shutters at the windows. It needed to be painted, and some of the screen doors were worn, but overall the impression of the place wasn't one of poverty so much as of a solid, honest house come to hard times. The clapboards, where the paint had worn away, was the color of driftwood. Dean was a tallish man with dark chestnut brown hair, blue eyes, and a charming smile.

Dean looked at the luminous dial on his watch and said, "They're counting down now at Yucca Flats. I set my watch by Pacific standard time. I got it from the telephone, right on the tone. You know, Raymond, they now have clocks that are accurate to a second in a thousand years. They do it with vibrating crystals."

The sky was an even, seamless gray.

"All right," said Dean. "Twenty, nineteen, eighteen, seventeen . . ."

Dean got down to zero.

"Cheap watch," said Dean. "It gains time." He shook it. "You know, Raymond, I always wanted a good watch, a real Swiss one. Waterproof. Shock resistant. With jeweled movement. Twenty, maybe thirty jewels . . . These things you buy at the drugstore last a week or two."

There was a pulse of light, the silence of it making it somehow more demanding. At first there wasn't much more than an almost unnoticeable glow, but it became a luminescence, the shape of it horizontal and then rising from the ground in one hard pulse. The sky just filled with light, not as if from the sun so much as with an increasingly perfect whiteness.

The man and the boy seemed dark, their shapes motionless as they waited by the fence, their heads tilted back while the light bled into the sky. Dean kneeled and put his arm around his son's waist. Then the light vanished, the speed of it and the motion almost magical, like a genie retreating into a lamp.

It was after watching light from the bomb on this morning that Dean first explained about why he went to Los Angeles.

"I'm not a firebug," he said. "Those are sick people. I'm an arsonist. There are good reasons for a building to disappear. . . ." Then he stopped, looking at his son. "I've trusted you, Raymond."

"I know," said Ray.

"Will you keep a secret with me? Because if you ever told on me, Raymond, they'd put me in jail. Do you understand that?"

"Yes," said Ray. "Do you like to burn them down?"

"Sometimes," he said.

In the evening, after a test, Dean and Ray watched the weather map on TV, which showed the cloud of dust and debris as it drifted over Los Angeles. The strontium 90 count was given on the School-O-Meter, which came at the end of the show and which also told parents how warmly their children should be dressed for school the next day.

Now, Ray was grown up, and his appearance showed this fact, so much so that he looked older than he was. A lot of people took him to be in his twenties, although he wasn't. Ahead of him, as he sat in the car, there was the Los Angeles City Hall, the thing white in the fog. The color was almost like the gas in a fluorescent tube, and, in the fog, the place seemed ethereal, a structure of light that at any moment, at the flick of a switch, could somehow simply vanish.

Dean drove past the train station, which was a Spanish-style building, and the tiles of it, the facade of it, the clock, and the silence of it all seemed, in the city light, somehow flat or deadly. It occurred to Ray, who was infected with the atmosphere of the evening, that the station was where all the trains from the East came to an end, as though there were no escape from Los Angeles.

They parked in Chinatown. It was after midnight and there weren't many people on the street, and the fire escapes on the buildings, the trash cans, the unlighted signs, the old S-shaped lighting fixtures that hung in snaky shapes above the doorways all emerged from the fog as Ray and Dean got close to them. The brick walls were wet, and in the sheen of them, in the shadows of the fire escapes, which looked like distorted black ladders, Chinatown seemed to have a resilience, as though there were no end to the things it could endure without being changed and without giving up its faintly sooty, faintly gritty vitality.

Dean locked the car and the two of them went down the block, their shapes receding, becoming darker as they walked through the scent of cooking garlic and onions, broccoli, chicken, beef, and the odor of simmering rice and hot oil. They passed a butcher shop with animals hung in the window, the eyes of the pigs protuberant, glassy, an expression of infinite fear still in them.

They passed some young men who stood against a wall, their hair longish and gleaming, the three of them wearing dark jeans and dark jackets. In the fog, they first appeared as figures of the imagination, but as Dean and Ray came closer, the shapes resolved themselves into silent human beings. The young men were still, their patience not a matter of killing time but of being somehow employed.

"Here," said Dean. "In here."

He stopped at a grocery store, a small place that had two windows in the front and a glass door between them, and in the windows there were cans piled up like a brick wall, their labels all the same and all printed in Chinese characters. The front of the building had been painted green, but now it appeared black, like a piece of paper used to cut out silhouettes. From a partly open door in the back of the place came a light, which fell onto the floor in a slash.

"Look," said Ray. "Maybe I'll wait for you out here."

"I didn't bring you down here to stand in the street," said Dean. "Come on."

Dean knocked gently on the glass of the front door.

A Chinese man looked through the door before approaching it, his entire aspect one of wanting to keep something between him and the foggy street. Then he came up and put his face close to the glass, looking from Dean to Ray. The man was thin, and he had an abrupt, quick way of walking, his shoulders twitching a little as though he had been carrying a heavy thing that he had just put down. He pulled the door open.

"Is Mr. Mei here?" asked Dean.

"Back soon," said the man.

"He's expecting me," said Dean.

"I don't know anything about it," said the man.

"Can I wait?" asked Dean.

"Sure," said the man. "I guess so. You could come back."

"We'll wait."

Dean and Ray stepped into the store, which smelled of the large sacks of rice, of dust on the canned goods, of soy sauce, and of smoked ducks, which were in a case at the back. Only some things in the store could be seen, the edges of canned goods, or the blades of knives that were hung up behind the butcher's case, and these and any other bright object, the nickel-plated cash register, for instance, looked like a collection of shiny metal thrown into water and seen by moonlight.

In the room at the back there was an oak desk and a chair on casters, the place not bare so much as frankly practical. On the wall there was a calendar, printed in Chinese characters and with a color photograph of a nude Oriental woman. There was an adding machine on the desk, an old one with a dirty plastic cover over it. There were a couple of chairs in front of the desk, and Dean and Ray sat down.

"Here," said the man who had let them in. "Cigarette?"

"Thanks," said Dean, reaching out for it.

"No thanks," said Ray.

Dean slid his foot over and kicked Ray.

"On second thought," said Ray, "I guess I would. Thank you."

The man held out a package of Kents, which was offered with an abrupt ceremony, not inhospitably but not totally friendly either, like a guard offering a cigarette to a condemned man. Ray and Dean each took one and lighted them at the man's Zippo, from which the flame rose in the shape of a leaf.

"That's a nice lighter," said Dean.

"It's just some old thing," said the man. "But I guess you need a dependable one, don't you? Or do you use a match?"

Dean looked across the desk. "What's it to you?" he said.

"You doing business with Mr. Mei?" said the man.

"Maybe," said Dean.

"Mr. Mei is ambitious, you know?" said the man. "He got big plans. Gonna be a big shot."

"Is that right?" said Dean.

"Yeah," said the man. He flicked his ashes on the floor. "But you know something? He isn't going to make it."

"Where does that leave you?" asked Dean.

"Oh," he said, "there are other people to work for down here. Plenty."

"I wouldn't know," said Dean.

"Well, there are," said the man.

They all sat for a while, their smoke hanging above them in one stale cloud through which Ray looked around the room, feeling his hands sweat. Dean reached over and put an arm on his shoulder, saying, "Are you hungry, Raymond? How would you like to go out to dinner later?"

"I'm not too hungry," said Ray.

"Say," said Dean to the man. "What's a good place to eat?"

"Everyone serves greasy noodles down here," said the man.

Ray sat back, his eyes down, feeling the silence that lay in the room like a smothering presence, and after a few minutes he blurted out to the man opposite him, as though only to breathe, "Foggy, isn't it?"

"This? You call this foggy?" said the man. "Sometimes down here you can't see your hand in front of your face. No one can see you then."

"I guess that's handy," said Dean.

The man just smiled for a while, smoking his cigarette, and then said, "Yeah. I guess that's right."

The man finished his cigarette and ground it out on the floor, and then Ray and Dean went on smoking alone, listening to the silence of the place. Ray looked around the room, at the adding machine, the yellowed walls, the photograph of the nude woman, who wore lipstick as red as the skin of a Delicious apple. She seemed to look right out at him, and Ray looked back, swallowing from time to time, and as he did so, as he tried to hold the cigarette so it wouldn't show how bad his hands were shaking, he wondered what he could ever say to the woman in the picture. There was a formality to her nudity, and a distance, too, in the hard smile on her lips, all of which at least gave Ray something to think about.

"You looking for an Oriental girl?" said the man who had given them the cigarettes. He followed Ray's gaze to the calendar. "I know a place where you can get one. Clean. Not expensive."

Ray shook his head, although in his heart, in the fear in the room, he thought about it. Then he shook his head again.

Outside someone walked on the street, the steps getting faster in front of the store. The door opened, and a short, heavy man came into the room, his gait, the dropping of his raincoat implying a barely restrained impatience. He was Chinese too, and he was in his late forties, dressed in a dark gray suit and a blue tie. He wore rimless glasses, the lenses covered with a mist from the fog. He cleaned them on a handkerchief and put them back on, his eyes bright and alert behind them. For a moment he looked at the other

Chinese man in the room, not harshly, just thinking things over, and then he turned to Ray, considering him too.

Ray stood up and put out his hand, saying, "My name is Ray Gollancz."

"Is this your boy?"

"Raymond," said Dean, "I want you to meet Mr. Mei Yaochen."

"Well, he has nice manners," said Mr. Mei, who reached out and took Ray's hand. "So now you help your father? That shows obedience."

"I don't know," said Ray. "We get along all right."

"Well, that's a good young man," said Mr. Mei.

"Yes," said Dean. "He's a smart boy. Have you got some money on you? Take three or four bills out. Go on."

Mr. Mei reached into his pocket and took out three twenties.

"Read off the serial numbers. One after another."

Mr. Mei read off the numbers, and then Dean said, "Raymond?" and Ray repeated them.

"Doesn't that beat all?" said Dean, smiling now.

Mr. Mei put the tips of his fingers together and looked at Ray. Then he said, "Let me see you do it again. I'll get out more bills."

"It's not a trick," said Dean. "Use any you want."

Mr. Mei reached into his coat pocket, where he had an elongated wallet that folded up like a book. Ray looked down at the linoleum floor, which was worn, the shapes on it looking like old maps of imperfectly rendered continents, and as he did so he thought of how he liked to remember numbers, in sets of six or seven or eight, the groupings themselves bringing a kind of reassurance. He repeated the numbers Mr. Mei read off. Mr. Mei listened and then looked at the other Chinese man and said, "Did anyone call?"

"I don't think so," said the other man.

"Don't you know?" said Mr. Mei.

"I went out for a minute," said the man.

Mr. Mei's eyes seemed alert, and although there wasn't much change in his expression, nothing that Ray could see, the atmosphere in the room, in a sudden rush, was transformed from the interrogatory to one of general malice. Upstairs someone flushed a toilet. There was a rushing sound in the walls and then a whine as cold water moved in the pipes. Mr. Mei said, "All right. There's a package up at the other store. Go pick it up."

"I'll go later," said the man.

Mr. Mei went on staring at the man, not moving, not blinking, only saying, "Now. Not later."

"Well, sure," said the man, "if that's the way you feel about it. Sure. Be right back."

Then he went out, leaving the three of them sitting in the silence of the office. Ray wanted to move around, or to just walk out into the store, but instead he looked at Mr. Mei, who was sweating, his forehead and upper lip covered with a shiny film. Mr. Mei looked at Ray for a moment too, as though he were considering him for the first time. His glance wasn't pleasant, and Ray looked away.

Mr. Mei then turned to Dean.

"I thought you were coming tomorrow," said Mr. Mei. "Why don't you come back then?"

"We were supposed to come tonight," said Dean. "I marked it on the calendar."

"Maybe tomorrow would be better," said Mr. Mei.

"It's a long drive," Dean answered. "You have to go over the mountains north of the valley and—"

"All right, all right," said Mr. Mei.

He looked at his watch, a thin gold one, the second hand of it moving in small, erratic jerks, the mechanism of the thing seemingly caught up as much as the men in the tension of the room. Upstairs there was the sound of a television, the voices of it coming through the ceiling as they only can from a television, not as distraction but as profound irritation. Ray couldn't decide for sure what program it was, but it had canned laughter that periodically came into the room, the raucous, false sound washing over all of them, although no one flinched or seemed to notice the sound at all.

Mr. Mei looked at Ray and said, "You want a watch like that? You want a fast car?" As he spoke, though, he kept glancing out to the street.

"It's a beautiful watch," said Ray. "I've never seen one like it."

"Dean," said Mr. Mei. "You got a smart boy."

"Look," said Dean. "Maybe I made a mistake. Maybe it was tomorrow night. . . . I could come back later or tomorrow."

Mr. Mei looked at his watch. It had a broad white face on which there were black roman numerals, and the neat order of them, the precise printing of them, had a soothing quality, as though the watch were connected to some ordinary business.

"I don't think you should go out now," said Mr. Mei, glancing at Ray too. "Anyway, we've got some business. It's a kind of show-room."

He gave Dean the address from memory and described the size and shape and the location of the building, his voice bored and distant, as though by describing it he had already made it cease to exist: it was the moment when a theoretical consideration begins to take an active, suddenly quite real form. It was a warehouse and showroom in Downey, and for some reason the place wasn't making any money. As it was described, Ray imagined each detail, each brick, just to have something to think about. Mr. Mei gave Dean two keys, one to the front door and one for the burglar alarm.

Mr. Mei offered seven hundred and fifty dollars for the job.

"I don't know," said Dean. "That's not much these days. . . ."

Mr. Mei looked at his watch.

"You, smart boy, what you think?" he asked.

Ray looked at the floor and put his hands together, feeling the slick, sweaty touch of his palms. He moved his eyes from his hands to Mr. Mei, and while looking him in the face he said, "I think it should be fifteen hundred."

Mr. Mei didn't smile. He just looked back to Dean and said, "All right. A thousand." He reached into a bottom drawer of the desk and took out a cashbox from which he took some bills, the ink on them the color of eucalyptus leaves. Mr. Mei counted out a thousand dollars and pushed it across the desk. The money that had been used to test Ray's memory, five twenties, still lay there on the edge of the desk, and Mr. Mei pushed them at Ray.

"Here," he said. "That's for being brave."

Ray pushed it over to his father.

"No," said Mr. Mei, "I gave it to you. Put it in the bank. Don't waste it."

Mr. Mei looked at his watch again, snapping his wrist around as he did so and licking his lips, his tongue making a quick pass there. His forehead was very shiny under the bare bulb on the ceiling.

"Well, all right," said Dean, "I guess that takes care of it."

Dean stood up and turned toward the door, beckoning to Ray, and as they went out to the front of the store, their shadows falling away before them in grotesque elongation, Dean's voice came in a quiet whisper as he said, "You get down when I tell you. Don't ask questions. Just get down."

Dean walked through the store, Ray behind him. Ray smelled again the comforting odor of rice and the clean roll of paper used to wrap the smoked ducks, and as he moved into the darkness, he heard some footsteps outside, the padding of them coming through the fog with a hint of profound isolation. Ray turned his head toward the door, and for a moment it seemed that the silence was a kind of liquid that flowed through the store and into the street, the stuff pierced only by the unbelievably fast sounds of more than one person running, although even with the speed of the footsteps there was an order or certainty about what was going on outside, as though men were moving along a perfectly straight line. Mr. Mei stood in the doorway of his office, the light behind him, his shape in silhouette as he cocked his head toward the street. Then he said, "Psst. Dean. Come back in here."

"What's the matter?"

"The boy too," said Mr. Mei.

Dean came in, and they all stood there, the air still and a little musty, the oak desk looking stained, the yellow-gray wall above them having on it the picture of a nude Oriental woman who sat on a piece of pink satin. The satin was a rosy, bright pink, and the woman smiled, showing her beautiful white teeth.

From the street there was a muffled crack, like someone breaking a stick in a barrel. The sound had about it a finality, as though it signified some enormous thing that was just beginning to make its appearance.

"Quiet," said Mr. Mei. "Don't move now. Stay in here."

Ray looked at his father, who stood by the wall, head pressed against it. Ray stood next to him, and Dean reached out and put his arm around him.

"It'll be all right," said Dean.

On Mr. Mei's lip the sweat stood out in small beads the size of pinheads.

"You know, Dean," he said quietly, "I have a piece of land up in Malibu. Up there you can see the swells rolling in from the Pacific. You know what's out there? At the horizon? Nothing at all. Just emptiness. I'm going to plant a garden on my land. Chinese vegetables. And some flowers, too. Some hibiscus. Some gardenias. Some citrus trees. Navel oranges. I've got it all planned. You'll be able to see the sea lions from my garden."

There were two more noises in the street, just as before . . . a little muffled. Then two people walked away from the front of the store, the sounds of the footsteps disappearing slowly, if not nonchalantly, into the fog.

"All right," said Mr. Mei. "You can go now."

Ray and Dean went back out to the store, passing the dark shapes of the shelves, the piles of cans, the cooler off to the side, which gave off a purple glow. They hesitated at the door, looking into the street, Ray's hands trembling against the frame. In the distance there was the sound of cars, their tires hissing on the damp pavement. The scent of seaweed and fish made the fog seem almost salty. Dean looked up and down the street, and Ray waited too, looking around and thinking of the gentle green swells of the Pacific.

The man who had let them into the store was lying between two cars at the curb, his feet making a wide V, his hands open at his sides, the fingers curled a little. On the street there was a dark stain, which mixed with the rainbowlike sheen of oil visible in the glow from City Hall. Lying next to him was the package he had picked up, a shoe box from which a few bills now leaked out. A couple had fallen out of the box altogether and had fluttered down into that dark stain and the colors of the oil, which had the shine of a fly's green body.

Ray turned and looked into the window, where Mr. Mei stood,

watching from the darkened store, his hair lighted by the room where he did his business.

Ray and Dean walked through the fog, the street completely deserted, the odors of the restaurants stronger than ever, not to mention that fishy scent of the Pacific, and as they went their breath trailed away in long shreds of mist. Their gait was a constant, hurried one, like men just about to break into a run, and they didn't waste time looking from side to side. It seemed to Ray that the shadows in the doorways up ahead didn't suggest a human being lying in wait so much as a receptive darkness, as though people could simply disappear if they stepped into it. Ray and Dean went down to the avenue and turned right, into a wedge of orange light that fell from the overhead sign of a restaurant.

"In here," said Dean. "It's okay here. It's not for tourists."

They sat down at a long table that was covered with green Formica. It was a small restaurant, with about ten long tables with eight or so chairs at each one. A waiter came up to the table and gave them two menus and some chopsticks. Once he glanced toward the street, but that was all.

Dean looked at the menu when he spoke.

"What you saw in the street," he said. "That just didn't happen. All right?"

The menu was in Chinese characters, and Ray stared at them, going over them again and again as though repetition would make them somehow understandable.

Dean looked up now.

"We've got other things to worry about," he said.

"All right," said Ray.

"It was just bad luck," said Dean. "That's all."

Dean ordered for the both of them, pork with scallions, shrimp in garlic sauce, pork fried rice, wonton soup. Ray looked out into the street, seeing people pass from time to time, their shapes emerging from the fog and then disappearing again, like some memory that refuses to be recalled.

Two young men with long dark hair and new running shoes came into the restaurant. They just stood around by the door, looking at

Dean and Ray. The front of the restaurant had a short counter with a menu taped to it, a cash register, and a stool, and on the wall there was the same calendar with the photograph of a nude Oriental woman, although here a piece of paper covered up all but her face. The two young men wore new blue jeans, sport shirts, and short jackets made of a shiny silklike material. They waited with a nonchalance and a silence too, their certainty being a sign, as far as Ray was concerned, that he had seen something he shouldn't have.

"Jesus Christ," said Ray. "Who are they?"

Dean didn't look over his shoulder, but he said, "I guess just some neighborhood kids."

The soup came, and Ray tried to eat a little, but after a while he stopped and put down his spoon.

"Just remember," said Dean. "We didn't see anything. Okay?"

"Sure," said Ray. "Maybe we should get out of here."

"I don't think so," said Dean. "I think we should just eat our food like a couple of tourists who couldn't care less. So eat up."

"Okay," said Ray.

He took another mouthful of soup. It was hot and it burned his mouth, but he took some more, keeping his eyes down.

"It's just as well," said Dean. "There are some things you have to know. We can talk about them."

"Is your soup hot?" asked Ray.

"Yes," said Dean.

"Do you remember when we used to get up and watch the light from the bombs at Yucca Flats?" Ray asked. "You know, we'd get up early in the morning. It would be just the two of us."

"I remember," said Dean.

"That light was something," said Ray. "It was like we were watching the beginning of the world, like we were looking through a billion years. It was as though it had rolled right off God's hand."

When Ray glanced up the young men were still at the door, their eyes on Dean's back and on Ray's face.

"I don't know about that," said Dean. "I used to have ideas like that when I was your age. But after a while you see it's just some light."

The waiter brought the food in stainless-steel dishes on a stand and with a cover. He brought two plates and some tea and water and then he got right away from the table.

"Listen," said Dean. "Here. You want some of this shrimp? It's great." He put some on Ray's plate. "Start eating."

The shrimp were small, but they had been cooked quickly and looked almost transparent. The sauce was sharp and brought out the taste of the shrimp. Ray hadn't used chopsticks before, and he held them as Dean did, but he had trouble, especially with his hands shaking, in picking anything up, but he tried again, the tips of the chopsticks slipping apart and crossing over as Ray poked at the shrimp on his plate.

"There are some things you've got to know," said Dean.

"Like what?" asked Ray.

"You've got to remember we're not being paid for smoke damage," said Dean. "Any jackass with a match can do that. What the owner of a building is paying for is heat, flames, and ashes."

"Okay," said Ray.

He managed to get a piece of shrimp on his chopsticks, the thing balanced awkwardly where the two pieces of wood came together like the top of a capital A, and as he lifted it toward his mouth he looked up. The two young men, who were leaning against the counter, stared right at him, their glance not interrogatory so much as coolly judicial and implying that they had made up their minds about something. Ray looked down and saw that he had dropped the pink, almost transparent shrimp. He began to poke at it again.

"There are rules," said Dean.

"Tell me one," said Ray.

"Never, and I mean never, hang around to watch a building burn," said Dean. "Do you understand that?"

"Yes," said Ray.

"That's for firebugs. We're not firebugs. We're arsonists."

"Do you use gas?" asked Ray.

"No," said Dean. "That's for some kid who gets paid fifty bucks to burn down someone's house. We use kerosene. It burns just as hot but it has a higher flash point. That means you've got a better chance of not setting yourself on fire if you use kerosene. Here." Dean put some pork fried rice on Ray's plate. "You're not eating. I thought I told you to enjoy yourself like you just came in to have dinner."

Ray looked up at the young men.

"I'm not real hungry," said Ray.

"Eat," said Dean. "Listen. Say you've got a place with plaster-board walls. You kick a hole in a wall. Then you take a newspaper, a daily edition of the *Los Angeles Times*, and you roll it up, just like you were going to hit a dog. You stick it in the hole, and when you've got it in there, you stick a candle in the middle of the roll. How much of the candle you leave out depends on how long you want it to burn before the fire starts. Put the paper above an electrical socket. It looks just like some cheap wiring shorted out."

Dean stopped and looked at his son.

"Are you getting this?" said Dean.

Ray tried to get some pork fried rice on his chopsticks, and then he put them in his mouth, tasting wood more than anything else. "I think we should get out of here," he said.

"I told you about that," said Dean.

"I burned my mouth."

"Drink some ice water."

Ray took a drink of water, seeing the ice cubes bob on the surface, the thin tinkling of them against the side of the glass making a pure, small sound, like a silver bell, that Ray concentrated on until he felt a little better. Then he put his glass down and looked across the table at his father.

"All right," he said. "Go on."

"You know, Ray," said Dean, "what I really do well? What I do better than anyone else?"

"What?" said Ray.

"I can make a building disappear faster than anyone else. A good-burning fire expands two thousand percent in four minutes, but I can make it do better than that. Once, I got rid of a bowling alley. Listen to this."

Ray glanced up and looked into the eyes of the young men, who had sat down beside the counter.

"They're still there," said Ray.

"Stop looking," said Dean. "How many times do I have to tell you? Listen. Here's how I did the bowling alley. I unrolled paper towels on the alleys, and then I covered them with lacquer. The paper kept it from running all over the place, kept it right on the wood. Then I left a fuse, a windup clock with a black-powder cap stuck right where the hammer was going to hit the bell. You know, a black-powder cap like ones used for a black-powder rifle."

"I know what you mean," said Ray. He got some more rice on his chopsticks, but it spilled off. He tried again, keeping his eyes down.

"That burned so hot," said Dean. "I mean it was so fast and so hot, even the foundation, which was concrete, just turned to ashes. Let me tell you, that sucker burned."

"Uh huh," said Ray.

"Use chopsticks like this," said Dean. "Put one here, in the crotch between your thumb and first finger. Hold that one still. Use the other against it. That's it."

Ray ate for a while, feeling the softness of the shrimp between the tips of the chopsticks, tasting the scallions with the pork. He ate only a few bites before he put the chopsticks together and set them down on the side of his plate.

"Let's go," Ray said.

Dean turned now and looked over his shoulder at the young men by the cash register. They seemed to be perfectly still and patient, not hurried, not anxious, nothing at all, really, aside from being constantly alert.

"I don't know," said Dean. "Finish your food."

Ray stared back at him.

"No," he said. "I can't eat."

"Jesus, Ray," said Dean. "You didn't see anything. Neither did I. Isn't that right? So just wait for these guys to leave."

Ray picked up the chopsticks again and put them in his hand the way Dean had showed him.

"Yeah," said Dean. "It's amazing what you can do with just newspaper. You make it into balls, big floppy balls, and leave them in an open space. The flames come through there like you wouldn't believe."

"Look," said Ray. "Let's just walk back to the car."

"With those two following us? Come on."

"At least we'd know where they were," said Ray.

Dean grunted.

"Listen, " he said. "You want to set a fire at the bottom of a wall. You get better draft there. A long hall is good, because of the draft. Sometimes you might have to make a draft, you know, by opening a window or a door."

Outside, the fog had gotten a little thicker, and now it pressed up against the window with the gray color of a dirty sheet. Every now and then a car went by, the headlights looking like golden blurs, like enormous puffs, passing with the hiss of tires on the wet street. Ray watched the cars go by, his eyes following them with a searching, intense expression, or maybe envy since they seemed to escape so easily.

Only the people walking very close to the window could now be seen, and there were times when they passed in just a swirl, a disruption in the gray-white murk outside, but as Ray looked up, one of these disturbances seemed to hesitate, and out of it there appeared a face that for an instant seemed to hang there, cut off from a body, like a mask hung on a hook. Ray looked closely, his recognition of Mr. Mei coming with a rush that was indistinguishable from inspiration.

Mei Yaochen came into the restaurant and turned to the young men, speaking once to both of them, and then they stood up, not saying a word and no longer looking at Ray and Dean. They turned and walked away from the counter, turning out of the yellowish light of the restaurant and disappearing into the street. Then Mr. Mei turned and looked at Ray. Finally he smiled and walked over and said, "Dean. Good food here? You like greasy noodles?"

"It's all right," said Dean.

"What about you, smart boy?" said Mr. Mei. "You can eat now. All right? Okay? No trouble now."

Mei Yaochen smiled.

"Don't worry," he said. "You working for me. I'll take care of you. Everything fine."

He spoke to the waiter, who stood just a few yards away, and then he said, "You going to Downey tonight, Dean?"

"I guess so," said Dean. "It's a good night for it."

"Good. Good," said Mr. Mei. "You take care."

Then he walked into the fog. Dean asked for the check, but the waiter told him it had already been paid.

"No trouble," he said. "He paid."

The waiter pointed to the fog outside, the mass of which hung in the street, the headlights of an occasional car floating through it with a slow, constant beauty. Ray picked out a few cold shrimp and ate them and a little rice, and then Dean said, "All right. I guess I better show you how it's done."

═

They got into the car and Dean started the engine. He let the windshield wipers run back and forth over the glass, the water collecting under the blade and running away from the corner of the windshield. Somehow, the water running down the side of the windshield reminded Ray of the tears of a man who has been about to cry and who has been fighting it, but who then closes his eyes and makes the tears run down the side of his face. Dean pulled into the street, saying, "Jesus, this fog is thick. A night like this, cars pile up on the freeway. Forty, fifty, a hundred. Who the hell knows how many once they start piling into each other."

They got on the freeway.

"Are you scared?" asked Dean.

"So what if I am?" said Ray.

"Listen, Ray," said Dean. "You aren't ashamed of me, are you?"

"No," said Ray. "Of course not."

"I do this real well," said Dean. "There have been a lot of great torches. Jimmy Avery and Max Hillboro in Chicago, Charlie Blue in Atlanta, Joachim Solarius in the Bronx—"

"How far is it to Downey?" said Ray.

"About twenty miles," said Dean. "Listen, anyone can start a fire and it looks like it was set. The guy who does it jams the lock so the firemen can't get in. The fire burns better this way, but it causes trouble for the owner. Especially, say, if the main power switch has been turned off so the fire alarm doesn't work. Well, Raymond, you see this?" He had a bag on the front seat, and now he took out of it a heavy spring and a rubber band with a hook on it. "This throws the main switch back on when the fire is going good enough to melt the rubber band. All that's left in the rubble is an ordinary spring."

Dean put the spring away.

"You know who invented that?" said Dean.

"Maybe someone in Chicago. Or Boston," said Ray.

"No," said Dean.

"I don't know," said Ray.

"I knew you'd never get it," said Dean. "It was me."

They found the building in Downey. It was newish, made of cinder blocks and topped with a metal roof, and it sat by itself in the middle of a large empty parking lot, the lines on the asphalt for parking spaces seeming white and neat. There was a streetlamp on a standard near the front of the building, the purplish light falling onto the asphalt with the color of a new bruise. Dean parked at the side of the building, in a shadow, and then he got out, taking with him the bag he had on the front seat, which stank of kerosene. Ray got out too.

Dean opened the door with the key he had gotten from Mr. Mei, walked inside, and turned off the burglar alarm. The building was a toy factory and showroom, and the place where the toys were displayed was fifty yards long and twenty-five wide, the scale of it like an arena. It was covered with wall-to-wall carpet and had adjustable stands, like dressing screens, on which there were toys, new-style Frisbees, dolls, puppets, crayons, games, trucks, model airplanes with gasoline engines, sets of Legos. In an open place there was a car, large enough for a child to sit in, that ran on batteries. There was a metal stand with spokes, about the size of a beach umbrella, and on each spoke there was a cardboard duck. The spokes turned and the ducks could be knocked off with a toy shotgun that shot darts.

Dean and Ray went down the aisles, their feet silent on the wall-to-wall carpet, their eyes moving over the airplanes, dolls, cars, the new odor of which was overwhelmed by the stink of kerosene. They came to a train set laid out on a table, the tracks shiny and running over small black railroad ties, and around it there were trees, houses, a grassy knoll, and a pond, which had been brushed on with blue paint.

"A Lionel," said Dean. "A real Lionel. I used to go up to the hobby shops when you were a kid and look at the Lionels."

He reached down and turned on the transformer and then moved a lever on it so that the train started to move, the grind and click of it small in that enormous room.

"Right around Christmas," said Dean.

He looked up now, his glance one of angry regret. He put down his bag and stood by the table, his finger touching the texture of the model grass, a green dust that had been spread over some glue.

"I never really wanted one," said Ray.

"No?" said Dean. "How can you tell me that? We come here to do something we could both get thrown in jail for, and you tell me lies?"

"All right," said Ray. "Maybe I wanted one. So what?"

Dean picked up a bottle next to the transformer, a dark amber–colored one like those from a pharmacy. Inside there were some small white pills, about the size of a child's aspirin. He dropped one of them into the smokestack of the train and turned the lever on the transformer, the movement of his wrist quick. The train went around in circles, and soon a wisp of smoke came out of the smoke-stack, the strand of it trailing away from the engine. It got thicker, stronger, the trail of it lingering now, and as they watched, Ray said, "I guess that's the world's first polluting toy."

Dean went on staring at it. He shut the engine off, and Ray and his father stood opposite one another, the toy's smoke rising between them.

"I guess that's right, Raymond," said Dean, staring at his son. The smoke had an acrid odor. Dean looked around at the toys and said, "Let's burn this shit up. Maybe we'll feel better."

There was a small room at the back of the building, and Dean went into it, saying, "Here. This is what we want. It's a long ways from the power switch." Dean kicked a hole in the plasterboard wall, just above a socket, which was next to a metal shelf where chemicals and photographic developer were stored. He took a copy of the *Times* from his bag and rolled it up and shoved it into the wall and put the candle in.

"You see?" he said, his voice argumentative now. "Like this. Not too tight. You want the paper to burn. If it's too tight it just smolders, and then someone comes in here in the morning and finds just a black streak on the wall."

He opened his bag and showed Ray five condoms, all filled with kerosene, each so full it was as round as a cantaloupe.

"These are better than balloons," said Dean. "Balloons are always breaking. Tie these to the light fixture. There's a ladder. I'm going to put my gimmick on the power box. You'll need a flashlight. Here."

Ray worked quickly, tying the large, whitish globes to the light fixture, the scent of kerosene around him. He finished the last one and climbed down, then put the ladder away. He stood in the doorway of the room, watching as Dean came across that large, dark space, the beam of his flashlight pointing right at his feet. As he came toward Ray he walked backward, and he was stooped over a little. He held a gallon bucket of lacquer that he was spreading over the wall-to-wall carpet, the glistening path of the stuff, as bright as saliva, wandering one way and another under the displays of toys.

Ray held a match in his hand, and as he watched his father, he thought of what would happen if he lighted it early. He just stared for a moment, feeling the weight of being trusted. His father put the can neatly on the shelf that held the chemicals and the developer.

"You see?" said Dean. "We close this door. The fire starts in here, gets the kerosene going, and then it burns through the wall to the lacquer, which by then will have plenty of carburetion and . . . that's all she wrote."

Dean struck a match and lighted the candle.

"All right," said Dean. "Let's go. Let's go!"

On their way out they passed the train and the painted pond, over which swayed shadows cast by the flashlights. Dean didn't stop to look now. They came up to the burglar alarm again, which Dean turned back on, and then they stepped into the purple darkness of the parking lot.

Dean started the engine and drove out of the parking lot, his face damp now, clammy, as he looked back once at the rear of the building, where there was a slight glow, a yellow flicker that had about it all the promise of dawn. They drove into the street, from which, up above in the distance, they could see the lights from the freeway. They looked like globes, bright, almost glistening, and seemed to float in the air by some force of nature, like ball lightning.

"Here," said Dean, handing the keys over. "Get rid of these." Ray threw them out the window, the silvery things turning and looking, for one second, like a drop of rain seen in a headlight.

They drove north, through Hollywood and the Cahuenga Pass. The valley was filled with lights, but here there weren't so many golden avenues. Instead, there were a lot of blocks that were defined only by the purple streetlamps. The collection of these squares, marked off by purple dots, manifested an only partial, or incomplete order, more like an idea for a suburb than the place itself.

The car went up toward the Tejon Pass. There wasn't any fog at all up there, and the stars were out, a clutter of them against the sky like bits of foil spilled on tar paper. The constellations showed clearly, the certainty of them bringing a chilly relief, or at least a reminder of some long-term perspective. In Bakersfield, they drove through the quiet streets, the houses of which were blue-black against the dawn. Here and there a light was on in a house, and the buttery glow seemed warm and safe.

Dean parked in front of his house. There was a light on in the kitchen, although in general the place had a sleepy, closed-up quality. Ray started to go up to the door, but Dean stopped him and said, "Let's go around back."

They sat on the back porch, facing the sky, which looked like a piece of smoke-colored silk. Here and there a bird began to sing, and occasionally one would fly across the yard, appearing small and dark, fluttering.

"It was about this time we used to watch the light from Yucca Flats," said Dean.

Ray nodded.

"Yeah," he said. "It was right at six. I remember."

"Sure," said Dean. "Sometimes I wish they were still doing it. Just so we could be together like that."

"We're together," said Ray.

"Are we?" said Dean. He rubbed his hand across his chin and cheeks, where there was a shadow of his beard. It was dark on the sides, but around the chin it looked like salt and pepper. "Well, maybe. What did you think of L.A.?"

"I don't know," said Ray.

"What's that supposed to mean?" said Dean.

"I think you better be careful down there."

"I thought it was going to be 'we' down there," said Dean. "From now on."

Ray watched the eastern sky.

"If you make a mistake, they aren't even going to be able to find what's left of you," said Ray.

"That's only part of it," said Dean. "Isn't it? I mean about not liking L.A."

"Yeah," said Ray. "That's only part."

"Listen," said Dean. "I want you to give it another chance."

There were more birds now, swooping through the yard, their paths not straight but gently rising and falling, their flight describing a telephone line that droops a little between each pole. Ray looked at them and then turned to his father.

"All right," he said.

"That's good, Ray," said Dean. "Jesus, you know I love you, don't you? You're my flesh and blood."

Ray nodded.

"Okay," he said.

"Please, Ray, please," said Dean. "Just give it a chance."

"All right. Let's go in. It's cold out here."

"Don't turn away from me, Ray," said Dean.

"I said okay," said Ray.

They both stood and went into the kitchen. It was a largish room, painted yellow, a place that had an old, white Kelvinator, a round oak table, some plants hanging in a window, a sink, and some dishes in a rack next to it. Marge Gollancz, Dean's wife, was wearing a green cardigan sweater over a housedress as she sat at the table drinking a cup of coffee. Pearl, Ray's sister, was there too. She was twenty-one, finished with school, and she was looking through the morning paper. When Ray and Dean came in, Marge pushed a strand of hair away from her face and smiled and said, "Thank God. You're all right."

Dean looked at his son and said, "Well, let's hope so."

Then Dean took some money out of his pocket and gave it to his wife.

ABBADABBA
BERMAN

━

Marge Gollancz was ten years older than Dean. As time passed, Marge felt the burden of those years, especially when her husband spent time (in a motel or in some out-of-the-way bedroom) with another, usually younger, woman. Marge had a constant antagonism to the passage of time, all of the evidence of which (a new wrinkle, a crease, a darkening of the skin, or one of her husband's infidelities) she cursed out loud, usually when she stood before the mirror in the morning, examining her face as though it were something she had bought against her better judgment, the imperfections only proving her original suspicions.

She had been over thirty when she married Dean, and she had believed, in the beginning, that his good looks and his easy smile weren't just superficial gifts, like being able to roll his tongue or wiggle his ears, but were signs of his soon-to-be-revealed success.

She persisted in this, even when she had evidence to the contrary, and if there was a reason for her toleration of the time he spent with other women, it was a belief that Dean was somehow on the verge of proving she had been right to believe in him after all. Now, she was over fifty.

Dean usually met women who had come to Bakersfield for a visit. He walked past a house where someone's out-of-town sister or cousin was sitting on the veranda. He smiled and raised his cap. And that was all, at least for a while. But when he passed again, the woman was sitting closer to the front of the porch, or maybe even on the first of the steps that ran down to the garden, her hair seeming slightly intimate (some strands out of place, say); or there was, in the way her slightly damp hands hung over her knees or in the look in her eyes, evidence of the amount of time she had spent waiting to hear the steady sound of his shoes on the sidewalk.

In the past, when a neighbor said something to Marge about seeing Dean with a young woman, or when Marge had reasons of her own to suspect this was the case, she had begun to argue with Dean, not about the young woman but about whether or not a woman would make a good president. Now, though, when she had her suspicions, she just looked at Dean and said, at the dinner table, "Well, who is it? Can you tell me her name?"

A week after Dean and Ray had come back from Los Angeles, Marge put a tuna casserole in the oven. She cooked it with crumpled potato chips on top, and it was one of the things Dean didn't like. Marge said, "Well, who is it? Can you tell me her name?"

"There's no one," said Dean.

"How can you lie like that?" she said. "You aren't even a good liar."

"I'm not lying," said Dean.

"How can you say that?" said Marge. "Do you think I am blind?"

"No," said Dean. "It's over."

"Can I trust you?" said Marge. "Is it really over?"

"I told you," said Dean. He looked down at the food. "There's nothing more to say."

Then Dean left the table and went up to the attic, where, resting on two sawhorses, there was an instrument case in which there was a trombone. The case was lined with satin, and the trombone sat in it like an enormous, golden paper clip. Dean had learned how to play the trombone in high school, and he had bought this one on his second wedding anniversary. He took the case downstairs to his bedroom and, leaving it on the bed, flipped up the latches. Then he picked up the trombone and put the mouthpiece in and began to play. He played "Georgia on My Mind," "Rock of Ages," "Met the Devil at the Crossroads," and some other sweet or sad music.

The music had a faraway, romantic sound, like a band heard over water on a summer evening, and just as at such a time, when lovers, sunburned and tired from swimming, heard such music, the yard around Dean's house had an almost palpable sense of youth and glamour. Soon, though, one of the neighbors, a man by the name of Carson, opened a window and then turned to someone in the depths of his house, raising his voice when he spoke. He said, "Hear that? I guess Dean Gollancz has got himself another piece of ginch somewhere. Sounds like she's left him flat, too. They always do. Takes a while sometimes. He always plays that way when the thrill is gone."

This was Friday night, early in the evening, and Ray heard the trombone coming from Dean's bedroom as he dressed and as he combed his hair in the bathroom. Then he went downstairs and out the door, where he still heard it, but after a while, when he had got down to the end of the block, there was only the hush of the street.

He had asked a young woman, Mary Wilcox, to a movie, and when he waited downstairs in her house, he thought he could still hear that trombone, and he started humming, but then when Mary's father said, "What's that you say?" Ray stopped and said, "Just clearing my throat. Warm night, isn't it?"

Mary's father grunted, and then Mary came downstairs. They went to a movie, a double bill, and then they went to have a Coke in the luncheonette that was in the middle of town, and when they passed the pawnshop, they stopped and looked into the window, in which there was a display of pistols, all of them arranged in a circle, their barrels pointed toward the center. Each one had a lock in the trigger guard, and almost all of them had wooden or plastic grips textured with hundreds of small pyramids. Ray and Mary just looked at them for a while, both of them thinking about the times someone in town had come to the pawnshop and bought a small pistol, just the thing to go into a handbag or a pocket, and had killed a husband or a wife who had happened to be caught at the wrong moment. Then they looked above the pistols, where instruments were hung from the ceiling, tubas, trumpets, clarinets, guitars, trombones, and in the back there were drums and cymbals.

"Look at all of those instruments," said Mary. "What would you play if you had your pick?"

Ray looked at the trombones hung at the back of the shop, but he didn't say anything.

"Me," said Mary, "I'd like some cymbals. I'd wallop them plenty." She laughed. "Better than a trombone."

"What's wrong with a trombone?" said Ray.

"Come on," said Mary. "Only some kind of charity case plays a trombone."

"My dad plays one," said Ray.

"Oh," said Mary. "Well, I didn't mean anything."

They walked back along the tree-lined blocks, the leaves shimmering in the streetlights. Here and there a cricket sounded, and there was the scent of early summer, a mixture of wet ground, grass, and, in California, the exciting, distant odor of gasoline. Ray took her hand as they walked along, and in the shadows of her yard she gave him a hard, quick kiss, coming close to him, almost bouncing against him, and then she stepped back, leaving him with the lingering, beguiling odor of her newly ironed clothes, the taste of her mouth, and the memory of the quick heat there had been between them. Then she said thanks and went up the steps and into the house.

Dean was a printer, and his shop was in a warehouse a few blocks from that two-story house of his with the gray clapboards and the screen with the holes that let the moths in. Above the glass door of the shop and across the front window there was a sign that said, DEAN'S PRINT SHOP. He printed whatever came his way, wedding announcements, invitations, flyers, letterheads, envelopes, brochures, and small catalogs.

One evening after work Dean sat at the kitchen table with his checkbook, the one from the shop having three checks on a page and looking solid if not prosperous. Dean went through the pages carefully, adding the figures up and then staring out the window. He took a small box of kitchen matches and put it on the table, giving it a flick with his finger from time to time, the small rattle lingering in the kitchen.

It was summer, and Ray worked in the shop, cleaning the press, watching it when it was printing, delivering small orders, answering the phone, or running the small copying machine there. The morning after Dean had balanced his checkbook, he came in and said, "I'm going to talk to Mei Yaochen. Tonight. Maybe tomorrow."

"Are you?" said Ray.

"Yeah," said Dean. "You coming along?"

"I said I was, didn't I?" said Ray.

Dean looked at him. "You could be a little more enthusiastic," he said. "You don't have to come."

"I said I would," said Ray.

Dean sighed and leaned against a counter.

"Ah, Raymond," said Dean. "I was just thinking about the Big Time. You know what that is?"

"No," said Ray.

"It's a place where you're in charge. Where you're feared a little. People get nervous when they talk to you. If you want something, you can get it."

"Is that right?" said Ray.

"Sure," said Dean. He spoke now like a fan remembering a football player who has been retired for a while, his voice relaxing with the pleasure of it. "Now, you take Otto 'Abbadabba' Berman. He was a smart man. The brains behind Dutch Schultz . . . yeah, you'd have to say Abbadabba was in the Big Time. And Herman 'the Baron' Lamm. Now, the Baron held up banks, but he had the jobs planned. You know? He had a jugmaker, someone who knew the inside of the bank. Yeah, he was Big Time, too."

Ray opened a new package of paper for the copier and knocked the pages together neatly.

"What do they have to do with us?" asked Ray.

"Nothing," said Dean. "I just kind of like to think about them. That's all. There was Harry Pierpont. Fat Charley Makley. Yeah, and Walter Devitch, too. In the Big Time, they wear silk suits. Five hundred dollars, maybe six hundred. Handmade shirts. Wing tip shoes. Beautiful ties. I'd like to get some nice ties. Silk ones. A black silk shirt and a white tie. That's style, Ray."

Ray looked at his father.

"It just makes me feel better, Ray, imagining it."

"You thinking about a bank or something?" asked Ray.

"No," said Dean. "No. I'm no good for that. No, I'm content. I got a skill. I'm good at it."

"What about Mei Yaochen?" said Ray. "Is he Big Time?"

"Well, Raymond, no one knows," said Dean. "At least not yet."

In the afternoon, Dean closed the shop early, hanging a sign in the window that said, BE BACK IN TEN MINUTES. He took Ray to a men's store downtown, a large place that smelled of wool and newly vacuumed carpets and the faint odor of cigar smoke. There Dean held shirts and ties up to Ray, who was almost as tall as Dean now. Ray put on a jacket and the silk lining slipped over his shirt, while behind the slick, engulfing sensation there was the weight of the wool. They looked at shoes, too, some French-toed ones that Dean called "Puerto Rican fence climbers." They didn't buy anything, though, since Dean said nothing had any style.

"Yeah, the Big Time, Ray. Some people get all the breaks."

Ray had a friend, Eno Lamar, who was a young man with red hair and blue eyes. In the hot evenings of summer Eno stopped by to visit, and usually when the air brought with it a scent of dampness and a sharp tang of growing things, Eno began to make plans. He thought he should get into aluminum siding, in which he was going to make a bundle. Sometimes he brought the business opportunities section of the paper and read them aloud to Ray, who thought about each one, trying to decide what it would be like, for instance, to have a Chicken Delight franchise.

Eno worked in the print shop sometimes, too, when there was a little extra work. While Ray and Eno were working, Dean explained the day's news to them ("The Russians are up to something, you watch. The Russian is a cagey bear"), gave his advice about the best way to clean a press, and told them his theories (that the Garden of Eden had been in the New World, somewhere near Guatemala, and that the best way to treat a cold was by inhaling hot air to kill the virus). And Dean knew, too, who was doing what in town, not so much the romantic side, about which he had no interest at all, but other things, such as who was taking barbiturates and which old woman in town was killing stray cats. This was "the world behind the mask," as Ray put it. If anything, Dean saw the boys' company as a compliment and evidence, too, that they were growing up, since they seemed to be more interested in his opinions than they had been just a few months before.

The next evening, when the light was bluish and warm and the houses seemed mysterious, Ray sat on the front porch with his father. Eno came up the street and turned into the yard, where he stopped in front of the steps.

"Hi, Ray," said Eno. "Mr. Gollancz."

"Hi, Eno," said Dean. "Getting into trouble?"

"Me?" said Eno. "No. What about you?"

Dean stared into the street. "No," he said.

They sat quietly, looking into the street. After a while Ray took a breath and said to Dean, "Listen, I'd like to talk something over with you."

"What's that?" said Dean.

"Maybe we should take a walk and talk things over."

"Are you thinking of joining the army, or some other piece of tomfoolery?" asked Dean.

"No," said Ray. "Something's come up."

"What?"

"I took a test in school this spring. . . . I did pretty well on it and they're saying I should apply to some school," said Ray.

"Where?" asked Dean.

"In the East," Ray answered.

"You mean college?" said Dean. "You mean the kind of place

those shitheads who live in the north side of town go to? They drive those German cars. You'd think Detroit was good enough for those boys, wouldn't you?"

"Let's take a walk," said Ray.

"Listen," said Dean. "I thought you were going to go into the printing business. Isn't that what we'd always planned?" He paused and looked at his son. "Maybe we'd do some other things too."

Dean turned from Ray to Eno and said, "What about you? Are you thinking about going to some college too?"

"Naw," said Eno. "The future's in aluminum siding. Any fool can see that. All you got to do is think about the price of paint. Not to mention labor. Painters are going to price themselves right out of a good thing."

Dean stared at Eno, thinking about it, but then he turned back to his son.

"Well, maybe we should take a walk, Raymond. Maybe we should get this straightened out."

"It wouldn't cost anything to go to college," said Ray. "There are scholarships. They think I could get one."

"Is that right, my Whizzaro?" said Dean. "You know what I think of those guys on the other side of town? I think they're assholes." Dean turned to Eno. "You coming too?"

"I wouldn't miss it for anything," said Eno, but by then Dean and Ray were already moving toward the sidewalk. The three of them went together, leaving behind that weathered house. The street-lamps hadn't come on yet and the air had a warm, summer quality. It smelled of dusty leaves, and the temperature of it seemed to be the same as human skin. The light was bluish and soothing.

"All right," said Dean, "talk."

"I already told you," said Ray.

"You should think about aluminum siding," said Eno. "I swear I'm going to make a bundle."

Dean went straight ahead.

"Are you looking down on me, Raymond?" he said.

"I didn't say that," said Ray. "This is getting out of hand."

"You don't understand a goddamned thing, Raymond. You think

that somehow you can just escape this?" Dean pointed at the houses, the trees, the sky. "Well, I'll tell you something. You can't. You and I are in it together."

Ray stopped and looked at his father.

"That's the truth, Raymond," said Dean. "Do you think otherwise? Well, answer me."

Ray turned toward his father, both of them standing still in the street.

"Don't push me around," said Ray.

"Here," said Dean, "take my hand."

He put his right hand out.

"Go on," said Dean. "Take my hand!"

Ray reached out for it and they stood there, like two men greeting one another, and as they did so, Ray felt the warmth and the thick roughness of his father's hand. "You feel that?"

"Yes," said Ray.

"What is it?" asked Dean.

"Like there's something running between us."

"That's damn right," said Dean. "You won't escape that. Ever. It runs from my heart to yours. Don't you ever forget it."

"I thought you'd be proud of me," said Ray.

"Is that right?" said Dean.

"Look—"

"No," said Dean, "you look. I've worked hard, and you've never gone without. Do you understand that? I've taken some chances, too. Do you know what I mean? Jesus, there's been some times in L.A. . . . I mean some . . . times . . ."

Dean took a small box of matches from his pocket and began to rattle them, the sound dry in the cardboard of the box. For a while they walked quietly, Dean looking down at the sidewalk or straight ahead, as though he were alone.

"I got nothing against learning," said Dean. "You want to learn something, there's a library right here in town. Go and read. It's not the learning I don't like, it's those assholes on the other side of town. They turn up their noses at people like us."

Dean put his head back now and sniffed.

"There's nothing in that world for us, nothing in those colleges. You can tell just by looking. Look at the clothes they wear. No style."

"Maybe there's more to it than the clothes," said Ray. "Maybe it's something you can't see."

"Jesus," said Dean. "It's just like the light we used to watch. You were always saying there's more to it than just the spectacle. Like it came off of 'God's hand.' . . . But it didn't come off God's hand. It was a bunch of guys with slide rules. It's best to keep things simple. Say someone has got a building that isn't useful anymore. It disappears. No metaphysics. If it's done right, you can take the building away in a sandwich bag. There's no mystery to it. So, keep it simple. There's nothing for us where people are going to be snotty."

"Maybe there's more to it than just clothes," said Ray.

"Ach," said Dean, raising a hand in disgust.

"If you listen to me," said Eno, "you'd get into aluminum siding."

"What the hell do you know about aluminum siding?" said Dean. "You know something? You need electricity to make aluminum. And you want to know something else? It's going to cost a goddamned fortune to make electricity soon. Then what are you going to do?"

"What about the price of paint?"

Dean made a quick, impatient gesture with his hand, opening it and waving Eno's objections away.

"There's solar power," said Eno.

"Solar power," said Dean. "Why, you poor dumb bunny. The next thing I know you'll want to find some swami. Or go to see an astrologer. Solar. The next thing I know, you'll be talking about reincarnation."

Then all three of them turned through the soothing blue light. They went along a tree-lined street on which there were older, well-kept houses, mostly white ones that had verandas and carefully tended yards. Ray worked here after school or in the summer, mowing and watering the lawns and keeping the hedges trimmed square as a cardboard box.

They came up to Mrs. Harold's house, where Ray had worked the previous fall. There was a glider on the front porch, and as the three of them approached the house, they heard a squeak as someone moved back and forth in the shadows of the porch.

Dean heard that sound, and as he passed the house, Ray smelled the scent of perfume or bath soap, or some powder maybe. That delicate odor hung in the air, and there was a gentle and repeated appearance of the hem of a white skirt as Mrs. Harold's niece, who was visiting from San Francisco, went back and forth on the glider, in and out of the shadows of the porch, and her legs, shaved and oiled, had a sheen to them in the evening light.

Dean stopped. The sound of the glider became a little more languid. Soon the young woman stopped altogether, the silence, the cessation of that gentle swinging coming into the yard like a weight. Mrs. Harold's niece stood up and smiled in the half-light of dusk, her teeth flashing once as she did so, her lips dark against her pale face.

"Hello," said Dean.

"Hello," said the woman on the porch. "Beautiful night, don't you think?"

"Yes," said Dean. "We usually get a few days like this toward the end of the summer. You're not from around here, are you?"

"No," she said.

"Just visiting?" he asked.

"Yes," she said, and smiled again, her teeth white in the evening's shadow. "I haven't seen much yet."

"Well," said Dean, "I hope you like it here."

He started to walk again, his eyes swinging away from the porch as he did so, and as he took the first step he glanced at his hands and then at Ray. For a while, Dean just stared at his son. Then he turned around and took a step back, facing the young woman on the porch.

"My name's Dean," he said. "Gollancz is my last name. If I can help you with anything, you let me know, hear? Nothing's too small to ask."

"Well, thank you," she said. "My name's Grace Skip."

Eno put his elbow against Ray and gave him a little shove.

"Good night, Grace," said Dean.

"Good night," she said.

Dean and the boys went down the street, Ray feeling that elbow in the ribs again, the shove of it coming not only as a triumph but as a question too, which was, All right, but what next? They walked in silence, going around the block and heading home, Dean's steps lighter, almost cheerful now.

As they walked, Dean said, "Harvard. Dartmouth. Yale. Well, what do you say, let's think about something more pleasant for a while."

"Sure," said Ray.

"You know," said Dean, "I'm feeling great. Just great. Like Ab-badabba Berman working the numbers."

For a while Dean was quiet, glancing back toward the street they had just turned out of. Soon he started whistling "Sweet Georgia Brown." At home, the three of them sat on the front porch, each with his forearms over his knees, all of them staring into the beautiful blue-black shadows of the evening.

"All right," said Ray. "So we disagree about the appearances of things. So what?"

Dean grunted.

"You could say that," said Dean. "Yeah. That's pretty accurate, isn't it?"

"RED RIVER VALLEY"

＝

In the morning, Dean walked up to the corner, to the stationery store, which had a number of out-of-town newspapers, and there he looked through them, lingering over stories of arson from Los Angeles, San Francisco, Seattle, or even Las Vegas. There were photographs, too, and Dean looked at the flames with a careful estimation of just how they had come into being. It was always a giveaway, as far as Dean was concerned, if the owner of a house that burned had been away recently, especially on a trip to Las Vegas, or Jamaica, or any other place where gambling was allowed. Then, Dean looked at the paper, or the picture of a burned-out building, and said, "Vegas. And suddenly the guy's got problems with the wiring . . ."

"What's that you say?" said the owner of the stationery store, a man by the name of Sonny, who sold pornographic pictures from behind the counter and who let underage kids buy beer and cigarettes. He was about sixty, had gray hair, and wore a T-shirt that showed a plane flying away from a mushroom cloud. Underneath the plane there was a caption that said, NOW IT'S MILLER TIME.

Dean turned and looked at him. Then he said, "You know, I was just thinking. There were two old guys sitting on a park bench in Miami. They're retired, you know? One says to the other, 'How did you end up down here?' and the other says, 'There was a fire in my store. I collected the insurance and came down here. What about you?' 'There was a flood in my store and I collected the insurance.' And you know what the first one says?"

"No," said Sonny. "What?"

Sonny looked around at the gray walls of the place, the piles of paper, the pencils that weren't selling very well.

" 'How do you start a flood?' " said Dean.

"Is that right?" said Sonny.

In the dining room Marge said to Dean, "So, you've started again, haven't you?"

"Excuse me?" said Dean, looking up from the tuna casserole.

"You heard me," said Marge. "Where did you meet her this time?"

"Her?" said Dean, his fork still held off the plate.

"Yes, that's right," said Marge. "Her. Where?"

"I don't know what you're talking about," said Dean.

"Oh, God," said Marge. "So you're going to play dumb. Well, you know what, in your case that's not hard, is it?"

"What did you say?" said Dean, putting the fork down now.

"You heard me," said Marge.

Dean sat there, looking across the table at her.

"Please," said Pearl.

"I think you owe me an apology," said Dean.

"Me?" she said. "Apologize to you?" Then she started crying, not putting her head down or anything else, just closing her eyes and bobbing her head a little.

"Listen," said Dean.

Dean looked at his son and daughter, at the table, on which there was food.

"All right," he said. "I'll take care of it."

"Will you?" said Marge. "Will you promise?"

He put his head down.

"Yes," he said.

Dean showed up in the morning at the shop, looked over the list of jobs with Ray, and then he went out the door and got into his Chevrolet, which he drove along the back streets to Mrs. Harold's house, where he picked up Grace Skip and went toward the south side of town, which was mostly a collection of car dealerships, fast-food restaurants, and motels. The signs for the motels were on enormous stilts, and beneath each one, THE RED COACHMAN, THE LAMPLIGHTER, THE SUNSHINE INN, there was the word VACANCY, in front of which there was a small, neon NO. All of the NO signs were off. The parking lots were almost deserted. The dustiness of the buildings, the peeling paint, and the cheap scent in the more expensive places didn't bring dreariness to mind so much as the erotic valor on the part of the people who contemplated, in the full, unkind light of a late-summer day, facing one of those rooms, which smelled of disinfectant and barely disguised cigarette smoke.

At the shop, Ray sat down and started filling out the applications for those eastern schools. He sat down at the box with a lighted top that was used to check negatives before making a plate, but now he put a letter he had received from one of those eastern schools over the illuminated glass. The paper was heavy, cream colored, water-marked, and it had a texture, too, horizontal lines that had the pattern of venetian blinds. Ray picked up the sample book for paper and looked up the stock the letter came on, and although he couldn't find the exact paper (which somehow made the supply house Dean dealt with seem a little hickish), he found one that was close to it. Eighteen dollars for five hundred sheets. But finding out how much it cost did him no good at all or, if anything, confused the issue. So he simply stared at the paper, which sat there like a puzzle. It had a scent like soap, and the weight of it was pleasant to the touch, and there was something about the polite formality of it, the distance of it, that Ray couldn't dismiss, and as he thought about the fragrance of the paper, which seemed clean and still alive, like some flower in a cold chest, Ray remembered that moment with his father when, in the stink of lacquer, a mistake could have been made (like a match being struck at the wrong time) and the warehouse would have burned too soon. Ray imagined the flames, or the black shape his father would have made in front of them: perhaps, in that horrible moment, if things had gone wrong, Ray would have seen the despairing look on his father's face as he stood for that first moment when the flames spread around him. The paper seemed to be an antidote to that moment, or to the possibility of things ending in red, gold, and orange flames, tipped with wisps of smoke.

Ray ran his finger over the embossed printing and read the directions for an essay the application required. He went around the shop doing his chores, telling himself that he should take the paper into the parking lot behind the building and burn it, but instead he began to write a piece about "London in the Great Plague and Fire," imagining the city in flames, the masses of smoke so enormous as to make the sky black too, so that the entire vista was orange and yellow blazes, each one shaped like a leaf, or an impenetrable darkness. Ray added details about how the fire spread through buildings the frames of which were made of old, dry wood covered with plaster.

Then he filled in the rest of the applications and dropped them in the mail, the envelopes falling away from his fingers with a dry tick. He dropped them in and said, "All right. I'm not going to hang around to watch any fires." Then he went back to the shop and put his head down on the desk.

In two weeks Mrs. Harold's niece went back to San Francisco, to her job and her boyfriend there, her time in town (and in those motels or on those long, private drives up into the mountains between Bakersfield and Los Angeles) all disappearing into thin air. Dean came back to work, thinking things over and sitting on a pile of paper while looking through the printers' trade journals he had missed during the last few weeks.

In the evening, Dean, Marge, and Pearl and Ray had dinner

together, all of them sitting at the table and eating a pot roast made as an obvious celebration by Marge, who knew, without a word being said, that the young woman had gone. After dinner, Dean went upstairs and took out of his jacket pocket a pint bottle of liquor, and when he had broken the seal and had a sip, he got out his trombone, lifting the thing from the case and fitting the mouthpiece in, and then he played "Clementine" and "Red River Valley" while that neighbor, Mr. Carson, came to the window, listened for a while, and then said to someone inside his house, "Well, that sounds like Dean's beginning to get over her, whoever she was, the poor son of a bitch."

Ray came in and sat down on a chair and listened. The slide of the trombone moved in the shadows of the attic, the golden tube slipping in and out of the darkness, which seemed, as Ray sat there, to be filled with a miasma of his father's own character, a collection of faults and insistence that brought Dean back to this same moment, which always came as a surprise, and as Ray listened to the music he stared into the darkness, as though the things he needed to know were right there in front of him. In the sound of the instrument, which Ray felt in his chest, there was a sensation almost of a current, or currents, and in them he could distinguish only a few strands, such as his own ignorance, and his love for his father, both of which made it difficult to get a good look into the shadows of the attic. Dean put his hand on Ray's head and smiled and said, "Ah, Raymond, if you only knew how much I wish things were different than they are."

ZZZ, ZZZ, ZZZ

≠

It was late summer now and a young woman moved to town from Santa Clara. She was in her last year at school, in the same class as Ray. Her name was Iris Mason, and she came to school in her fashionable dresses, her hair perfectly done, her stockings new and making a little swish when she crossed her legs, her feet in high-heeled shoes. She sat at her desk and pushed aside the things she was supposed to be reading, put her notebooks on the floor with disdain, and opened up the makeup kit she brought along and flipped out its mirror on a little folding arm. There, in front of it, she worked on her hair, leaning her head to the side and brushing straight down. Then she put on her makeup, carefully doing her eyelashes with a thing like a little guillotine. She went about this with a methodical calmness, and when one of the girls in the class asked her what she was doing, Iris said, "Oh, wouldn't you like to know?" her voice not harsh or arch or anything.

When Iris spoke this way, the girls looked as though they'd been slapped, one of them saying to another, "That slut. Just look at her."

Ray watched her as she came into a room, and when she left a class he went after her, coming close, beginning to speak, but then passing without saying a word. Sometimes he went into a bathroom, and there, in front of a mirror, he smiled and said, "Hi, I hope you enjoy your stay," as Dean had said to Mrs. Harold's niece, the ease of it, the softness of Dean's voice then, the look in his eyes, which showed something like humor, the entire atmosphere of the man, the expression of quiet complicity all still just eluding Ray as he stood in front of the mirror. When he saw Iris again, he just glanced at her and passed by.

Once, after school, he found her sitting on a bench in the warmth of the afternoon sun, and as she turned her face to it, he came up to her and said, "You're not from around here, are you?"

"What?" she said.

Ray blushed and said, "My name's Ray Gollancz."

"Hi, Ray," she said, looking up at him.

"Well, if I can help you with anything, you let me know, hear? Nothing's too small to ask. I hope you enjoy your stay."

She just looked at him.

"Are you for real?" she said.

"Yeah," he said.

"You're blushing," she said.

"Maybe." He shrugged.

"Well, you know what you're supposed to say now?" she asked. "You're supposed to say, 'How about a Coke?'"

"How about it?" he said.

"I'll think about it," she said.

Then he turned and walked away, already talking to himself, shaking his head with mystified grief and embarrassment.

Each day she slid into her desk, her presence somehow already making the piece of furniture look inappropriate, or like some antiquated, half-forgotten memory, if only because she was all grown up and ready to escape. So she sat down, the desk reduced to the point of silliness as it confined her for a few hours every day.

Dean often came to pick Ray up from school, and when he did so he parked his van illegally at the curb, which had been painted a bright yellow. One day as Dean waited, watching students come out of the building, he was pensively brooding about the fall, the passage of time, and lost opportunities. As Ray came down the steps and walked toward his father, Iris got up from the concrete bench where she had been sitting. It was a yellowish, hazy day in California, and the air was still and as warm as cozy sheets. Iris wore a pair of blue jeans and a man's shirt, and she strolled across the sidewalk, her gait a slow, unselfconscious saunter that had about it something of the intimate warmth of the air.

She came up to the van, and as she noticed that it was parked illegally, she smiled, as though the fact that it was someplace it shouldn't have been were a kind of introduction. And when she stepped off the curb in front of the van and looked into the windshield, she faced Dean, her eyes set on his, her lips in a pleasant, almost conspiratorial smile, the corners of her eyes wrinkling a little. She looked through the window on the driver's side and said, "You know you aren't supposed to park here, don't you?" But as she spoke she went on smiling, and then she stepped into the street, not turning to see if a car was coming.

"Who was that?" asked Dean.

"A new girl," Ray said.

"She looks old enough to be a teacher," he said.

"She's a student," Ray said.

"Is she?" said Dean.

They drove quietly now, Ray thinking about Iris walking in that warm, smoky air. It seemed then that her smiling through the window at Dean had been an isolated incident, a coincidence, but that was before the next afternoon, when, in that same light and smoky heat, Iris walked past the shop, behind the window of which Ray stood, drinking a soda. Dean looked up, wiping his hands on a rag, and then went back to the press, which he had taken apart to clean, but as he picked up the first roller he started whistling "Met the Devil at the Crossroads."

So Iris sat in the classroom, dismissing it and *The Canterbury Tales* (although she had a brief interest in "The Wife of Bath's Tale") with a flick of a makeup brush, her entire aspect one of a prisoner who doesn't believe in good behavior anymore. Ray watched with amazement. She worked on her hair and nails, the file making a faint zzz, zzz, zzz as she did one finger and then another. She winked and smiled, the faintly puckered lips and those greenish eyes imbued with a secret she shared with Ray.

After class, she came up to him in the hall and said, "Say, sometimes I need a ride home. Do you think your father could take me?"

"Sure," said Ray. "But why don't I just walk you home. How would that be?"

"I'd rather ride," she said.

Iris lived in a house on the west side of town, in a neighborhood of plumbers, restaurant managers, and short-order cooks. It was a large, two-story place with an acacia tree in front, the crown of it spreading into the air at the side of the roof. Weeds grew in the front yard, and in them there sat some new Adirondack chairs and a table to match, the furniture still hung with small manila price tags. There were new curtains in the downstairs windows, too, at least in the front, but in the windows at the sides of the house there were the pull-down shades left by the previous owner.

Iris's father worked for an insurance agency in town, and her mother was a hostess in a restaurant, for both lunch and dinner. The house had the sleepy quality of a place that has been left in a hurry, the screen door open a little, some trash from the car left on the driveway, a newspaper on the front step.

One afternoon, when Dean arrived to pick Ray up, Iris came up to the van. Her skirt was tight at the knees and she walked with short steps, but she came up and stood next to the window, where she smiled now, her expression frank and a little urgent.

"Hi," she said. "My name's Iris Mason."

"I'm Dean Gollancz."

"Listen, Mr. Gollancz . . . ," she said.

"Dean," he said. "You can call me Dean. . . ."

"Dean," she said. She looked right at him and said, "Dean, I'm late. I should be home now. I'm new here and I don't know any of the people here with cars. . . . I know your son, though. Hi, Ray."

Ray sat in the passenger seat.

"Hi," he said.

"Jump in," said Dean. "I'll take you home. No trouble. Where do you live?"

She stood by the open window of the van, her cotton blouse smelling clean and bringing the scent of a linen closet. Then with a smile and with an obvious considering of possibilities, she came around to the passenger side and opened the door, her hands taking the handle with a jerk. Ray was pushed into the back of the van, not so much with a wave of Dean's hand as just by the approach of Iris. She sat in the front, dumping her books into the space between herself and Dean. Dean began to talk, his voice friendly and unhurried, relaxed, not saying anything particular, or even new, but soon they were both laughing. And by the time the van pulled up to Iris's house, there was between them the beginnings of a compact, even though it was as delicate and as fine as cobwebs, and as frail too.

The van stopped in front of that house with the weeds growing in the garden. Then Iris turned and said, "I can't thank you enough, really," and Dean said, "Anytime," his eyes filled with the bright glance of having just stopped laughing. Iris blushed and got out, slamming the door hard, swinging it into the frame from her shoulder.

In the evening, at dinner, Marge sat across from her husband, watching him. She wasn't certain yet, but there was something in his walk, in the way he looked out the window, in his whistling, even in the way he slept, his back toward her, that made Marge begin to wonder about where he was spending his spare time. They ate in the kitchen. There was a radio on the table, which was tuned to the stock market report, the voice of the announcer bringing into the kitchen a sense of competence. Dean nodded, saying, "Hear that? Chevy's stock is up. Hell, you couldn't pay me to drive a damn Chrysler."

When it was over, Marge turned the thing off.

"I think we've got to talk," she said.

"Sure," he said, although he lowered his eyes.

"We're having a little trouble this month."

"Like what?" said Dean.

He ate his dessert, his spoon clinking against the bowl from which he ate a canned peach in syrup.

"There're some extra bills and—"

"Well, they're just going to have to wait," said Dean.

"I don't know if they can," said Marge, "because some of them have been waiting from the month before last."

"What the hell is happening to the money?"

"I don't know," said Marge.

"What do you mean you don't know?" he said.

"I don't know," said Marge. "Maybe there just isn't enough."

"What's that supposed to mean?" said Dean, putting down his spoon.

"I just mean we're having some trouble, that's all," she said.

"And it's my fault, is that what you're trying to say?" he said.

"I didn't say that," said Marge.

"It's what you think," he said. Then he turned toward Ray and said, "And what about you? Are you turning on me too? What are you doing about those schools?"

"I've applied," said Ray.

"Have you?" said Dean.

Ray nodded.

"Well, shit," said Dean.

"We're at the table," said Marge.

Dean ignored this now, looking at his son. "I thought you were going to work with me."

"Nothing's been decided about that," said Ray.

"Nothing's been decided around here," said Dean. "No one knows a goddamned thing."

Then he looked down, saying nothing.

"I didn't say anything about you," said Marge. "I said something about needing money."

He nodded and looked from Marge to Ray, just staring now. Then he said to his son, "You think you're smarter than me, don't you?"

"No," said Ray.

"Well, let me tell you something, Mr. Good Test Taker, there's a lot more to being alive than some shitty multiple-choice test."

"We're at dinner," said Marge. "Watch your language."

"Language?" said Dean. "I've got some language all right." He turned back to Ray. "Well, we need some money. Are you going to help me get it?"

"Yes," said Ray.

"Don't take him," said Marge. "Not now."

Dean hit the table, making the spoon in the bowl with the canned peach clink.

"Goddamn it," said Dean. "I've had it around here. No one understands a thing anymore. How come everything has to change?"

"I told you to watch your language," said Marge.

Dean picked up his spoon, and then dropped it into the bowl.

"All right," he said, turning to Marge. "I'll get the money."

No one said a thing, and then Dean went back to eating.

"Go on. Eat. Let's not let it go to waste," he said.

"I'll go with you," said Ray. "We'll get the money."

Ray and Dean walked up to the corner, to Sonny's stationery store, where they went in, Dean going up to the counter and saying, "How many quarters you got? You have five dollars' worth? I got to make a phone call."

Sonny counted them out, piling them up in five neat groups, which Dean swept into his hand, saying to Ray, "Come on." They went along the long rack for out-of-town papers and magazines, Ray glancing once at the Swedish Reader series, on the covers of which there were blond women in black garter belts. "Listen," said Dean. "Everything's got to be done with cash. Leave no records." Then he stepped into the oak telephone booth at the end of the magazine rack, one of those with an accordion door and a light that went on when the door was closed. Dean dialed and said, "I know what it is," and then put the money in, slamming one coin in after another, turning once as he did to look at Ray. Through the closed door Ray heard Dean say, "Is he there? Tell him it's Dean. From Bakersfield." A little later Dean said, "Hi. How are things? Well, I was just wondering if you had anything for me. No, it doesn't have to be big. Hell, a booth in a parking lot is all right. I'm not real particular now. Well, sure. I know. Time is a consideration. No, I'm not saying you don't understand. All right. Yeah. Well, if that's the best you can do. Okay." He hung up and pushed the door open.

"It's going to be a few weeks," said Dean. "Doesn't that beat all? You know, Raymond, I'm tired of being ashamed." They walked past the magazine rack and into the street, saying good night to Sonny. "Jesus, do I need something to pick me up," said Dean.

At school there were days when Iris's seat was vacant, not only in one class but in all of them, and Ray went from one to the other, hearing voices talk about "The Miller's Tale," John Milton, William Shakespeare, or quadratic equations and equal and congruent triangles, and while he heard the drone of the voices he looked at that empty seat, which seemed to follow him from one room to the next.

At lunch Ray walked from the school to the shop, where he rattled the locked door once, and then went to the parking lot behind it, to the van that sat on the gray, smoke-colored asphalt. The late-summer light, which was filled with dust, seemed to fall in lines that streaked from the top of the shop building to the ground. Ray stood, looking at the van, not entirely certain he wanted to go ahead, but then, with a jerk, he pulled the door open and started the engine. He drove to the block where there was that house with the weeds growing in the front yard, and there, not right in front of the place but parked discreetly up the block, was Dean's car.

Ray sat for a moment, just looking at it, tapping his hand against the steering wheel. The yard was quiet, the overgrown flower beds appearing still and somehow guarding a secret, and the windows of the house, with their new curtains, had about them the air of something that is almost smirking in its exclusion. Ray looked at it, and then he turned around and drove back to the shop, where he abandoned the van and then walked through the slanting light of the afternoon until he came to Sonny's Stationery, and there, standing in front of the wire racks, he went through the *Los Angeles Times*, the *Seattle Herald Dispatch*, the *San Francisco Examiner*, and the papers from Utah and Oregon, taking them down with a jerk and glancing at the accounts of fires. He stopped when he came to the story of a "suspicious" one.

The newsprint had a slight dampness, something like the moisture of a fresh rose petal, and in the dewy promise of it, as though the paper were some living thing, in the cool touch of it, Ray thought of his father, of the man standing at the same rack and going through the same papers, and as he looked at a photograph of a warehouse that had vanished into smoke and ashes (foundation included), he did so with the recognition that the fires portrayed in the pages had the same attraction for him as they had for his father, since both he and his father stood here and looked into the papers out of a keen sense of having been excluded, not to mention that Ray did so with the apprehension that things were somehow getting out of control.

In the afternoons, Dean was at the shop, although his movements were subdued and at times he stopped and stared out the window, or just stopped and held a stack of paper or a roller from the press or a can of solvent. At school, Iris came into the class and sat down, still immaculately dressed and still moving with a gait that had a tidy, crisp swing to it. When she looked at Ray it wasn't with a wink, or anything like it, but with curiosity and with seriousness too.

There were days when Iris simply disappeared from school, calling in sick. She waited behind those pulled-down shades in the upstairs of her parents' house until Dean drove up the block and stopped at a discreet distance.

Ray found a book of matches in Dean's car from an ice cream parlor in a town twenty miles south, and because of it he knew that after Dean and Iris had finished in that house with the weeds in the yard, they had gotten into Dean's car, both of them tired and hot and sweaty and perhaps even sore, and then driven twenty miles, both of them not so much mystified by how the entire thing had happened as reassured by the power of it, which, once let loose, had an enormous scale of its own, and when they got to that ice cream parlor they both had gone in and had a long, cool chocolate milk shake, each of them tasting the ice cream and looking into the other's eyes with a sweet, delicious, and undaunted acknowledgment of a forbidden pleasure.

Ray went on working in the shop, but now he walked from school, and when he was doing his chores, sweeping up or cutting paper or answering the phone, Dean avoided looking at him directly, and when they went home they were silent, both of them walking along, arms swinging, eyes set on the horizon or on some distant object. Now, when they were together, they hardly spoke at all aside from the necessary words about a job, and in their usual silence, in Dean's wistful and obvious return from Iris's bed, there was something else, too, which was a kind of argument, an insistence that had to do not only with a young woman (who made Dean feel a little better for a while) but with buildings disappearing in a sudden flash of flame: it was as though Dean believed all his trouble in getting what he wanted from his son was only a failure of will, and that if Dean's will were demonstrated clearly enough, if he took what he wanted in the open, or at least in a way his son was forced to see, why then his word, or his desires in other things, would be respected too. And when on those rare occasions Dean looked into his son's eyes and saw a fury so deep as to have a color, a variety of black-purple in the pupil, Dean took it as a sign that he only had to be more willful, more insistent than before. The two of them went through the days, working in the afternoons, walking home together, the air around them heavy with a miasma that was compounded of anger, desire, willfulness, and a constant brooding about flames.

Once, just at dusk, when they came up to the house, Dean turned to Ray and said, "Why don't we go and sit out back. What do you say?"

Ray looked at him.

"It's a nice night," said Dean.

"Yes, I guess it is," said Ray. "All right. Let's sit."

They went back to the steps of the rear porch and sat down. The sky was gray and crimson, and there were a few birds flying, hurrying someplace before dark. Dean draped his arm across Ray's shoulders, and Ray let it stay there, the weight of it reminding him of affection directed to a child. They watched the fading light, the yard and houses turning into black facades, the light bleeding out of the sky, and around them it was quiet, a silence that was disturbed only by the almost hallucinatory beating of their hearts. Then Ray pushed the arm away. He went on looking at the sky for a while, until it was completely dark, and then he stood up.

"Thanks, bub," said Dean. "For sitting with me."

"Sure," said Ray. "It was a pretty night."

"But I guess it hasn't changed anything between us, has it?" said Dean.

"No," said Ray. "I guess not."

It took about three weeks for a new car to pull up in front of Ray's house, and it didn't arrive with the slow, careful speed of someone who has business to do (like selling life insurance, for instance) but with the squeal and jerk of someone who has decided that threats aren't really good enough. The car stopped in front of the house, angled to the curb a little, the rear end sticking into the street. Iris's father got out of the car, his jacket open, his tie flapping over his shoulder in the wind of his own hurried, half-running locomotion.

Ray looked out the upstairs window and then said, "Father, there's someone here to see you."

"Oh?" said Dean.

Dean waited in the upstairs hall, standing in his bathrobe, which he was wearing because he had just gotten out of the shower. Then he turned and went downstairs, walking slowly, his hair dark and shiny, slicked back.

Iris's father walked up to the porch, and as he stood there, breathing hard, he didn't knock so much as pound, bringing down his open hand with a repeated, angry whack, the sound exaggerated because the screen door wasn't fastened, the edge of it slamming against the frame every time he hit it.

Dean walked into the living room and opened the door.

"What's the trouble?" he said.

"Who are you?" said Iris's father.

He was in his late forties, dark, and bald. He was overweight and he was breathing hard, panting like a runner after a race.

"Dean Gollancz," said Dean.

"Well, you know who I am?" asked Iris's father.

"No," said Dean.

"I'm Robert Mason," he said.

"Pleased to meet you," said Dean.

"Are you?" said Mason. "I'm Iris's father. You know Iris, don't you?"

"Yes," said Dean.

Mr. Mason took deep breaths now, throwing up his chest as he did so, sucking at the air. His chest rose with the effort, and his skin was the gray color of a dead fish.

"I've had three heart attacks," said Mr. Mason.

"I'm sorry to hear that," said Dean.

"Is that right?" said Mr. Mason.

"I said I was sorry," said Dean. "Come in. Would you like a glass of water?"

"Yes," said Mr. Mason, "I think I better. It would serve you right, you know that, if I dropped dead right here." He went on panting, and then he reached into his pocket and took out a pillbox. "I've got to take some nitro. I've got pains."

"Do you want a doctor?" asked Dean. "Or an ambulance?"

"No," said Mr. Mason. "Get the water."

Dean went into the kitchen and brought back a tumbler of water and held it out. Mr. Mason took it and put the pill into his mouth and drank, throwing his head back.

"It takes a little while to work," he said.

He still stood there, just as angry as before, but after a while he didn't pant so hard. He put a hand to the middle of his chest and pressed there with the heel of it.

"Maybe we should get your car out of the middle of the street," said Dean. "If someone comes by here fast like they do, why, they're going to hit—"

"Leave it there. I'm not worried about the car," said Mr. Mason.

"Well, sure," said Dean.

"How do you know Iris?" said Mr. Mason.

"My son goes to school with her."

"That's right," said Mr. Mason. "That's right. What are we going to do about it?"

Dean sighed.

"I guess it's got to come to an end," he said.

"That's right, that's absolutely right," said Mr. Mason. "Where is he?"

"What?" said Dean.

"That son of yours," said Mr. Mason.

"You want to see my son?" said Dean.

"That's right. That's absolutely right. My wife and I knew Iris was seeing someone during the day. Sometimes she even stayed away from school. We have proof of that. At first she wouldn't say who it was, but then I held her feet to the fire. I shook it out of her." He started panting again, his eyes large now and bright. "We had evidence, too."

"Evidence?" said Dean.

"Stains," said Mr. Mason.

"What kind of stains?"

"On the sheets," said Mr. Mason.

He started panting harder again.

"Oh," said Dean.

"She said it was your son. The neighbors saw him hanging around once or twice in your van, too."

Dean looked at Mr. Mason. He said nothing at all. There was a clock on the mantel and for a moment the only sound in the room was that steady ticking. Then he said, "Just a minute."

He turned and climbed the stairs, not hesitating at the landing in the middle but just turning there and coming the rest of the way up, his hair still slick from the shower, his eyes looking up as he climbed. Mr. Mason went on breathing heavily. Dean stood at the top of the stairs.

"You were wrong, Raymond," he said, "he doesn't want to see me. He wants to see you." He leaned close to Ray. "Listen, if word got around in this town that I was spending time with a high school girl, I'd be ruined."

"Maybe you should have thought of that before," said Ray.

58

"Maybe you're right," said Dean.

They looked at each other, neither one of them flinching.

"There are two things you can do," said Dean.

"What's the first?" asked Ray.

"You can go down there and start whining about being accused of something you didn't do," said Dean.

"What's the other?" asked Ray.

"You can go down there and take this like you had some backbone. You decide." Then he turned and said, "Come on."

He took two steps and stopped, his eyes a little wide now. He stood that way for just a minute, and then he turned around and went back up to where he had been before, his face opposite his son's just as it had been before.

"Say, you weren't going over there too, were you? You know, some afternoon when I thought you were out running cross-country?"

Ray waited, looking at his father.

"Well?" said Dean. "Answer me. Were you going over there too?"

Mr. Mason went on breathing downstairs.

"I guess you'd like to know, wouldn't you?" said Ray.

"Yes," said Dean.

"Well," said Ray, "there are two things you can do about it."

"What's the first?" asked Dean.

"You can start whining about it," said Ray.

"What's the other," asked Dean.

"You can take not knowing like you had some backbone," said Ray.

Dean swallowed and stared at his son.

"That's all you've got to say?" said Dean.

"Yes," said Ray. "Why don't you get out of the way."

"Listen," said Dean. "This is no time to get angry."

"No?" said Ray. "Why the hell not? Get out of my way."

They went downstairs, Dean first, Ray following, their heads bobbing up and down at each step, just like men filing down out of the seats of a stadium after a baseball game. Mr. Mason stood in the middle of the room, his head back, the light from the hall in his eyes.

He looked pale, and he was still breathing hard as he stepped forward, his hand out, the fingers reaching for the front of Ray's shirt.

"Just what the hell do you think you're doing?" said Mr. Mason.

"Nothing," said Ray.

"You call what you been doing nothing?" he said. "You know what you need? You need to join the army. That will straighten little bastards like you out—"

"Watch your language," said Dean.

"What do *you* call him?" asked Mason, turning toward Dean.

"That's between Raymond and me," said Dean.

Mr. Mason gasped a couple of times, now turning back to Ray.

"Did you ever think about getting her pregnant? Do you care about her?"

"Yes," said Ray.

Dean watched Ray closely now.

"Yes what? Do you care, or did you think about her getting pregnant?" said Mr. Mason.

"Yes that I care," said Ray.

"What the hell would you do if she got pregnant? What about that, smart guy?"

Ray stood there blinking.

"That's right. That's how much you thought, isn't it?"

"Well . . . ," Ray said.

"Are you contradicting me? How dare you? What do you think it does for a beautiful young woman to end up pregnant? I bet you don't feel bad at all, do you, you little piece of filth."

"I told you to watch your language," said Dean, stepping up to Mason, glaring at him now, already clenching a fist.

"All right, all right," said Mason.

"Maybe she takes birth-control pills," said Dean. "Maybe that's the way it was. Maybe there wasn't even any chance of her getting pregnant. Maybe you didn't know a goddamned thing about it."

"How would *he* know that?" said Mr. Mason.

"Maybe she told him," said Dean.

Mason turned toward Ray and stepped close, his chest heaving, the sweat on the gray skin of his face now glistening unhealthily.

"All right," said Mason. "I want the truth. You hear me? I want to know exactly what happened. Is that the way it was?"

Ray looked from Mason to Dean.

"Well?" said Mason.

"It's the moment of truth, Ray," said Dean. "Tell us how it was."

"Yes," said Ray, "I guess that's the way it was. . . ."

For a moment Mason just stared. Then he took a large hand-kerchief from his back pocket and wiped his head, and when he was done he stood there holding the white piece of cloth. He rubbed the center of his chest again and said to Dean, "Sometimes I don't know what things are coming to."

Dean looked at his son.

"Yeah," said Dean, "I know what you mean."

"I used to sell a hell of a lot of life insurance," said Mr. Mason. "I sold it by the bale. Now I seem to have lost the touch, you know? It just went like that." He snapped his fingers and looked at Dean. "I don't get it."

Dean sighed. "Yeah," he said. "I've got money worries too."

"Do you?" asked Mason. "Cash flow?"

"You could say that," said Dean.

Mason closed his eyes for a moment, but when he opened them, he looked at Ray again and said, "All right, maybe she told you. But what about the morality of what you were doing?"

Ray shrugged.

"Well, so much for morality," said Mason. "I bet you don't know the meaning of the word."

"You'd be surprised about that," said Ray.

"Don't you get smart," said Mr. Mason. "Listen. You stay away from her. If I catch you with her, or even hear of it . . . I swear, you'll live to regret it."

Ray stared at him.

"You don't understand, do you?" said Mr. Mason. "If I have to come back, I'm going to bring a gun. Don't you understand? I'll kill you."

"What did you say?" said Dean.

"You heard me," said Mason. "I've got a forty-five. I've got a box of ammunition. I'll bring them next time."

"How dare you!" said Dean, taking a step toward Mason.

"You want him alive, you keep him away from Iris," said Mason. Then he turned and went out, slamming the door behind him, the sound enormous in the living room. Dean looked at his son for a moment, the two of them hearing that lingering BAM!

"Do you think he's serious?" asked Ray.

"Well, I'll tell you," said Dean. "Where these things are involved, you never can tell."

Ray looked at his father.

"So, does that change things?" asked Dean. "Do you want to run out there and tell Iris's father about how there's been a misunderstanding?"

"No," said Ray.

"Why?" said Dean. "This is tailor-made. Jesus, you could have me sweating."

"We'll settle things between you and me," said Ray. "That's all. It's a private matter, isn't it? I'm not going to whine to anyone. If you think that, then you better think again."

"Well, well," said Dean. "I'll be goddamned."

"It's between you and me. That's all," said Ray.

"I'll be goddamned," said Dean. "So that's what you're made out of?"

Ray stared at him. The two of them stood in the living room, the place having a faintly domestic, closed-up quality and the lingering odor of cooked chops and baked tuna casserole. Dean turned quickly and went through the door, onto the porch.

"Wait," he said. "Just wait a minute."

Mr. Mason made a limping, slow passage across the lawn. The light was yellow and it hung in the yard like smoke. Mr. Mason stopped, one hand on the open door of the car, one foot on the curb, the other in the street, and when he turned, his face came around in one furious swing. The street was empty, almost peaceful, the trees on it absolutely still.

"Wait," said Dean.

Mr. Mason put a hand to his chest.

"What is it?"

"It wasn't my son," said Dean.

"No?" said Mr. Mason. "Then if it wasn't him, I'd sure like to know who it was. I've had it with this. You hear me?"

"Yes," said Dean.

"Who was it?"

"You're looking at him," said Dean.

Mr. Mason stared for a moment, his gaze solid there in the yard with the yellow grass and the lime-colored shrubs. He slowly took a handkerchief from his pocket, drawing it out by the corner like a magician.

"Don't make me laugh. You're almost my age. What could she see in you?" said Mr. Mason as he looked at the trim, handsome man who stood on the porch. "You won't save him that way. I wouldn't have thought you capable of such a story."

Then he turned and got back into the car, slamming the door and looking at the house, Dean, and Ray with an appalled disbelief. He started the engine and gunned it, the exhaust coming in a smokeless rush. The car pulled away and then slowed down at the corner, the taillights glowing before it turned and disappeared into the pale air.

Dean came back inside and sat down on the sofa. Ray sat down too, and for a while they thought things over, both of them blinking in the same way, the shape of their hands identical as they hung from their knees, both a little surprised now.

"Can I ask you a question?" said Ray.

"Sure," said Dean, who was staring into the yard, the dark netting of the screen door making the grass, the trees, the dusty street, the smoky air all seem veiled, like skin through fishnet stockings.

"Did you know that after Mason yelled at me he wouldn't believe you'd been seeing Iris?" asked Ray.

Dean looked over now and said, "What a dirty mind you have."

"Answer me," said Ray.

Dean looked at the screen door, and then he turned to look at his son. He just stared, sucking on his lip.

"Ray," he said after a while, "I guess the truth is, yeah, the possibility occurred to me."

Then he laughed.

"Well?" said Ray.

"Well what?" said Dean.

"Are you going to leave her alone?"

"It might be a lot more exciting with her old man packing a gun," said Dean. "But, yeah, it's over."

Dean stood up.

"Where are you going?" said Ray.

"Oh," said Dean. "I just thought I'd go upstairs. Haven't played my trombone since I don't know when."

THE PAINTED
JUNGLE

Iris was out of school for a week, although when she came back she was still carrying her makeup kit. The small hinged box with the fold-out mirror seemed somehow used, or travel worn, like a suitcase that has been handled roughly and yet still implies all the romance of travel, one that hints of out-of-the-way islands with puffs of clouds overhead, of green, fogbound coasts. She had her books, too, but she still dismissed William Wordsworth or Robert Herrick with her small eye-shadow brush, and when the girls asked her where she'd been, she said, "Wouldn't you like to know?"

Ray waited for her after school. When she saw him, she walked right toward him. She said, "You know you aren't supposed to bother me anymore."

"Anymore," he said.

For a moment they looked at one another.

"Well, what is it?" she asked.

"I was wondering if we could have that Coke?"

"Why?" she said.

"I'd just like to have a Coke with you," he said.

She looked at him for a moment.

"Didn't my father threaten to kill you?" she said.

"I'm not worrying that much," he said.

"No," she said. "That's wrong. He came home and took out that gun and showed it to me."

"Well, there's only one thing to do about that," said Ray.

"What?"

"Let's go have a Coke."

She looked at him again.

"Let me think about it," she said.

Two days later Iris came into a room where the words "Explaining God's Will to Man" were on the blackboard, and as she went to her seat she looked right at Ray. Then, a few minutes later, Ray felt a slight, repeated tickle, which at first was so light he ignored it, but then it came again and again, and when he made a quick turn of exasperation, he saw a note, the thing pushed against his side by one of those girls who used to ask Iris where she had been, the piece of paper being pressed against him with the words, "It's from her." Ray unfolded the piece of paper and saw, written in a scrawl across the pale blue lines of the sheet, "Do you have any idea what would happen if I got caught again?"

Ray sat there, hearing talk about Milton and the conspiracy in heaven, and while he did so there came over him a thrill, the cold, prickly touch moving over his back and into his scalp. He slowly tore a sheet of paper from the notebook, the sound it made coming like a languid unzipping, and then he wrote, his hand shaking a little, "Yes. He said he'd kill me. I don't think he'd hurt you, though."

So she went on thinking, not looking at him when she had the chance, and going her own way when she was out of those dusty, chalky buildings, her entire gait upright, correct, certain now, even when there was good reason to be other things, like frightened, or cowed, or maybe just quietly angry.

The next day he felt that same insistent tickle, and when he opened the folded paper he saw, in that same scrawl, a message that said, "All right. How about tomorrow? You know where the house is, don't you? In the morning, about ten o'clock."

In the morning, just before ten, Ray went along those cool, tree-lined streets that led to the house with those fancy curtains in the downstairs window and the weeds in the yard. It was a clear day, the sky pale blue, the color of light coming through snow, and in the air there was something, some anticipation so great as to come with a pleasurable itch or sting or just a keen pressure that Ray felt generally, all over his skin, but mostly in the pit of his stomach.

He knocked on the door. She answered, and as she stood in the doorway she said, "We haven't got a lot of time."

He stepped in and they closed the door together, their hands touching as they both pushed the thing shut, the air rushing out of the frame and over their fingers.

"My parents are going to check on me at one o'clock. Come on."

They went upstairs into a girlish room with ruffles around the bottom of the bed and with prints of flowers on the walls, Iris saying, "Here. Let me help you. Here. Here. Take your socks off."

He stood in the cool room, now feeling the touch of her, the powdery sensation of bare skin. Then she pulled him down so he sat next to her, and as she did so she said, "Don't make noise. You aren't a screamer, are you?"

"I don't know," he said.

"When you feel like screaming, you just look into my eyes. Come on. Here. Isn't that nice?"

"Yes," he said. "Oh, yes."

"Oh, sugar, say something nice now. Just something nice."

"I never felt so good," he said.

"Nicer," she said.

"Oh," he said. "Anything. You tell me."

"You say it," she said.

"I love you," he said.

"Why?" she said.

"Because you're outside all the rules," he said.

She closed her eyes.

"You don't mean it," she said, "but it's nice to hear."

"I mean it," he said. "Do you believe me?"

She looked at his face now, her eyes narrowed.

"I'll be able to tell if you care," she said. "Look in my eyes. Just watch. Oh, sugar. You just watch for a while."

Outside there was the sound of a car in the street, the engine slowly idling by. She put her hands over his ears. The sheets and pillows had a slight, definite odor, of her hair, of sweat, of bad dreams, of lazy mornings, of the things she had brought up to bed to eat, toast and sugar and butter, all of it mixing together until the blend was so complete as to include just about everything. There was the sound of another car in the street and they both turned toward it, still feeling that warmth between their skin.

Iris got up and went into the bathroom. Through the door there was the sound of running water, and then she came out, where she stood against the white door and looked at him. Then she walked across the room and sat down, getting back under the sheet and whispering, "Did you mean it? Did you?" Ray put his head against hers, but as he began to speak, she touched his lips with her fingers, saying, "That's all right. . . . You don't have to say anything. I keep forgetting that if I ask no questions I won't hear any lies."

"I wouldn't say it unless I meant it," he said.

She shook her head. Then she closed her eyes and curled up next to him, just touching him.

"Don't," she said. "I don't want to start thinking it's true. That gets to be a lot of work."

They went downstairs. She took a Coke out of the icebox, pulled the tab, and the syrup-colored foam rose up from the opening in the can.

"Here's your Coke," she said.

He sat in the kitchen, at the table. The room smelled of breakfast, of coffee and toast, the scent a little stale. Both of them noticed the silence of the house, the quiet domesticity of the place having the aspect of some sea where they were adrift.

"You don't mind if I talk about your father, do you?"

"No," he said. "Unless you're going to tell me how we're different or the same or—"

"No," she said, swallowing. "I won't talk about that. No. It's just that Dean was . . ."

She stopped and looked at Ray.

"He was always talking about the Big Time," said Iris. "It was like a place you could go to . . ."

"Sure," said Ray. "The Big Time. Like Abbadabba Berman . . ."

"Harry Pierpont," she said.

"Homer Van Meter," said Ray.

"Fat Charley Makley," she said.

"Baron Lamm," said Ray.

"Walter Devitch," she said. "Those are the names. He always was trying to figure out if Harry Pierpont was more Big Time than Walter Devitch. . . ."

"I know," said Ray.

"It was pretty sad," she said. "Or tawdry."

"No," said Ray. "Don't say that."

"Oh?" she said. "I guess you want to stick up for him."

Ray sighed.

"Yeah," he said. "That's the best way of putting it."

"I don't know," said Iris, shaking her head. "Sometimes I think he's just not too smart."

"I told you about talking like that," said Ray.

"You heard me," said Iris. She looked him right in the eyes.

"Maybe he's smarter than you think," said Ray. "Did he talk about Chinatown?"

"No," said Iris.

Ray nodded, as though having something confirmed, but he still sat there, shaking his head.

"Hey, listen," she said. "I'm sorry. I didn't mean to make you angry. Okay?"

"Sure," said Ray. "Fine."

"What's that about Chinatown?"

"Nothing," he said.

Iris sat there, her eyes moving from Ray's to the window beyond him, through which there was the yard. It was so still as to seem to be a part of the peacefulness of the entire neighborhood at this hour, as though a clear, serene cloud had settled into the streets. Then she looked down and said, "Dean's going to die in this town. What could be worse?"

"A lot," said Ray. "There are some other places he might die."

"Like where?" she said.

"That's his business," said Ray.

She put a hand to her hair, brushing it out, absently running her fingers through it. The Coke was cold and the can was sweating, and Ray ran a finger along the side, making a mark in the condensation. Then he shrugged and said, "What are you doing tomorrow?"

"I'm going to see you," she said.

He picked up the can of Coke and tasted the syrupy sweetness. "What time?" he said.

"In the morning," she said. "Same time. I think we can get away with another day. Then we'll figure something else out."

She sat in the kitchen with its domestic odor of toast and butter and bacon, but there was desperation in her glance as she thought about taking chances (and serious ones, too, given the pistol that her father had taken out and shown her). Ray stared back, the two of them realizing that there was a difference between appreciating danger (as they had done before Ray had actually come to the house) and danger itself. They both waited, each feeling a shakiness in the legs and hands (from the time they had spent in that room upstairs). Ray said, his expression showing that he wanted to smile but was not quite able to, "Well, what is there to be frightened of?"

"Not much," she said, her expression about the same as his.

Then she looked away and went to the counter, where there was a small pad and a pencil, which she used to write down a short note, and when she held it out there was a certain mixture of vulnerability and daring. She held out the paper and said, "Here. Do you want it?"

Outside a car drove up toward the house, its tires making a dry tearing sound on the asphalt. The puttering of its engine had about it all the menace of the ordinary, workaday world (which seemed so interested in forbidding a moment such as this one). They both turned toward the car, Iris's fingers pressing down on the kitchen table until her nails turned white at the tips. Outside it was a cool, clear morning and there was in the air an innocent anticipation of the oppressive smokiness of a California winter. The car passed the house and continued up the street. Iris still held the piece of paper out, saying, "Do you?" Ray took it, his fingers just brushing the edge of the small sheet (in which he felt her trembling and her determination too). So he took the paper, seeing only that there was something written on it, and then he folded it up and put it into his shirt pocket. Then he reached down and picked up the light, cool can and had a sip, concentrating on the syrupy sweetness of the fuzzy stuff inside.

Iris stood up and they climbed the stairs again, although this time they didn't go into the room with the skirt around the bed and the love seat with the pink slipcover, but farther along, into a room at the end of the hall that overlooked the street and in which there was a double bed, a telephone, two identical bureaus. Everything about the room had a subdued, tired domesticity, the place having an air of the loss of romance and a deadly resignation, which Iris went through as though it were a stagnant pond. She stood in front of a closet, the door of which she swung open, and on a small night-stand, which had been put at the end of the clothes, there was something that looked like a blue-black shadow and that, with the light of the room falling on it, revealed itself to be that pistol, next to which there was a clip, handy to be shoved into the butt of the thing. Iris held the door open and showed that blue-black shadow even though it made her vulnerable, doing so as a matter of honesty and wanting there to be no misunderstanding on this score.

Ray looked inside and then back at Iris, directly into her face, saying, "All right. I understand," and reached over with one finger and pushed the door shut. It closed with a hush of air. Iris closed her eyes and swallowed.

They both turned away, back to the hall, and as they went down the stairs, Iris said, "Think about it. You don't have to come back here."

"All right," he said. "I'll think about it."

He went out the door and into the cool air, and then he walked downtown, passing the stationer's, the liquor store, the soda fountain, and stopping in front of the pawnshop, where he looked at the instruments hung in the window over the array of pistols, the two appearing there as a perfect balance between beauty and trouble. The trombones had the elongated shape of a flower, a daffodil, say, and there was in the tarnish of them and the slight dents here and there the evidence of things gone wrong, of escapes from windows and back rooms, of quick exits, if not just of the general rough handling of the unexpected. He reached into his pocket and took out the slip of paper, on which there was written, "Did you really mean it, sugar?"

So now they began in earnest, not coming right out and admitting it, but nevertheless working up to it slowly. They started with small, only mildly dangerous things, running across the street together when they should have waited (that quick taking of steps before the rush of chrome and steel and the sudden noisy honk of the horn following them into the bedroom, too, where it brought them a little closer together), but soon it was more than just that. Outside of town, on the road to Los Angeles, there was a straightaway that came to a dogleg turn. They discovered it, or the effect of it, almost by accident. They drove out of town one night, just to get away from things, Iris lying to her parents about where she was going and Ray borrowing his father's car, which Iris got into with a frank familiarity, saying, "Let me drive. I'm all tense." She got behind the wheel and moved the seat up and put her long fingers over the keys in the ignition, and then she started the engine and drove south, seeing the red glow from Los Angeles in the distance. She went fast along the road, pushing the speedometer up, sixty-five, seventy, and faster in that stretch before the turn, and as she approached it she looked over at Ray, seeing the alarm in his eyes, and something else too. She pushed the accelerator down, the terror of the moment sweeping over her, and in it she had the sense of pushing through the things that confused her or made her doubt him, and for a moment, as the yellow sign whisked by (on which the shape of the road ahead was shown in an enormous black S), she was able to believe, if only because he was with her and willing to go along, no matter what, that he meant what he said. She just looked at him, and then slowed down, taking the curve as it should be taken, glancing over at him from time to time and already wanting to get into a room where they could have some privacy. Neither one of them said a thing. And on the way back, when she approached the turn again she went faster than before, glancing at him and seeing that same half-crazed determination, which left both of them shaking, Iris saying, as they came out of the turn, "Listen, I've got ten dollars in my handbag. Have you got any money? There's a motel on the outside of town. Well?"

"Yes," he said. "Stop there. I've got the ten dollars."

They pulled up at the place and Ray went into the office, up to the counter, where he filled out the registration card in a scrawl, paying with her ten dollars and his (her bill having a scent from the small bag in which she carried it) and then picked up the key, not embarrassed at all, just walking out the door toward the parking lot in front of the rooms, where Iris was waiting, biting her lip as she tried to keep that sense of being able to believe him from slipping away after all. So they went into the room, where there was a chlorinated odor of sheets that hadn't been washed so much as sterilized, not even caring about it and the cheap furniture or the green, deadly color of the drapes. All of these things disappeared as they sat down next to one another, fumbling and desperate, Iris saying, "All right. I believe you."

There were moments when Iris watched him, her expression appearing almost disinterested, but in fact she was really more concerned than ever. They met in a department store, or a bookstore, or in the darkness of a movie theater, and as Iris revealed some small, seemingly bland detail of her life (such as buying some makeup), she looked at him as though daring him to give some hint, or to show that it wasn't just danger that was keeping them together but understanding too. He looked at the tube she held in her hand and said, "It's a disguise, isn't it, a way of getting away?"

"Yes," she said, looking down. "That's right."

One afternoon in the fall, when it was hot and the sky was a leadlike blue-gray, they went south to a river that flowed out of the mountains between Bakersfield and Los Angeles. The river was deep and blue, and they parked and walked along a railroad trestle, and when they were over the water, Iris took off her jeans and blouse and threw them onto the small beach a hundred feet below, and as she stood there, the hot wind blowing around her, she said, "Well, are you going to jump?"

Ray took off his clothes, rolled them into a ball, and threw them onto the small beach below. It was a long way down and the clothes made a flapping descent, like a parachute that won't open. In the distance there was a flat plain, which was almost a yellow color, something like butter. In the air, about halfway down (with the wind giving him an idea of just how fast he was moving after all), he looked up and saw her on the trestle, her expression one of terror and delight (if only because, for a moment, both of them were breaking through that sense of being cut off, or so love starved as to be unable to really trust someone else). And in the watery explosion that surrounded him when he had hit the river, Ray heard another sound, an aquatic rush that came with a concussion he felt in his chest. She hit the water too, her hands reaching out to him through the white, bubbly chains that rose around them in that cold, blue water.

So they went along, Iris not only taking, but giving too, since Ray began to let her have glimpses of his own moments. He left a catalog from one of those eastern schools where she could find it and even the scores of the tests he had taken, Iris looking at them and the school catalog and saying, "Sure. It would be nice to get out of here. Wouldn't it?"

Ray was using his father's car so often that Dean said, "Hey, listen. Don't you think it's time you got one of your own?"

Ray looked at him and nodded, saying, "Yes. I guess you're right," and then he started looking through the paper, circling the cars he could afford.

He and Iris drove out in the afternoons to look them over, Volkswagens, Chevrolets, Dodges, until they finally came to a 1954 Mercury. The owner of it was going into the army, and he stood in front of the open hood, beneath which there was a flathead V-8 engine with two four-barrel carburetors, not to mention that there was a Moon tachometer on the dashboard and a four-speed transmission, the lever for which operated through a hole that had been cut in the floor. It had Moon racing cams, too. The owner described the car with sadness if not regret, and Iris looked at Ray and said, "This one."

Ray had the money in his pocket (which had come from those afternoons when he had worked in the shop), and he began to peel off the twenties, putting them down on the trunk of the car, where Iris held them with her thumb to keep them from blowing away.

Dean went on waiting for a call from Chinatown, and when he heard Ray's car, with that throaty exhaust, pull into the driveway, he said, "Jesus, why couldn't you have bought a car that's easier on gas?" Then, in the evening, he looked out the window and said, "I wonder what's happening in Chinatown. What do you think, Ray?"

"I don't know," said Ray.

"It better not be too much longer," said Dean.

Iris's father went on watching her. He took out the pistol again, breathing hard, the heavy piece of metal seeming to make him feel there was some control in the world after all. Iris's mother came home from work, tired and angry and somehow confused that things had turned out the way they had.

In a darkened movie theater, Iris whispered to Ray, "I'm thinking of getting out of town."

Ray looked over at her.

"I think things are getting out of hand," said Iris.

"Do you?" he said.

"I'm feeling bad all the time," she said. "I'm having bad dreams."

"Tell me about them," he said.

"No," she said. "That's all right."

"Where are you going to go?" he asked.

"Guess," she said.

"L.A.," he said.

"That's right," she said.

"What do you know about L.A.?" he said.

"It's got to be better than here. Someone's going to get killed here."

Ray shrugged.

"I don't know," he said.

"Well, I do," she said. "Listen. Let's take a chance."

"Doing what?" he asked.

"Let's go to L.A. for a couple of days," she said. "My father's going to be away. I'll make up some excuse to my mother."

"What's the chance of getting caught?" said Ray.

She looked over at him with the same expression as when they had been approaching that turn at ninety miles an hour or when he had been standing in the wind a hundred feet above the water.

"All right," he said.

She looked straight ahead again.

"I don't know anything about L.A.," she said. "But I'm going to move there. I'm going to get out of here and move down there."

"I know something about it," he said.

"What do you know about?"

"Chinatown," said Ray.

"How do you know about that?" asked Iris.

"I've been down there," said Ray. "That's all."

"What were you doing?" she asked.

"Business," he said.

"What business?"

Ray shrugged.

"Why won't you tell me?" she said. "Don't you trust me?"

"Look," he said. "We'll go to Los Angeles for a few days. You can see if you want to move there. Let's leave it at that."

"Sure," said Iris. "Okay. Next week. All right?"

Then they both sat in the darkness, watching the movie, a black-and-white movie about a spy, and in it there were shots of Berlin, which was damp and rainy, and when people spoke, their words came in misty shreds, and as Iris watched she went on thinking about Chinatown. From time to time she whispered again, "Don't you trust me? Don't you?"

They left for Los Angeles on a morning just before Christmas, and as they came into town, going along the Ventura Freeway through the valley, they passed houses on which there were cardboard sleighs and figures of Santa Claus and on which the edges of the roofs were lined with lights that, during the day, had a dull, washed-out quality. The lights gave the houses the air of someplace that was fixed up for sale, like a used-car lot. There were some sickly looking palm trees, and some eucalyptus trees that, while healthy, had the odor of medicine. Iris looked at them and then turned to the hills, dismissing the valley as though it were just some aberration.

"Why don't we drive through Beverly Hills?" said Iris.

"Why?" asked Ray.

"Can't we just do it?" she said. "What's the big deal?"

"I don't know where it is," said Ray.

"I just want to see something that looks nice," said Iris. "That's not too much to ask, is it?"

"No," said Ray. "I'll ask in a gas station about how to get there."

Iris sat in the car, looking at herself in the mirror, fluffing up her hair, or taking an emery board from her bag (in which she had a change of underwear, a nightgown and a book, a makeup kit), the gesture one of already beginning to escape, as though this were the way she started to face up to the bewildering conglomeration of cars, streets, shopping centers, nurseries, and liquor stores, all of which, she now realized, had to be understood. So they drove over Laurel Canyon and then turned west, toward the beach, and as they went, Iris said, "Look. There's a bus. Do you think we could get a map of the routes?" Or, "I saw some used-car lots in the valley. I wonder how much a secondhand car is?" the questions coming as a kind of reconnoitering, a quick study of the place, and as she spoke, Ray looked over at her, hearing in her voice a constant desperation. It was one Ray recognized as being so close to his own (to get someplace where he was free) that there were times, especially when they were driving a car too fast or finding some other terror, when it seemed to him there wasn't any great difference between the two of them at all, and at these times, when he reached over and touched her, or just leaned his shoulder against hers, there seemed to be no definite boundary between them. And while this had a smooth, wonderful quality to it (especially when they found a place to be alone), it had its own terrors, too, as though he were somehow vanishing in her presence.

Now, though, with each bit of information about Los Angeles

(where the beach was, or where an emergency room was), she seemed to be not pulling away so much as getting ready to disappear (taking some of him with her when she went), and Ray drove along, looking at the billboards, or the restaurants on Sunset, or even pointing out a garden in Beverly Hills where the statues, life-size ones of nude women, had something like pubic hair pasted in the right spots, and as he went all he wanted was to find a way to make that sense of separation disappear, if only for an hour or ten minutes.

They checked into the Golden Palm Motel, which was near Chinatown. It was a plain, two-story building shaped like an enormous U. When Ray and Iris pulled in and parked by the office a woman who had arrived recently from southern Ohio was washing her clothes in the swimming pool. There were two children with her, both blond and pale like their mother, and when they had helped her wring out the clothes, the manager of the place came over and told her she couldn't do that anymore. Then he turned to Ray, who had come up to the pool, and said, "Well? What do you want?"

"A room," said Ray.

Ray filled out the card. Inside, Iris looked the room over, opening the drawers and going into the bathroom, her glance and examination still one of reconnoitering, as though even knowing about what was here might be useful.

"Why don't we just rest here for a while," said Ray.

"No," she said. "There isn't much time. Where do you buy a newspaper? Do you know? Is there a state employment office?"

It was dark when they began to look for something to eat. It was cool and misty, and the lights showed as enormous puffs of color. Ray started walking, taking Iris's hand, not really thinking of going to Chinatown but doing so anyway, almost as a way of fighting back, or of finding something, like driving a car fast, that would have its usual effect. Ray looked at the familiar streets, the signs and restaurants, the butcher shops and groceries, the telephone booths with roofs like pagodas, his saunter slow and almost nostalgic until he came to the store where he had gone with his father.

The place had been fixed up, and the new green paint, the brass doorknob, the gold and black ideograms in the window gave the store the air of a newly minted coin. In front of it, where the dead man had been left in the street, there were some oily stains where the crankcases of parked cars had leaked. The glass of the windows was still the same, clean and old and having a sheen like a large soap bubble, and inside, the cool edges of the stacked cans all seemed to hold some lingering quality, some sharp reminder of the man who had died in front of the store.

"Why are you stopping here?" asked Iris. "The place looks closed."

"Yeah," said Ray. "I guess so."

"Well," said Iris. "Let's go. I'm hungry."

Ray nodded.

"There's a restaurant right up around the corner."

"You know the neighborhood pretty well," said Iris.

"Not really," said Ray.

"Oh," she said. "This is where you did business, isn't it?"

Ray looked in through the window. "Yes," he said.

Iris looked in the window too now, her breath making a small, white mist on the glass.

"There's a gangster named Mei who uses this store. Mei Yaochen," said Ray.

"Do you know him?" asked Iris.

Ray shrugged. "What difference does it make?"

"A lot," said Iris.

Her voice still had that same distance as when she had talked about the bus routes, places to live, the state employment office. For a moment he wished he could use something as benign as a fast car, but as he stood there he realized they had gone beyond that.

"Well?" she said.

Ray reached out and touched the glass of the window, hesitating now if only because he wanted not to begin, and for a moment he thought maybe she'd let him drop the whole thing, but she stood there looking at him, her stance, her arms crossed under her breasts seeming to say, Well, are we in this together? Is there anything we will pull away from?

"Let's just forget about this," said Ray. "It was a mistake to come here."

"Tell me about the gangster," said Iris.

"Let's get out of here," said Ray. "We can go back to the room."

"You're scared, aren't you," said Iris.

"Yes," said Ray. "I think we should turn around and get out of here."

Iris swallowed and stepped closer.

"There aren't any real gangsters with guns and fancy suits, are there?" she said.

Ray went on breathing slowly, the mist drifting away from his lips, and as he looked at her he thought, Count to ten. Be careful. And, as Iris looked at him, there was something in his restraint or hesitation that had its effect. She stepped a little closer.

"Maybe they don't carry guns," said Ray. "That's not what makes them dangerous."

"What does, then?"

Ray shrugged.

"You don't know what you're talking about," said Iris.

Ray put out his hand, and she pulled away.

"My father and I came to this store," said Ray. "That's where I met Mei Yaochen."

"What did you do for him?" asked Iris.

Ray swallowed.

"We burned down a building," he said.

"You mean you were a firebug?" said Iris.

"No," said Ray.

"But you burned a building," said Iris.

"We didn't watch," said Ray.

"What difference does that make?" said Iris.

"A lot," said Ray. "We were arsonists."

"Oh, God," she said.

"We were paid to make a building disappear," said Ray.

Ray stood there, looking at her.

"Look," he said. "Let's get out of here. You asked about the store. I told you what I know."

They ate in a Mexican restaurant, a place with seats that had deep tucks in them, and on the wall there was a painted jungle, a mural in which there were palms and other trees, snakes, parrots, and small animals Ray had never seen before. They looked like raccoons and hung from trees. The jungle appeared in an array of palm fronds, fanlike, green and dark green behind bunches of bananas, purple banana flowers, and strings of orchids; and the depths of the jungle, the deep shades and bottle green shadows, obscured things that so obviously waited in them, snakes and insects, say, or wild pigs. "Perfidia" was playing on the jukebox.

Iris's eyes were the color of mossy stones under water, and as she ate she looked at him, thinking it over but still coming back to something that was like jumping off a bridge: her glance seemed to come from some cool, shiny depths. And as they ate it occurred to her, with a thrill of discovery, that Ray wasn't confessing to having burned down some building as much as bringing something else to the struggle between them. Before, they had only flirted with physical danger, with fast cars and heights and cold water, but now they faced more possibilities, and more frightening ones too, since here they had begun to play with corruption . . . and as she considered this she felt as though they were hovering so far above a river that she couldn't even see into the depths below. She squirmed on her side of the booth, making the leather squeak.

"Maybe we should go right back to the room now," she said.

"Okay," he said. "Fine."

She looked up at the mural above them, at the arc of shiny leaves, the coiling of a python on the forked limb of a tree, the face of a jaguar peering through the fronds of a palm.

"What do you know about the gangster?" asked Iris.

She licked her lips, and Ray noticed that there was a slight trembling in her hands.

"I heard a story," he said.

"What did you hear?"

"There was a man who lied to Mei," said Ray.

"You mean the gangster?" said Iris.

"He wouldn't like to be called that," said Ray.

"All right," said Iris. "The man in the store, then."

"Yes," said Ray. "A guy lied to him. I don't even think it was a big lie. But Mei took the liar out in a boat, a cabin cruiser he kept in San Pedro, and when they were out in the Pacific, down toward Ensenada, Mei cut the man who had lied, put him into the water, and towed him behind the boat on a rope. There are sharks down there."

Iris looked at Ray.

"Yeah," she said. "I guess the water is warm down there. I can imagine the shark part."

"Can you?" said Ray. "Well, when the sharks arrived, Mei pulled the liar close and said, 'You can still be saved. Just say the right thing now and I'll forgive you.' The guy in the water took a mouthful of seawater and sprayed it onto Mei's pants. Mei went on staring, not moving, not saying a word, the man in the water looking back. The two of them had a perfect understanding. Then the liar turned away, toward the sharks, and shoved off from the boat."

"What was the perfect understanding?" said Iris.

"That there wasn't any chance of being saved," said Ray. "The idea of it was part of the punishment."

Iris nodded and looked down at her plate. Ray watched her with a kind of discomfort, certain now that they were going a little faster.

After dinner they went for a walk. It was cool, and City Hall was as white as chalk dust, illuminated by the lights on all sides. Iris liked the clean, pure quality of it in the evening air, and she said it made her think that she'd really get a chance as soon as she moved to L.A. City Hall was beautiful, wasn't it? They walked along El Varo Street, where there were booths in which glass was blown into figurines and models, the molten strands of it as delicate and as shiny as a string of glue from a tube. Iris watched the trembling of them as a glassblower made a three-masted ship, the thing looking as if it had been carved out of ice. Then she took Ray's hand and said, "Let's walk up toward Chinatown," her touch having an urgency about it, as though any pulling away now would be a betrayal, or somehow an admission of failure.

They passed some restaurants, the phone booths like pagodas, the butcher shops and apartment buildings, the alleys where there were fire escapes, the shadows of which fell over the walls as in some dream of a spiderweb. The windows of the restaurants were filled with light, and inside there were people eating or waiting to eat, a few of them talking but many alone, reading a paper or staring into the street or at nothing at all.

Ray and Iris came up to the store. At first they circled around it a few times, first turning a couple of blocks before it, and then only one, and finally when they came up to the place, Iris stopped in front of it and looked at the new gilt lettering.

"Do you think he's here?" said Iris.

"I don't know," said Ray.

"Come on," she said. "Knock on the door."

Ray's breath trailed away from his mouth as he tapped on the door. After a while a man came from the back, his face coldly disapproving as he looked through the glass. He was about fifty or so, wearing a white shirt and a pair of dark pants, and when he opened the door he said, "Closed. All closed."

"Is he here?" said Ray. "The man in the back. There."

Ray pointed to the doorway in the rear of the store.

"You tell him Ray Gollancz is here," said Ray.

"All closed," said the man. "No one here."

"Tell him," said Ray.

"Place open up the street," said the man. "Go on."

Mr. Mei came into the doorway of the back room, and his shadow fell across the floor with the shape of a coat hung on a hook. Mr. Mei spoke in Chinese, and the man opened up the door and said, "All right. Come in."

Ray and Iris went through the dark store, the edges of the stacks of cans shiny from the streetlights, the accumulation of the silvery arcs looking like fish scales. The office at the back was the same as before, gray-yellow walls, a nude woman on the calendar, the same desk, on which there was an adding machine. There was some money, too, divided into bundles that were held together with red rubber bands. Iris reached out and took Ray's hand and stared at the money.

"Who's this?" said Mr. Mei, raising his chin slightly in Iris's direction.

"A friend," said Ray.

Mr. Mei sat down and lighted a cigarette, tossing the match into an ashtray.

"Well?" he said.

Iris took one look at Mr. Mei, at the office, and said to Ray, "Maybe we shouldn't have come. Maybe we should go now."

Mr. Mei stared at them through the rising smoke from the cigarette, his expression one of alert consideration.

"Why don't you sit down," said Mr. Mei. "There are so few times when people come just to talk." He glanced at Iris. "Isn't that what you came to do? Or did Dean send you?"

"No," said Ray. "We came alone."

Mr. Mei looked around the room. Then he said, "All right. Sit down."

"This is Iris Mason," said Ray. "Mr. Mei Yaochen."

"I pleased to meet you," said Mr. Mei. "Any friend of Ray's is a friend of mine."

Iris swallowed and nodded.

Ray pulled up two of the oak chairs, the grain of them showing as stripes, almost like a tiger's. Iris sat down, tucking her legs back, putting her hands neatly in her lap.

"Would you like a drink?" said Mr. Mei.

"No, thanks," said Iris. She turned to Ray and said, "Please. I want to go."

"No?" said Mr. Mei. "Usually when someone comes to visit he has a drink. Tea. Whiskey."

"Whiskey," said Ray. "Thank you."

Ray put his foot out and touched Iris's.

"All right. Yes. Please," she said. "Whiskey."

"With a little soda?" asked Mr. Mei.

"The way you have it is fine," said Iris.

Mr. Mei spoke to the man in the store, who brought glasses with a little whiskey in the bottom, the color of it reddish, the film of it clinging to the side of the glass where it had swirled around.

"We didn't think you'd be here," said Iris.

Mr. Mei raised a brow.

"We don't mean to intrude," said Ray. "We were just walking

down the street and I was wondering if you were here. That's all."

"There's nothing special?" asked Mr. Mei.

"No," said Ray.

"We're just down here for a visit," said Iris.

"Oh?" said Mr. Mei. "You're from up north?"

"For now," said Iris, "but not for long."

"You're thinking of moving to Los Angeles?" said Mr. Mei.

"Yes," said Iris.

"You'll like it here," said Mr. Mei. "The coast is beautiful. Have you ever seen it from the ocean?"

"No," said Iris. She shook her head.

"I have a boat," said Mr. Mei. "I keep it in San Pedro. Sometimes I get out, down as far as Mexico. You should come sometime."

"That would be nice," said Iris.

She looked at Ray now and reached over with her foot, pressing against his.

"It's always good to have a friend in a new town, don't you think?" said Mr. Mei.

Iris reached out for the small glass of whiskey that was on the oak desk in front of her, and as she picked it up, the tips of her fingers quivering a little, it slipped out of her hand, the reddish fluid falling onto her skirt. It was a tight skirt, and the stain seeped into the material over her thighs. She jumped up and brushed at herself, and Ray stood up too, giving her a handkerchief as Iris said, "How clumsy. How stupid," and brushed at herself. Ray picked up the glass and put it on the table.

"Maybe we better go," he said.

"Please," said Mr. Mei. He spoke Chinese to the other man in the store, who picked up the empty glass and put down another, which had whiskey in it. "You're my guests. Sit down."

Iris sat down again, glancing toward Ray every now and then. Her eyes seemed dilated, the pupils almost purple, wide and shiny. She took a sip of the bourbon and said, "I think I'd like to go so I can change."

"Of course," Mr. Mei said. "But you can wait for just a minute, can't you?"

She nodded.

"Anything you say," she said.

Mr. Mei looked at Ray.

"Los Angeles is a hard town to get a start in," said Mr. Mei. "You've got to have a car. Cars cost money."

Ray took a sip of the bourbon, trying to think of something to say. On the wall was the calendar with the photograph of the nude woman, who looked down with a cool aloofness. Mr. Mei smiled. Ray began to mention the fogs they had in Chinatown sometimes, but then he stopped, thinking of the man who had worked for Mr. Mei and who had talked about the fog, but this just made Ray more desperate to find the correct thing to say, as though a few words, like magic, could make everything all right. Upstairs, someone was snoring, the sound of it repetitive, grating, and a little blubbery too. A fly went around the room in a circuit that was like an enormous figure eight. Ray blurted out, "Dean's waiting for you to call. Do you have anything for him?"

Mr. Mei looked across the desk.

"I'll call him soon," he said. "So, he sent you after all. And I thought we were just being friendly."

"No," said Ray. "I don't want to meddle. He didn't send me. It just came out."

"All right," said Mr. Mei. "Okay. Let's forget it."

Iris held her drink in her lap with both hands, the fingers pressing against it.

"You know, Ray," said Mr. Mei, "this morning I was reading Marcus Aurelius. Marcus says that a man should look to what is excellent in the universe and to what is excellent in himself."

Ray nodded.

"Yes," said Ray. "I guess that's right."

"And you know why?" said Mr. Mei. "The two are related." He looked at Iris.

"That's nice," said Ray.

"I want you to know I am a civilized man," said Mr. Mei. Then he turned to Iris and said, "Get in touch with me when you come to L.A."

"Yes," said Iris.

"We'll go down to San Pedro." He went on staring at Iris for a moment and then said, "All right. You can go now."

Mr. Mei looked down at the table in front of him, at the ledger that was there, the figures in it written in a blue ink, the color of a tattoo, on the white paper. Iris stood up and went to the door, going through the small grocery, her shape small and delicate as she went around the piles of sacks of rice, although there was a table she hit as she stumbled in the dark, the pain of it making her take up her breath quickly, but she said nothing, trying to get to the door. In the street, she took Ray's hand and said, "Let's go back to the room now. Right now."

They walked through the mist, Iris taking his arm, and from time to time she looked at the shadows in the street, and at the people who emerged from them, her hand jerking at Ray as she said, "Didn't you see the way he looked at us? Oh, Jesus." They came to a liquor store, and in the window there were clear, ice-colored bottles of gin and a clean white light that fell into the mist of the street, and as they stood in the slanting rays of it, Iris said, "Please. I want something. They'll probably sell it to you, won't they?"

Ray went in and bought a bottle of bourbon, and then they walked back to the motel, where Iris went into that anonymous room, which now seemed different than before, the bed, the chair, the bureau with a desk that was built against the wall, the small refrigerator—all appearing somehow ominous, as though they carried with them some contagion, some association with the secrets that were known only in the store in Chinatown. Iris took one of the two glasses in the room and put some bourbon into it, and then she sat there, drinking and saying, "Look at my hands. Oh, Jesus, that's so much worse than driving fast or anything like that at all." Then she sat, drinking steadily, saying only, "I don't have to go there, do I?"

"No," said Ray. "I wouldn't do that. I wish we had just come home rather than taking the walk."

Iris nodded and went on drinking.

"I just wanted to get up and get out of there," she said. "You know?"

"Yes," said Ray.

She got ready for bed, taking off her clothes, which she tore a little, swaying and showing Ray a bruise on her hip where she had bumped against the table in the store in Chinatown.

"God, how clumsy," she said.

She pulled up the sheet and rolled over, saying, "I had too much to drink."

In the morning, Iris got up and went to the bathroom, getting a drink at the faucet, her small-breasted, bony-hipped shape visible in the half-light of dawn. She came back to bed and slept again. When she woke, she was hung over and her fingers were shaking. She pulled back the sheets where Ray slept, her hands unsteady as she ran her fingers over him, and said, "Please, please, please . . . let's . . . all right? Let's . . ." The light in the morning was dim, brownish, her skin showing as a pale glow. Now, she thought about the night before, which brought with it that sense of the two of them alone standing in the face of danger, and in the heat and itchy anxiety of the moment, in the power of her own quaking hangover, she was more frightened and more intrigued than ever. She opened her eyes and looked at him, not quite licking her lips but rubbing them together, as though she were thinking of some fond, wonderful thing that she let herself remember only on special occasions.

She got up and brought back a glass of water, into which she put ice from the small refrigerator, standing in the gray-brown shadows of the morning as she did so. She put her head back and drank, letting the water slip out of the sides of her mouth, the ice cubes rattling in the glass and then bouncing against her lips and falling over her shoulders, the bright, silver things bumping against her breasts and falling onto the bed with a thud. Then she put down the glass and sat on the bed again, still shaking just as much as before, her face set in an expression of furious insistence. She picked up the ice and rubbed it across her lips, making her lips cold, all the while leaning toward him, and then said, "You were scared too. I could tell. Just the two of us. I could trust you then, you know that?" She let him feel the perfectly shaped, full and cold kiss. Then she stretched out and said, "You think I'm kidding, don't you? Come here." Her lips were still cold, and her touch in the warm room had that anxious, hung-over quiver.

Around them there was the odor of that clean, anonymous room, in the bathroom of which there was the odor of Spic and Span, and outside there was the sound of cars on the street and of a distant siren. There were birds flying outside the window, and the shadow of their wings on the curtains made a dark, quick fluttering.

They went out for breakfast, but neither one of them ate much. Iris kept looking out the window at the cars and trucks that went by on Santa Monica Boulevard, and as each one went by, Ray felt that things between them had changed: She looked back at him and tried to smile, and this was the worst. It was as though she believed that the moments of trust were getting in the way, and that because of them she might stay in Bakersfield one day, or one hour, or one minute too long.

So they started the long drive home a day early, Iris sitting with her handbag on the seat between them, the two of them looking like married people now, or at least just people who, for better or worse, had come to some decision. Ray drove the speed limit, hearing the throaty rumble of the flathead V-8, which had been bored and stroked, and which had the two four-barrel carburetors. The needle of the tachometer hung in one place, nervously trembling there. Iris said she had learned a lot and that she thought she'd be able to handle Los Angeles all right.

So it wasn't even a surprise when, a week later, Ray went to meet Iris in the morning (when her parents were gone). The air of the street, the yellow sunlight, the mustiness of the neighborhood, the silence of it all brought a mixture of anticipation and dread. He went up the walk, between the weeds, and then knocked on the door, lightly at first, just a discreet tapping, but soon he knocked harder, getting no answer. The house sounded hollow.

At the side of the door there was a piece of paper, the same as before, lined notebook paper, and when he opened it up he saw in her large scrawl, "I don't want to forget that you meant it, sugar, when you said you loved me. The difference between you and your father is that he didn't mean it. Iris. P.S. This is the best I can do. Because at least this way we'll stay away from that pistol." Then he

stood knee-deep in the weeds while he looked at the upstairs windows and remembered the scent of her bed, which smelled of her
hair and skin, of powder and of sleepless nights, of the sweat of
worry and the sweat of heat, and of the lingering, buttery quality of
her snacks.

It took a couple of days before he found out what had happened,
and by then almost everyone knew that she had packed her things,
that makeup case and the rest, and had gone to Los Angeles, taking
her father's car and leaving it where it had run out of gas, not
because she had run out of money, not yet anyway, but because she
couldn't stand being in it any longer, even if it meant she'd have to
put out her thumb, which she did, taking her bags with her, getting
into the first car that was going south into the reddish haze of Los
Angeles, the concrete and palm trees, the blue mountains surround-
ing the place, the air there, the colors, the endless clutter of the
houses and stores, shopping centers, the African quality of the hills
with their money-colored trees, all of it representing a kind of
dangerous hope.

That night Ray went up to the attic, where he stood in front of
that enormous trombone case, the thing black in the light of one
sixty-watt bulb. Ray flipped up the snaps and lifted the lid, the
weight of it surprising, the black top rising with a horrifying familiarity. The instrument sat in that red velvet, the surface of it bright,
polished, the reflections in it all an elongated smear. Dean came into
the room.

"Raymond, what's going on?" he said.

"Nothing," said Ray.

"So," said Dean. "That's the way it is? What's her name?"

"I'd just as soon keep it to myself," said Ray.

"All right," said Dean. "Come on."

"Where are we going?" said Ray.

"Are you contradicting me?" said Dean. "I said come on."

They went downstairs and through the kitchen, where Dean took
down his jacket and shoved an arm through the sleeve of it and said,
"Put yours on. It's cold."

On the town's main street they stopped in front of the pawnshop.
In the window there were pistols, the revolvers and automatics

spread out fan style, all of their barrels pointing at one spot. Each one had a lock inside the trigger guard. They had different finishes, some simply blued, although others were made of stainless steel and some were nickel plated, the reflections in the metal of these last having a festive quality, like streamers on the surface of a silver balloon. But as they lay on a green cloth behind the glass of the cabinet there was about them, in their shapes, in the metallic gleam of them, and especially in the holes at the end of the barrels, the sense of something twisted and confined, some power, like a tree pulled down to make a snare, that more than anything else was simply waiting for the right moment to make itself known.

Ray stared at the pistols.

"Be careful in this town, Raymond," said Dean.

"Why does it have to be so complicated?" said Ray.

"Your guess is as good as mine," said Dean. "Jesus, I'm no philosopher."

Above the pistols there were instruments hung from hooks— trumpets, clarinets, guitars (some of which were electric, the amplifiers looking gray and dusty), saxophones, flügelhorns, bugles. There were even some stringed instruments—violins, cellos—and a few woodwinds, too—oboes and French horns.

"You'll get over her," said Dean.

"What if you're wrong?" said Ray.

"What?" said Dean.

"Maybe you don't ever get over some things. Maybe you just carry them around."

"No," said Dean, shaking his head. "No. You'll get over her."

They went through the door and into the shop, where the air was a little dusty and cool. There was a steel-mesh fence that ran around the room over the counters, and at the back of the shop there was a little window through it, beyond which the pawnbroker sat, smoking a cigar.

"All right," said Dean. "Pick one. Go on."

"Pick one what?" said Ray.

"An instrument. How about a clarinet? Have you ever heard Benny Goodman play 'Stomping at the Savoy'?"

"No," said Ray. "I don't want a clarinet."

"No?" said Dean.

"I'm not saying anything against Benny Goodman," said Ray.

"By God, you better not," said Dean. "What about a saxophone? Gerry Mulligan is my idea of a musician. No one, and I mean no one, has the richness of tone—"

"I'm not saying anything against Gerry Mulligan either, but I don't want a saxophone."

"Well, well. What about a trumpet? Are you going to have the gall to turn away from a trumpet? Now, Chet Baker—"

"I never heard of him," said Ray.

"Well, let me tell you," said Dean. "Chet Baker's rendition of 'Look for the Silver Lining' is one of the high points of American music." Dean raised his hands and seemed to hold an invisible trumpet, and while he held it to his lips, he whistled and then sang, ". . . whene'er a cloud appears in the blue. Remember somewhere the sun is shining . . . and so the right thing to do is make it shine for you. A heart full of joy and gladness . . ."

Ray looked at the trombone.

"Jesus, Ray, you don't want a trombone, do you?"

"Yes," said Ray.

"All right," said Dean. He turned to the pawnbroker. "That one. That trombone. My boy wants it."

Ray walked down the main street of town, past the movie theater, the soda fountain, the bookstore, and as he felt the weight of the instrument in its case, he thought, San Pedro. Jesus Christ, not San Pedro. She wouldn't go there, would she? Not out in the boat.

"What's the matter now?" said Dean.

"I was just thinking of going after someone," said Ray.

"Who?" said Dean. "A woman?"

"Yes," said Ray.

"Did she leave you?" said Dean.

Ray nodded.

"Don't bother," said Dean. "That's my advice."

FANTASIE FOR
TROMBONE

The telephone call came at night, after nine. Dean was sitting in the kitchen, listening to the radio. When the conditions were just right there was a station he could get out of San Francisco, and it broadcast music from Brazil, or a blues festival live from Tokyo, and from time to time it had on some musicians from New Orleans who played trombone, not to mention that there were times when the station put on classical music, too, in which there was a part for a trombone. It was difficult to get the station. Usually, a large mass of high pressure had to be coming out of the northern Pacific, and after it had passed San Francisco the station came in. Then Dean listened to Sigismund Stojowski's Fantasie for Trombone and Piano, Hugo Alfvén's "Vallflickans dans," or Guy Ropartz's *Pièce en mi bémol mineur*. So, Dean was looking for it, the static coming into the kitchen with a sound like heavy rain, when the phone rang. Marge

93

answered and said, "Just a minute." She covered the mouthpiece and said to Dean, "It's him."

Dean turned off the radio and stood up. He took the phone, held it against his ear, his eyes set on some distant place.

"Hello?" he said. "All right, I guess. I could use some work. Is that right? Good. Good. I'll be down to see you. Thanks."

Then he hung up.

"Don't take Ray," said Marge.

"Why not?" said Dean.

"He's got a chance," said Marge. "Maybe he'll get away from this."

"What do you mean?" he said.

"He's applied to that school. Some people here in town think he's got a chance to get in."

"Which people?" said Dean.

"Sabrina Hawthorne," said Marge. "She knows about testing—"

"Testing," said Dean. "Well, you know what I think about testing."

"Leave him here," said Marge.

"Whether he comes or stays is between him and me," said Dean.

"No it isn't," said Marge. "It's between you and me."

Ray came into the room, his finger stuck in the book he was carrying.

"Was that Mei?" asked Ray.

"Yes," said Dean.

"All right," said Ray.

"Ray," said Marge. "Please. Don't."

"I said I'd go," said Ray. "We've got some unfinished business."

"Is that right, Ray?" said Marge. "I wish you'd listen to me. That's all."

"I bought you a dark jacket and some black pants," said Dean.

"Where are they?" asked Ray.

Marge sat down at the table and dropped her hands into her lap. Around her the clean kitchen, the curtains in the window, the hum of the icebox had a lingering quality, like some memory of a happier time. She shook her head and then looked up at Dean.

"Don't," she said. "I've forgiven you a lot. I won't forgive you for this."

"We need some money," said Dean. He turned to Ray. "Tomorrow night."

"Money," said Marge. "Jesus, I hate it. I'd like to get my hands on a pile of it so I could burn it."

Ray came and sat opposite her, picking up one of her hands, and said, "We'll be careful."

"Oh, go on. Just get out of here."

The next evening, at dusk, Dean and Ray got into that anonymous Chevrolet and began the drive south. Ray sat silently, looking through the windshield, and when they were on the flat, straight section of the road outside of town (where there was that sharp, dogleg turn) he saw the reddish glow of Los Angeles, and in the crimson haze Ray imagined there was some constant turmoil, which, if nothing else, seemed appropriate. Ray looked across the seat and thought about the time Dean had been amusing himself with a high-school girl Ray was interested in.

In the San Gabriel Mountains there were accumulations of snow, enormous banks that were getting dirty with the exhaust from the cars and trucks. On the seat between them there was a paper bag in which Marge had put two meat loaf sandwiches, wrapped in waxed paper, and a thermos of coffee.

Dean and Ray appeared after dark on the side street in Chinatown, their shapes moving with a steady, slightly stooped gait, like men carrying buckets of water. Dean tapped on the door, and the same man, dressed in dark pants and a white shirt, let them in. Mr. Mei sat in his office, a cigarette in his hand, his jacket off and hanging on a new addition, an oak coat tree with brass hooks.

Ray sat down and accepted his bourbon, swirling it around in the glass and thinking of how Iris had sat here, her legs crossed, her eyes on the man on the other side of the desk. The atmosphere of the room was the same as always, which is to say one of perfectly distilled anxiety blended with the effort required to stand up to it. So he sat there looking at the desk, the walls, the new coat tree, the plastic cover over the adding machine, and as he glanced from one object to another, as he tried to take the keenest estimate of these things, he wondered if there would be any change, any sign, a fingerprint, a hint of perfume, or a stale, sweaty funk of desperation, or any palpable indication that Iris had shown up here recently, by herself, if not desperate then certainly ready to come to terms of some kind. Ray didn't like to think of her sitting here, in her blue jeans, her white blouse, her hair brushed out, her hands tightly clasped over her knee. He thought of her turning in the bed next to him, restless even in her sleep.

"Some developers in east Hollywood aren't doing so well," said Mr. Mei.

"Is that right?" said Dean. "I'm sorry to hear that."

"Are you?" said Mr. Mei. "That's generous."

Mr. Mei was almost cheerful, and Ray looked at him closely, going over the man's face the same way he looked around the room, and wondering, too, if there was anything conclusive about Mr. Mei, a hint of smugness, or pleasure, or maybe even a wistful quality, that indicated Iris had arrived here alone.

"Yes," said Mr. Mei. "You know, someone thinks he can put up a two- or maybe even a three-story building. He goes to the bank and borrows the money to do it. He thinks he's going to get a doctor, a dentist, a lawyer, and an accountant in there. Maybe a psychotherapist. It's going to be a nice professional center. But the neighborhood changes. There are people coming in from Mexico, from all over. The next thing the guy knows the bank is breathing down his neck. Yeah, they're having some trouble out there."

He turned to Ray.

"What are you looking at?" Mr. Mei asked.

"I was just listening," said Ray.

"You've got an attentive boy, Dean," said Mr. Mei.

Ray glanced around the office, at the chairs, even the dust on a filing cabinet.

"Is there something you want to ask me?" said Mr. Mei to Ray.

"I was just wondering," said Ray. "If anyone has paid you a visit?"

"Many people visit me," said Mr. Mei. "I try to do my best for them."

Then he turned back to Dean and said, "Yeah, well, it's funny the way a neighborhood changes so fast. It's hard to find a nice one these days. Unless you go up into the hills. It's hard to meet nice people."

"I asked you a question," said Ray.

"Young man," said Mr. Mei. "I don't know what you're talking about."

"Would you tell me if you'd seen her?" asked Ray.

"I'm not sure it would be any of your business," said Mr. Mei.

"Maybe I have obligations," said Ray.

"Your father will tell you what your obligations are," said Mr. Mei. "Or I will."

"That's right," said Dean.

"And anyway, if I had a business meeting with someone," said Mr. Mei, "that would be a private matter."

"What kind of business is there?" asked Ray.

"For a young woman?" said Mr. Mei. "Oh, there are service jobs in Las Vegas. Mexico. There are army bases in the Philippines that require hostesses."

"Ray?" said Dean. "Did you bring your girlfriend here?"

"Yes," said Ray.

"Oh?" said Dean. "Well, if she wants to come back, that's her business."

Ray put the glass down, leaving the bourbon in the bottom.

"Let's talk about the building, for Christ sake," said Dean.

Mr. Mei gave them the address and passed over some keys, the new, silver shapes appearing on the oak table in a liquid flash. Dean scooped them up and put them in his pocket.

"Fifteen hundred," said Mr. Mei. "All right?"

"No," said Ray.

"Oh?" said Mr. Mei. "I thought your father was in charge here."

"Fifteen hundred is okay," said Dean.

"It's worth more than that," said Ray. "How much are you making?"

"That's not your business," said Mr. Mei.

"Are you getting part of the insurance?"

Mr. Mei blinked now.

"Dean," said Mr. Mei. "Do you want it or not?"

"Well, I don't know," said Dean. "That's a good question, about the insurance."

"Listen," said Mr. Mei, glancing at Ray. "There is no room for losing your head. Or getting angry. I'm giving you some good advice."

He took out the metal, dented box he had in one of the bottom drawers and began counting the bills, putting them down a little harder than usual, glancing up at Ray again. "Fifteen hundred," said Mr. Mei. "Take it or leave it."

Dean picked up the money and said to Ray, "All right. Let's go."

Mr. Mei spoke Chinese and the man who had brought the drinks now came in with a glass for Mr. Mei, who took it and lighted a cigarette and then sat there looking at Ray. The room's stark, functional quality, like the office of a small-town lawyer, made for a spareness, and as Mr. Mei sat in it he seemed ascetic and dedicated. Ray stood at the door and said, "Good night."

"Good night," said Mr. Mei. "I'll see you again."

"Good night," said Dean. "Be sure to read the papers tomorrow. The press photographers love smoke."

The street was empty, and the stores, the office of a trucking company were dark, although above them there were some apartments, from which came a golden luminescence that seemed to be evidence of a life that was protective and dependable. Dean put his hand in his pocket and jingled the keys, and as he did so he said to Ray, "Jesus, Ray, be careful. Don't push Mei that way. You hear me? What's gotten into you, anyway?"

"I don't know," said Ray. "I'm jumpy, I guess."

"Well, get a grip on yourself," said Dean. "We got work to do."

The "professional center" in east Hollywood was empty, and had been empty for some time, aside from a month in the spring, when some H & R Block accountants had rented an office in the front, in the window of which there was still a sign that said, WALK-IN TAX SERVICE, although people didn't take it seriously now since it was ripped and dusty and hanging by only one piece of tape.

Dean wet the carpet in the hall with lacquer, spreading it with a careful but not necessarily slow motion: the silver fluid came out evenly, not too much, not too little. Ray held the alarm clock with the black-powder cap fixed to one of its bells. The stink of the lacquer was very strong and hinted of some other place, or other things, new furniture, or a woodworking shop. Ray's fingers were on the hands of the clock, which had been wound up, with the alarm set, and for a moment, in the possibility of the thing going off too soon (since it was in his hands), Ray simply stared, watching the lacquer fall onto the carpet and Dean's steady, bent-back, ass-backward progression down the hall. The possibility of the fire starting too soon carried with it a catharsis, the sensation of which was inseparable from the odor of lacquer. Ray held the clock and waited, his hands shaking.

Dean looked at Ray and said, "Put the clock down. Let's get out of here."

They went outside and got into the car, Ray exhausted now, no longer feeling anger or anything at all aside from a fatigue that was close to peacefulness. He reached for the thermos on the front seat and poured some coffee into the top, which he sipped slowly, looking at the approaching lines of the lanes of the freeway.

By the time they got home, Ray was almost groaning with amazement that he had gotten anything (like relief) from that moment of terror (of having a fire starting too soon). All he wanted now was to be loyal, plus of course to make up for the excesses of his resentment. In the days that followed, his amazement grew to the point where it had an almost physical weight (one that Ray felt sometimes when he was standing up or when he got out of bed in the morning). He put it to rest by saying to Dean, "Well, isn't it time to burn another?" Then the two of them walked along that dark street in Chinatown, both of them with their heads down, approaching that dark store where Mr. Mei waited, looking at them through the window, his suit appearing almost black. Mr. Mei had plenty of jobs for them now.

And there was something else, too, that entered into these trips to Los Angeles, and that was Ray's mixture of exasperation at having been deserted by Iris and his desire to find her. Nothing seemed clear about this, and on one of those long drives south Ray said, "Maybe you shouldn't let someone just walk out on you."

Dean turned and looked at him for a moment. Then he said, "Are you talking about the woman who left you?"

"Yes," said Ray.

"Forget it," said Dean. "She left you. Look, women have been leaving me all my life. You get used to it."

"I don't know," said Ray.

"Listen," said Dean. "I told you to forget it. That's the smart thing to do. There's nothing you can do anyway."

Ray shook his head, not believing this, and when they got rid of a building, when they lighted a candle in a roll of newspaper or put down a windup alarm clock (with the smell of lacquer around them), Ray did so with a fury, glancing at his father with an exasperated disbelief while at the same time suspecting there was some action he should take where Iris was concerned, the two ideas combining in such a way as to leave him looking to find, in the tension of a building about to burst into flame, some empathetic reflection of his own state of mind.

"Stop thinking about it," said Dean.

They got rid of one building, and then another, the supply of abandoned and insured motels, warehouses, and offices playing into Dean's hands. Each new place Dean agreed to burn was always larger than the last, the size of the jobs becoming part of the argument, since Dean had begun to use the fires and the excitement of them as a plea to keep his son from leaving him behind and as a desperate attempt to keep from admitting to himself that he was a small-time crook who was trapped.

The entire operation for Ray was like a drug in that, after a night when things seemed clear and bright (and when he took some relief from just the possibility of disaster), he was left the next day grief-stricken, ashamed, and somehow trembling, the cure for which was more of the same. So Ray went on, the entire thing working on him in a repetitive way, as regular as the tide, in that he went from anger, to relief, to shame, and then back to anger again. In between he sat at night thinking about those moments when he and Iris had been so scared and so excited they had begun to feel like one person. He hoped that in those circumstances where he hovered over the abyss of things going wrong, in that instant when a match might be lighted too soon, in the endless confronting of this moment, he and his father could come to some understanding, not to mention that he might be able to decide what he should do, even though he had been left behind.

They went south regularly, each night taking that brown paper sack of sandwiches and the thermos from Marge, who passed it over both as a blessing and as a talisman too, in that, as far as she was concerned, if they were eating a sandwich and having a cup of coffee, why then nothing that bad could happen.

"We haven't got a key tonight," said Dean.

"How are we going to get in?" said Ray.

"How?" said Dean. "Well, Ray, there's more to this than meets the eye."

They stopped in front of a warehouse. It was built close to another one, and the alley between them wasn't more than a few feet wide. Dean took a jack out of the back of the car and a piece of four-by-four. He put the jack against the wall and the four-by-four post against a doorframe of the building they wanted to get into. He worked the jack handle, and the doorframe began to creak like a sailing ship in a wind, and the wall seemed to give, too, at first not much, but then, with a sigh, the door simply fell away, leaving before them a dark portal, from the floor of which plaster dust rose like wisps of smoke.

"Always keep a piece of four-by-four in the trunk of your car. Be sure you have a jack," said Dean.

"Is that another rule?" asked Ray. "Like not hanging around?"

"Yes," said Dean. "Be sure you have a jack."

"All right," said Ray.

"Put it away when you're done," said Dean. "That way you won't trip over it on your way out."

Ray nodded. Around them there was that dusty mist, like fog, which rose from the broken mortar, or maybe just from inside the wall. It had the odor of dry cement, and as Ray and his father stood in it, their shapes a little vague, like men in a foggy river bottom, Ray said, "Listen, I think I've got to start looking for someone in L.A."

"Are you up to that stuff again?" said Dean. "Listen, you're wasting your time."

So they went in and spread kerosene around and left a fuse, both of them working fast, but even as the fluid with the blue tint splashed out of the can, Ray realized that something was changing, or shifting. They drove away from the building, which had started to burn a little too soon, the flash of ignition making the walls seem black as the windows filled with light and blew out, covering the sidewalk with shiny bits that looked like small, solid chunks of flame. Ray looked over his shoulder, where the roiling orange and yellow shapes rose out of the windows, the sparks crimson and winking, and as he did, he thought, That was a close one.

After a night in Los Angeles, Dean read the paper, and when he found the photograph he was looking for he showed it to Ray and said, "Look. You see? That place in Chula Vista? The warehouse. Look what's left. Twenty thousand square feet, it says here."

＝

Usually, the mail was delivered to Dean's house at about ten o'clock in the morning, and after the postman had put the letters through the slot in the front door, Marge picked them up and sorted them out, leaving them on the kitchen table. But this was Saturday morning, and while Ray and Dean sat over their coffee, they heard at the end of the hall that ran from the kitchen to the front door the tick as some letters fell from the mail slot onto the floor. Dean glanced up and Ray looked directly at him. They both sat there in the silence that came after that tick.

"Well," said Dean. "Go get them. What are you waiting for?"

They heard the whistling of the mailman and his steady, efficient stride as he turned and walked across the boards of the porch and then down the steps into that February morning.

"All right," said Ray. He stood and walked down the hall and picked up the envelopes, finding among them one of those made out of that heavy, watermarked, and even fragrant paper. Ray held the thing between two fingers, feeling the weight of it and looking at the logo and name of that eastern school. The envelope was white. Ray brought it into the kitchen and put it down on the table.

"Well, open it," said Dean. "Waiting isn't going to change anything."

Ray ripped it open and looked at it and said, "They want me. Full scholarship."

Ray looked down at the newspaper Dean had spread on the table, and in the middle of the page there was a picture of a burned-out building: there didn't appear to be anything left but a black spot, like a stain, on the ground. Dean stared at the picture too, and said, "That's one sucker that isn't going to turn up as smoke damage. We even got the foundation."

Ray nodded.

"I guess so," said Ray.

Dean looked up. "I can see it on your face," he said. "You're going to go. Just like that."

Ray held out the letter.

"Look at it," said Ray. "Look."

The paper started trembling a little.

"You didn't answer me," said Dean.

"I want you to look," said Ray.

"I can see by your face what's happening," said Dean. "You're going to go. I want you to tell me something, Ray. That is, if you've got the guts. Why are you going?"

"I don't know," said Ray.

"Sure you do," said Dean. "I never said you were stupid. Tell me. Come on. Are you just some chickenshit little—"

Ray took a step closer to his father.

"Stop it," he said.

"Well?" said Dean. "Tell me."

"There are times down there, in Los Angeles . . . ," said Ray.

"That you like it," said Dean. "Sure you do. It's a way of getting free for a minute. Isn't that right?"

"There are times down there," said Ray, looking at his father, "when I'm so pissed off, when I'm holding a match . . ."

Dean looked right at his son.

"And what?" said Dean. "Tell me."

"I'm afraid I'm going to light the thing before I should," said Ray.

"Goddamn it!" said Dean. "I apologize for anything I did. Take my hand on it."

"I'm not done," said Ray. "I thought if I went down there, if I went through that moment, that somehow things would be all right . . . that you'd know you could trust me, that even then you could depend on me. And that if you knew that, you wouldn't mind about this."

Ray held out the letter.

"Read it," said Ray.

"Goddamn it," said Dean. "You know what? You're a stranger. Nothing but a goddamned stranger."

They looked at one another, Ray still holding the letter out.

"All right," said Dean. "I don't want you coming with me anymore. It's that simple. You understand? I thought we had something together. I guess I was wrong."

Ray folded up the letter, creased it sharply, angrily, and put it back in the envelope.

"Well . . . sure . . . okay. . . . If that's the way it is," Ray said.

Dean went to Los Angeles by himself now, although soon the trips he made became less frequent and then a little less yet. Then there was an editorial in the *Los Angeles Times* about the number of fires in the city, and Mr. Mei decided that for a while anyway it was time to leave things alone. Dean stood in the kitchen, looking out the window toward the south, saying, "It sure seems to get dark early this time of the year, doesn't it? Maybe I'll go for a drive. Just to get out."

There was still a spring and summer to get through. The spring came with new grass the color of broccoli, and for a while the hills, which were usually tawny, turned green and had a cool promise. The leaves of the eucalyptus seemed darker than usual, and the younger trees had a pinkish blush over their bark. There was some wind, too, which had about it a hint of the enormous emptiness of the Pacific out of which it blew.

In the summer, Ray and Mary Wilcox spent time together, going into the hills and the fields outside of town, and when the days were hot, and the air was filled with the pressure of summer, they stretched out on the tall grass, letting the sun hit their bare skin, both of them approaching each other with curiosity mixed with the certainty that time was running out. There were moments, with the sun on Ray's shoulders and with his and Mary's perspiration mixed together on his stomach and chest, when he turned to look at the land, which shimmered in the heat, and in the fluid quivering of it there seemed to be a reminder of those flames in Los Angeles, where, if nothing else, Ray had begun to grow up. When they sat with the sun on them, Mary said, "So, you're getting out of here?"

"Yes," said Ray.

"Me too," she said. "I'm going to study computers. No traps for me. No kids. No husband. I'm going to have it all."

When he walked into the house, his skin having the scent of the afternoons he had spent, Dean looked up, his entire air one of being somehow cheated, if only because time has its own moments when it gives and then takes away (as it takes youth) with a frank brutality.

There were times when, on Saturdays, Dean left the house, walking along the streets of town, his eyes set on the distance, his demeanor one of defiance. On these afternoons, Ray said to his mother and Pearl, "Come on. Let's go out for a while." They would get into that anonymous Chevrolet and drive to the edge of town, where there was a drive-in, a place where there were carhops on roller skates. Marge drove and Pearl sat up front, and Ray sat in the back. The carhops wore short brown shorts, a white blouse trimmed in brown, a pillbox hat, and net stockings. Ray, Marge, and Pearl each had a sandwich and some french fries, which a carhop brought out, rolling up to the car with an aluminum tray. She would fasten the tray to the window.

"Oh," said Pearl one afternoon. "Those french fries are good."

"They'll ruin your complexion," said Marge.

"Complexion, shmection," said Pearl.

Ray sat in the back and watched the carhops as they floated between the cars and back to the place where they picked up their orders. They pushed off to the side with one foot and then the other, their locomotion having about it the quality of someone who is just floating above the ground.

"Ray," said Marge, "I'm glad you're going away."

"You think it's a good idea?" asked Ray.

"Yes," said Marge.

"Yes," said Pearl.

"The thing you've got to be careful about is the romance of things. Your father is a romantic. The Big Time. Abbadabba Berman . . . ," said Marge.

"Big Time, Shmig Time," said Pearl.

"What he does in Los Angeles," said Marge. "You know . . ."

"Yes," said Ray. "I know."

"So be careful about it," said Marge, "about the romance of anything. Romance is on the surface. Look behind it. All right?"

Ray watched the carhops. The automobiles were parked in two lines, one in which their headlights pointed toward the building of the drive-in, the other with their headlights pointing to the grass in the fields outside of town. The carhops had long muscled legs that were smooth inside their stockings, and the brown shorts were very snug over their hips so as to show the youthful shape of them. The carhops were very fast as they went between the cars, their legs swinging out as they gathered speed, their motion almost swooping as they carried the aluminum trays. There was, in their movement as they floated against the summer grass outside of town, in the tight shape of their hips, in the sway of their backs, a hint of order, and a skill too, like a man eating a spaghetti dinner while sitting on a chair balanced on a high wire. They glided from place to place, usually along a curved path so smooth as to imply a kind of mathematics, and in the swinging of their legs, in the muscles that contracted with an almost oily slither under the fishnet stockings, in the crispness of their blouses, in their steady, almost languid gaze, in their sudden and unexpected smiles, or in their winks and laughter there was an atmosphere of life delighting in itself. Ray watched them floating against the landscape as he held his untasted sandwich in his hand.

"I don't know," said Ray. "There's nothing wrong with romance."

"Wait," said Marge. "I've had it up to here with romance."

In the fall, Dean drove Ray to the airport. Both of them sat in the front seat, as though they were on their way to Los Angeles to get rid of a "professional center" or motel or warehouse that had outlived its usefulness. They didn't speak, though, and Dean didn't play the radio, either. At the airport there were No Parking signs in front of the terminal, but Dean stopped the car where the curb was painted yellow. He reached across his son and pushed the door open.

"Get out," he said.

There was the stink of jet fuel in the air. In the back seat there was a new suitcase, a secondhand typewriter, and the trombone. Dean said, "Well, this is the end of the line."

"Are you coming in?" said Ray as he got out of the car.

Taxis pulled up and let people out in front of the terminal. A driver of one of them rolled down his window and, while pointing at the No Parking sign, said to Dean, "Are you blind or what? Can't you read?" Dean got out of the car quickly and took a step toward the cabdriver, who put the taxi into gear and took off, not looking back.

"You see?" said Dean. "You call their bluff and they get out of your way." He went to the trunk of the car. "Look. I got something for you."

He opened the lid. In the trunk, among the jumper cables and a spare tire and some tools, there was a package. It was wrapped in brown butcher paper and held together with twine, and there was a small handle, like the kind department stores put on packages, looped over the twine. The package was about four feet long and it looked as if it might contain an instrument of some kind or maybe some athletic equipment, lacrosse sticks and a helmet, say, or a fly rod and some waders. Dean picked it up and handed it over.

"Here's a present," said Dean. "It's a jack and a piece of four-by-four."

Beyond the airport there was some flat land over which there was a clear blue sky. There wasn't a cloud in it, not a fleck of anything but that whitish blue. Ray looked from it to his father and said, "Okay. Thanks."

Ray reached out and took it.

"Come in, will you?" said Ray.

Dean picked up the trombone case and carried it in, and after Ray had checked his things, the jack and four-by-four included, the two of them stood by a window and looked at the large, brightly painted, and shiny airplanes, the things lifting into the air and trailing plumes of exhaust.

"What's rule number one?" asked Dean.

"Don't hang around after a fire," said Ray.

"That's right. Don't forget it," said Dean.

Dean put out his hand.

"All right. There's my hand," said Dean.

Ray reached out and took it, the two of them looking into each other's eyes, the sensation exactly as when they had taken each other's hand in the street and Ray had felt something running between them.

"Yeah, well," said Dean. "All right."

Then he turned and walked along the windows, beyond which the bright airplanes waited. He walked easily, his head turning from side to side, as though he were just out for a stroll. Outside, the airplanes taxied on the runway, the whistle and shriek of their engines muted by the thick glass.

Ray changed planes in Los Angeles. From the air the city looked dusty and sprawling, glittering. In the distance there were some fires burning, or maybe it was only smoke from an oil refinery, and as the streets and the miniature cars rolled by, Ray realized how frightened he was to be leaving it after all. The place seemed to have its own tug, its own attachments, the denial of which seemed, more than anything else, to represent a failure.

THE BURNING
RIVER

Ray was taught to row by Frank Beam, a tall man in his late fifties whose face had been scarred in an automobile accident. When Ray saw the shells on the river and had asked Beam about learning to row one, he had looked at Ray, the white, plasticlike scars on the side of his face giving Beam a fierce quality. Ray stood on the dock, with the Connecticut River behind him, not really understanding what it was about the long, narrow shells that attracted him. Beam glanced away and said, "All right. Be down here tomorrow. Wear something you can get wet in."

It was fall, and the mornings were cool and the maples and popples along the bank had turned orange and yellow. Ray stood on the dock, shivering a little, and as he looked at the glassy water, from which the mist rose, Beam came up behind him, his scarred face emerging from the fog by the river, his eyes definite, almost contemptuous, and then he said, "If you're afraid, it will make matters worse for you. Get a boat out of the rack."

In the boathouse, the racks for shells went from the floor to the ceiling, the light appearing in long lines on the lacquered hulls. The singles were narrow boats made from aircraft-grade spruce that was covered with mahogany. The mahogany was a sixteenth of an inch thick. Each boat had a seat that rolled back and forth, riggers that extended from the sides of the washbox where the rower sat, and stretchers, or shoes with laces, for the rower to tie in his feet.

Ray brought one out and got it in the water, and Beam showed him how the Latanzo oarlocks worked and explained about the sliding seat, the stretchers, and then Ray sat in the boat, which in its tippy movements, even as Beam held the stern, seemed so uncontrollable and alive as to make for a variety of panic. Ray sat in it, the oars on the water, Beam's face scowling at him. Beam held on to the stern and Ray tried to row a little, and then Beam let him go. Ray tipped over, hitting the cold water. It was so cold as to burn, and it made him pant as he swam back to the dock, his eyes set on Beam's. Beam said, "You were afraid. Or just unsure. Don't be afraid. Be certain. The worst that can happen is you'll fall in. You've done that once, so there's no mystery. Try it again."

Ray showed up in the mornings and Beam watched him, correcting him when he dropped a hand at the catch, or when he rushed the slide, and soon Beam was out in the launch, making Ray row hard for a long enough time to get tired and to make mistakes again, and then Beam said, his face furious, "You're trying to control it too much. That means you're afraid."

Ray went to the river at seven o'clock each morning, when the water looked like a mirror from which a mist was rising. He rowed, keeping the pressure on the balls of his feet, the entire sense of the shell moving through the water coming almost as an oiled, fleshy push, the surface behind him marked by the roiling of the puddles where the blades had been. The puddles went two by two, and as they spread, with the pattern of water where someone has thrown a stone, the concentric rings interfered with one another. The leaves were reflected in the water: it seemed as though the river were on fire, the soldering-iron orange of the maples mixing with the yellows of the poplars. Ray passed over what seemed to be a chaos of flames. The creak of the stretchers, the thump of the oars turning in the locks, the sliding of the seat had a hypnotic quality, and in it, with the fiery colors around him, and with each new advancement (rowing with more pressure, or at a higher rate), with each bit of fear that simply vanished into competence, he began to think about California.

☛

Pearl got married, and Ray came home for the wedding. It was held in a church in town, and the reception was in a Holiday Inn. There was a band, and the groom and Pearl danced a little awkwardly in front of the others. Dean was talking and laughing, even crying when he danced with his daughter. He and Ray stood at the side of the room, neither saying much.

"How's Mei Yaochen?" asked Ray.

"Him?" said Dean. "Oh, he's fine. Couldn't be better."

"How are things otherwise?" said Ray.

"Fine, fine," said Dean. "How are things with you?"

"I'm okay," said Ray.

"Glad to hear it."

In the morning, Ray walked downtown, where he passed the dry cleaner's, the gas station, the pawnshop, and then he turned and went along a tree-lined street, stopping in front of a house that had weeds in the yard. Iris's father had bought a new car, a convertible, and it sat in the driveway. Otherwise the house seemed unchanged. Ray stood in front of it and then went up to the door and knocked.

Iris's father opened the door, and Ray said, "Hello, Mr. Mason."

"Oh," he said. "It's you."

Mason's skin still had a gray quality, and he breathed quickly. He was wearing a pair of gray slacks, a green sweater, and a pair of slippers. It was ten o'clock in the morning and Mason was carrying a box of Kleenex. "I got a cold," he said. "Otherwise I'd be at the office. What do you want?"

"Can I come in?" said Ray.

"What for?" said Mason.

"I wondered if you had heard anything from Iris," said Ray.

"Her mother got a card," said Mason.

"Do you have an address for her?" asked Ray.

"Do you want it?" asked Mason. "Oh, God, doesn't that take the cake?"

"I was just wondering how she's doing," said Ray.

"Were you?" said Mason. He pushed open the door. "Come in."

Ray went into the kitchen and sat down. There was a cup of coffee on the table and a newspaper, and next to it there was a coffee cake. It had a brown glaze that was covered with slivers of almonds, and it gave off the aroma of cinnamon. Mason had torn away some of the crust, and beneath it was the butter-colored and fluffy cake.

"Sit down," said Mason.

Ray sat down.

"You'd think I'd know better than to eat this stuff," said Mason. "What with my heart."

"What did the card say?" asked Ray.

Mason looked away now and then went to the icebox, where he took out a bottle of grapefruit juice. He poured a glass and put it down in front of Ray, saying, "Here. Drink that. It's good for you."

"I've had breakfast," said Ray.

"You know," said Mason, "I never thought much about Iris's food. She ate junk like me."

Mason pushed the juice at Ray.

"Go on," he said. "Let me see you drink it."

"Tell me about the card," said Ray.

"Drink the juice," said Mason. "It's got vitamin C. It's fresh squeezed. I should have put some gelatin in it . . . that makes it even better. It's got trace elements, too, which are important for brain function. You've got to have iron. Calcium. I've been reading about it."

Ray nodded.

"Well," said Mason. "Are you going to drink it?"

Ray drained the glass.

"Good," said Mason. "I should have thought more about Iris's food."

"The card," said Ray.

"It said she was all right. Maybe she was going to travel," said Mason.

"Travel?" said Ray. "To where?"

"I don't know. Las Vegas. The Philippines. All kinds of places. She said she was just thinking about it."

Mason blew his nose into a Kleenex.

"I wish I could shake this cold," he said.

"Did she send an address?" said Ray.

Mason closed his eyes and said, "No. Doesn't that beat all?"

"Yes," said Ray. "I guess it does."

"You know what I'd like to do?" said Mason. "I'd like to cook something for Iris. I've been thinking about it. Some salmon poached in court bouillon. Broccoli flowers, you know, stir-fried, just so they get a dark green and are shiny. Small red potatoes. And for dessert, a chocolate cake. You make it like a soufflé, except you cook it in a big pan and then you roll it up with whipped cream. I'd just put it on the table."

They sat quietly for a moment and Ray looked around the room, at the sink and icebox, at the doorway, the silence of the place different now from what it had been on those mornings when he came to visit Iris.

"Well," said Ray. "I've got to go. Thanks for the juice."

"Sure," said Mason. "Take care of yourself."

Downtown the stores seemed a little foreign to Ray, even though he knew the names of the people who worked in each one. The air was warm and in it there were bits of dust, each a bright speck. The temperature and dusty light had a soporific quality, as though even time ran sluggishly here. Ray looked up the block at his parents' house, and as he walked toward it, through the drone of some late bees who flew on transparent wings, Ray tried to figure out what was wrong. There didn't seem to be anything out of the ordinary, although perhaps a car, which he recognized as Pearl's, had been left at an odd angle in the driveway. Ray walked a little faster, keeping an eye on the door, the windows, the trees that rose above the place, and when he came up to the porch Pearl said, brushing a strand of hair out of her face, "Oh, Ray, you're not going to believe this."

"What am I not going to believe?" said Ray.

"Dad's been arrested."

"For what?" said Ray.

"Arson," Pearl said.

Ray looked up at the gray clapboards of the porch.

"He was watching a fire he'd set and they picked him up," said Pearl. "There was a gas can in his car."

"He didn't use gas," said Ray. "He used kerosene."

"I wouldn't know about that," she said.

"Has he got a lawyer?" said Ray.

"I called one already," said Pearl. "I just wanted you to know."

"You mean he's going to be tried?" said Ray.

"Yes," said Pearl, "it looks that way. He's going to be . . . you know, arraigned in a couple of days. They can't prove anything, but, you know, they suspect him of more than just one fire."

✹

The arraignment took place in a courtroom that had pale green walls, a worn pinkish brown carpet, and a judge's dais made of blond wood. Dean came in from the side of the room, through a door beyond which prisoners were kept. He wore a dark blue jumpsuit that had written across the back (just like the name of a team) LOS ANGELES COUNTY JAIL. Ray had never seen his father without a shave, but Dean's face had a five or six days' growth, which didn't make him look so much like a bum, or shabby, as somehow reduced, like a walking version of something marked down at a fire sale. The thing that struck Ray was the whiteness of the beard around his father's chin and lips, the salt-colored whiskers looking somehow like everything that was inescapable. Dean was wearing handcuffs, iron-colored, drab things that had a long chain, the links of them clinking with an almost cheerful cling. Ray looked at the handcuffs and then refused to do so again, as though looking at them somehow validated their effect and made Ray a participant in the reduced state of the man who stood in the courtroom. Dean kept his head up and his shoulders square, as though he now believed in the difference between arsonists and firebugs not so much as a historical fact as an article of faith. Even though Ray didn't have to look at the handcuffs, he still heard them as his father was brought in from the room where prisoners were kept; and when his father stood up or sat down, his motion, the sound, the beard, the blue jumpsuit—all evoked a reduction, or the leavings of some kind of implosion, some pressure that simply made someone less than he had been before.

Ray sat in the first row, behind the rail. Dean kept his eyes on the judge or on the front of the courtroom or on nothing at all, so long as his eyes didn't face the section of the courtroom for spectators. Dean went about his business, getting up and sitting down and waiting patiently while the lawyer and the county attorney talked, his hands neatly folded in front of him. When the proceedings were coming to an end and Dean was going back into that small room where he had been before, Ray whistled a song they both played on the trombone, bringing up the volume as slowly as he could, the sound becoming barely audible. He went on until Dean jerked around, nodding as though he'd been asked if he understood. Then Ray looked down, hearing the clink of his father's chains.

In the hall, Dean's lawyer, a man who wore a pair of slacks, a tweed sport coat, and a Dacron shirt, turned to Ray and said, "We'll get the bail down. Don't worry. He'll be out in twenty-four hours. It'll be a while before the trial. Six months, a year? It'll be a while."

Then Ray went out to the airport, where the air was filled with the stink of kerosene.

≠

At the boathouse, Ray took a shell from the rack, and then he kneeled on the dock, reaching for the Latanzo lock on the outside rigger, opening it and dropping the oar in, doing it all with an insistence, or urgency, and then he stepped into the stretchers, tying the laces of them tightly. The trees were red, yellow, and orange, and as the maple leaves moved in the breeze they shimmered like coals in a stove. Ray rowed over the reflection of them, the colors breaking up into the blue, turbulent rings of the sky in the puddles left behind by the oars.

Ray squared the oars when his hands were over his feet, dropped the blades into the water without any splash, and drove off the stretchers, keeping the pressure on the balls of his feet, all of it making it hard to remember much of anything else, but in the pattern of it there were still moments when he was able to think, in a series of glimpses, of the things he had heard. At first the news from Pearl was that Dean had gotten out on bail, that he was working in the shop (and only in the shop) even though, with the lawyer, there was need for more money than ever before.

But there was something else Ray thought about. In the glassy water, in the movement of the boat, he thought of Iris as she had been when they approached a turn at a high rate of speed or when they were in bed and she would close her eyes and shake her head with amazement that she could ever have been so certain about another human being. While shaking her head she would start to cry, saying, "It's okay. Don't mind this. It doesn't mean anything at all." So now Ray went across the water, thinking of the flames of Los Angeles, of Iris's leaving her father's car at the side of the road, and of the dangerous hope that Los Angeles presented; and in it all, with each stroke, there was a mixture of exasperation and fury at his impulse to get away. He went on rowing, balancing over the treacherous possibilities of the depths.

＝

Pearl called, and when Ray picked up the phone and asked how she was, she said, "I don't know, Ray."

"What's wrong?" said Ray.

"Dad's got a girlfriend," said Pearl.

"What's new about that?" said Ray.

"Nothing," said Pearl. "Except this time it's a married woman. You know? I don't like the looks of it."

Pearl said the woman's name was Harriet Rainey. Harriet was thin and good-looking, in her middle thirties, with broad shoulders and a straight, small-hipped carriage. Her face had fine features, although they were rougher now than when she had been twenty-one. Her eyes were blue and she liked to keep a tan. She favored skirts and silk blouses, and she wore her medium-length, frosted hair in curls. There was a hardness about her expression, a fearless acceptance of the things she had seen, and her face showed some desperation too, and an attractive vulnerability that revealed itself as an unnourished capacity for pleasure. She sold sofas in a downtown discount house. Her husband was a truck driver.

In the beginning, Dean and Harriet had been discreet, or at least careful, but soon they were meeting in motels in the evening and going to restaurants in town, sitting in the middle of them, where they could be seen by everyone. There were times when they didn't come home until three or four o'clock in the morning, both of them wearing clothes that had obviously been put on in haste.

"I went to talk to him," said Pearl. Ray could imagine her shrugging. "You can imagine how that went," she said.

"Maybe I'll try," said Ray.

"I'm not so sure that's a good idea," said Pearl.

"I'd just like to talk to him," said Ray.

"Maybe later," said Pearl.

"What's the matter?" said Ray. "He'll talk to me, won't he?"

"I don't know, Ray," said Pearl. "I don't know. Maybe you should try some other time. All right?"

Ray went down to the river and sat by the bank. It was a still afternoon and the surface was as shiny as a polished mirror. Some leaves were washed up in the backwaters and eddies near the shore, the colors of them no longer bright red, but dull cinnamon colored, or bleached and pale rather than yellow.

In the evening he called his father.

"Hello," he said. "It's Raymond. I just called to say hello."

"Hello," said Dean.

"How are you doing?" said Ray.

"Okay."

"Look," said Ray. "I think we've got to talk."

"Well, sure," said Dean. "But I hope it's not to tell me what to do. Because you know what? What I'm doing is none of your business."

"Yes," said Ray. "I understand. I just wanted to say . . ."

They were both silent for a while.

"What?" said Dean. "What the fuck do you want to say?"

"I wanted to tell you to be careful," said Ray. "That's all."

"Who are you to tell me anything?" said Dean.

"Look," said Ray. "Just be careful. All right?"

Dean said nothing.

"I'm talking to you," said Ray.

"Are you?" said Dean. "Well, that's fucking great, isn't it?"

"Please," said Ray.

"Please what?" said Dean.

"Look," said Ray. "I'm sorry. That's all. Let's leave it at that."

"Not me. I'm not sorry. I'm pissed off. You know why? Somehow I ended up feeling like a piece of shit. So you know what, Mr. Test Taker? I'm going to enjoy myself for a while. What do you think of that?"

"I already told you," said Ray. "I think you should be careful."

"You keep your nose in your own business," said Dean.

"Look," said Ray, "I . . ." He stopped. "Maybe we should talk about something else."

"Sure," said Dean. "Like what?"

Ray looked at the blank white wall in front of him.

"Well, there are all kinds of things."

"Name me one," said Dean.

"Do you remember the mornings when we watched those bombs?" said Ray.

Dean said nothing, his reticence coming as the transcontinental static of the telephone.

"Or what about Abbadabba Berman?" said Ray. "Or Fat Charley Makley? Homer Van Meter? You remember them?"

"No," said Dean. "Not really. Not anymore."

So Ray rowed, hanging from the oars, feeling the pressure in his legs and under his fingers. There were still some leaves on the trees, and the water was bright with them, but here and there, through the last yellow of the poplars, there was the gray shape of the hills beyond the shores of the Connecticut. The gray reflection of them made the water look like the sea under an overcast sky. In the middle of the stroke, as the seat slid forward, Ray thought of Pearl's voice as she had said, "George Rainey went to the pawnshop and bought a gun. That's Harriet's husband."

"I know," said Ray.

"It's all over town now," said Pearl. "Everyone knows. Dad knows."

"I'll call him again," said Ray.

"That'll just make things worse," said Pearl. "You know that, don't you, Ray?"

On the river, he thought about Harriet's husband going into the pawnshop, the same one where Ray had picked out a trombone. He imagined George Rainey's hand reaching into the fanlike array of pistols and picking out a nickle-plated .357. With the thing in his hand, Rainey felt the cool tug of it. Ray thought of the pawnbroker, too, who took the lock off the trigger guard as though finally releasing some pent-up thing and pushed the pistol across the counter with a shove of approval.

≈

The weather got colder, and it was time to put the boats away. There had been ice on the river in the mornings, and at night there was the steady honk honk honk of the geese as they flew away from Canada. There were ducks flying, too, and there were times when Ray saw them in an eddy or a quiet pool. There was a beaver, which crossed from New Hampshire to Vermont, a wide V-shaped wake tapering away from its nose as it went. Ray stared at it, thinking about those pistols in the pawnshop, the sheen of the metal somehow melding with the molten, undulant reflection of the late-fall sun on the water.

Ray went to the dean of the school. He was a man of fifty, wearing a blue shirt, a green tie, and perfectly pressed khaki pants. He was bald, fluent, and smiled most of the time. The effect of the man was a steady and even pleasant diminishing of almost all things, and when Ray said he was going back to California for good, the man on the other side of the desk began to talk it over, but Ray shook his head and said, "I've got something to do."

BOOK II

THE HOUSE
AT ONE A.M.

Ray stood in front of the house with his suitcase on the sidewalk beside him. Even now he felt the effect of the airplane, and the steady thrust of the engines, the irregular sway of the wings, the constant blowing of air from a small tube came back in the same way the pounding of the hull of a sailboat comes back on dry land. It was cool, and the house seemed to sit under two enormous and shaggy creatures, which were trees against the night sky. On the front porch there was the glider that Ray's mother liked to sit on during the hot evenings of July and August, but it was too cold for that now, and even from a distance the glider seemed to have the dustiness of winter and lack of use. There was a light on downstairs, and through the filmy white curtains Marge had put up Ray saw a sofa, a chair, a magazine rack, a braided rag carpet, a reading light, all of which were arranged around a fireplace that Dean used to light on the cool evenings of January and February. Now it was black and empty. The room seemed comfortable, as dependable and as unchanging as a fossil, and for a moment Ray was struck by how ordinary it was. For a moment he stood there, and then he walked across the grass and stood on the porch, touching the glass, almost to see if it was real, if only because he wanted to go in and sit down with all the comfort of homecoming.

Instead, he went around to the back of the house. There was a light on in the kitchen too, and on the table there was a single place setting, a knife, a fork, a spoon, a glass, and a napkin, and in the middle of it there was a note, written in Marge's hand, which said, "Dean. There is a dinner for you in the oven," the note's handwriting showing a mixture of hope and fury, which was validated by the scent of the tuna casserole she had left.

Ray looked through the window here too, seeing the table, the counter, the draining board, the stove, and the old, white refrigerator, all of which seemed filled with a domestic promise of safety, although Ray knew precisely how much of an illusion this was. He put his things down on the back porch and sat, his forearms on his knees, looking east and remembering those mornings when he and his father had watched the light from the atomic bombs that had been set off in Yucca Flats, Nevada. The memory of the light brought with it a beauty, just a fleeting glimpse of what secrets there were behind the appearance of things, although the secrets seemed less benign than they had a few years before. Now, the light in the east, the false dawn of the tests, reminded Ray of fire, of things being out of control and having their own imperative, their own constant, unavoidable trajectory. Ray put out his hand for a moment, feeling the false security of the house behind him and remembering the illusion of the light, both of which left him looking to the darkness of the night for comfort, although he smiled, too, when he recalled those afternoons when he and Dean had gone downtown to the men's stores where Dean had held up a jacket, one lined with silk, and had slipped it over Ray's arms and shoulders, saying, "What do you think, Ray? Does that have any style?"

There weren't many stars out because it was a little hazy, but Ray went on looking at them, each one having the glitter of a purple sequin, the beauty of each seeming to be not only in the color, or the fact that each was uncorrupted, but that each was also incapable of being corrupted. Then he went back to thinking about the bombs, wondering how big they had been, the size of a trunk, of an orange? He stood and opened the door, putting his typewriter and then his bag down in the kitchen, where he waited, smelling the tuna casserole and looking at his mother's handwriting. He guessed that Dean would be back later.

He was careful with the screen door. It had a spring on it, and the memory of the squeak and bang came back now as something he could depend upon, a sound that had been there every day, not cheerful or anything really aside from constant. Then he looked in the oven, just to make sure: there was the tuna casserole, under a glass cover, made with potato chips just the way Dean hated it. Ray looked in for a moment, wanting to sit down on the floor, right there, but then he let the stove door close, just as quietly as he had the door to the porch. He had the impulse to take the casserole out of the oven and throw it in the backyard, as though it were the cause of the trouble rather than just one of the symptoms.

He went into the darkened hall beyond the kitchen, and as he stood there, only half lighted, it seemed to him that he was momentarily phantomlike, not himself so much as just a memory of how he had grown up here, and as such, he climbed the stairs, the pressure on the balls of his feet seeming to go through the years: he went through the shadows of the ladderlike supports of the upstairs banister. At the top he looked around, going first into his own room, which seemed smaller than he remembered, his bed, bureau, clothes in the closet seeming infinitely still. On the wall there were pictures of a mushroom cloud, a fireball, and the depths of the Galaxy, the stars there appearing in a purple miasma, the photographs bringing back all the old keenness of a desire for understanding.

In the hall, he stopped in front of his sister's empty room. There was almost nothing in it, and on the walls were the smoky outlines of where there had been pictures. Even now there remained something of Pearl's constant, unaffected ability to go on living and to do so without asking too many questions.

Marge could be seen in the dim light from the hall. She slept on her side, the blanket pulled over her shoulder, her head on the pillow. Her hair was gray, cut so short as to make her appear ascetic or self-flagellating, and in her sleep, which was silent, she seemed not to be resting so much as concentrating on some problem that just wouldn't go away. Ray stood at the foot of her bed, taking something (what, precisely, he wasn't sure) from the gentleness of the room, which was unlike a lot of the rest of the house. Around him there was only a silence, the weight of it and the finality of it making Ray linger, as though in the hiss of it there were some hint of the vulnerability everyone had to the effects of time. Outside there was the occasional sound of a car passing, but none stopped in front of the house.

Ray went downstairs again and into the kitchen, where he sat at the table opposite the empty place setting for Dean. The kitchen was quiet aside from the throb of the refrigerator, a repeated *unh, unh, unh* that always suggested a machine about to break down. From where Ray sat, he could see the pilot lights in the gas stove, the flames small and blue, surrounded on the top by a feather-shaped and yellow glow. There were many things that he had been ready to say, small speeches that in the East or on the plane had seemed to carry such weight and clarity, but that now seemed to have as much substance as the flame of the pilot light. In the absence of words the turmoil that was behind them was stronger than before. After a while he got up and made some coffee, and then sat opposite the empty place setting to wait.

It was one o'clock. The house at this hour seemed to be filled with something that was almost audible or palpable. Ray sat with the cup of coffee between his hands, his fingers symmetrical, almost as though in a gesture of prayer. Ray concentrated, trying to determine exactly what it was that filled the darkened house, and what was so maddeningly just beyond the tips of his fingers, his sight, or his ears. It seemed that it might even come from the objects in the room, and Ray got up and touched the stove, the rack in which there were knives, forks, and spoons. He opened a drawer in which there were tablecloths, checked ones and green ones that were used for every day, and the washed and soft cotton, pliable with use, seemed to convey the atmosphere of the house. He closed the drawer and stood still, his head cocked, his eyes looking toward the hall, and in the soft warmth of the shadows and in the patches of golden light, in the outlines of the shadow of the banister that lay on the wall of the stairs, there was the hint of the resilience that the people who lived here had brought to the house. Now, late at night, it seemed to meld with the shadows and become part of them, and for a moment Ray strained, wanting the sensation of it not to disappear, since when it did he would be left waiting with only a fierce impulse rather than his prepared speeches, which now, in the house, seemed to be the flimsy things they really were. Ray was unsure if this soothing presence really existed at all, or whether it was only a reflection of his lack of sleep, the long flight on the airplane, and his own impulse, which he now recognized for the first time, to have something dependable here, something recognizably ordinary and reassuring. But even as he stood there, wanting to go upstairs and to get into his old bed, he realized what an illusion that possibility was. Instead, he went into the hall, still holding the coffee cup, luxuriating in the softness of the silent house and knowing, too, that whatever it was, the precious thing he felt now would evaporate when someone else came into the house, if only because the house was exposed this way or capable of being understood only when someone who had lived in it stood alone in the hall at one o'clock in the morning.

Upstairs, Marge stirred in her sleep, turning over and murmuring, and then fell back into a deep slumber, her gentle breathing seeming to mix into the shadows and golden light. Ray turned and went back along the hall, into the kitchen, where he put the coffee cup on the table, the sound of it bringing him back to the task at hand. He couldn't even say, precisely, how things had gone wrong. He sat with the hard cup between his fingers, squeezing it, as though that would make things more obvious. The icebox began its slow, repetitive throb. Ray tried to find one clear, identifiable place to begin.

What was the thing that Dean had gotten out of the fires, aside from money? Ray looked around the house, now trying to estimate what the silence of it felt like to his father at one o'clock in the morning. The house, for Dean, might have had that reassuring sense of resilience, but this was probably blended with something else, a claustrophobia that came from the lack of possibilities and the certainty of being trapped. The walls themselves must have appeared to him as evidence of how there was no place to turn. Ray got up and went over to the icebox and put his hand against it, feeling the throb, and as he did, he suspected the first fire Dean had ever lighted must have been an antidote, a moment of piercing and short-lived freedom. How was Dean going to convey that to his son? It seemed possible to Ray, in the silence of the house at this hour, that his own impulse toward getting away was somehow related to his father's moments when burning down a building. He remembered taking his father's hand, and now, as he sat in the kitchen, watching the clock slowly mark the passing minutes, it seemed that what had passed between them was a desire, no matter for how short a time, to push away the constraints that seemed so deadly.

Ray went into the living room. There was only one light on, but Ray turned on another over a desk that was against the wall. It was a rolltop desk, stained a dark red, a color (like cordovan leather) that had been popular in offices in the late twenties and early thirties. The desk had belonged to Dean's father, a man who had failed as an insurance salesman and who had gone to work in Los Angeles for a mortuary, selling caskets. He had had soothing, even dignified manners (and an air of being both gentrified and genteelly down-at-the-heels), although he had taken to coming home at three in the afternoon to have a "toddy," as he called it, if only to fight back at the stink of formaldehyde that seemed to permeate even the showroom, and to fight, too, an afternoon letdown that came from being around those open caskets with their silk liners. The desk was about all that Dean had been left, and he sat here from time to time to do the bills or to balance the checkbook, seeming to take some consolation from the fact that his father had faced financial trouble from the same point of command.

Ray sat down and rolled the top up. In the pigeonholes there were papers, bank statements, notices of life insurance payments due, of health and house insurance, a clutter of domestic papers, the security of which was only partially or occasionally realized. There was a green ink blotter, a fountain pen, and a set of drafting compasses in a box lined with green felt. Ray opened the drawers, not even knowing what he was looking for but somehow doing so out of something more profound than ordinary curiosity and with the awareness that this was the thing one did to the papers only of someone who had died. In the top drawers there were blank checks and old tax returns, and in the bottom one there was a file that had written across it, with ink from the fountain pen that lay on the blotter, OPPORTUNITIES.

Ray lifted it out and put it on the desk, feeling the weight of it. He had never seen it before, not even when he had been a child and had sat here using the compasses to draw pictures of trains and airplanes. The folder was old, though, and inside there were bits of paper that were yellowed with age. Ray looked at one and then another, lifting some of the old pieces of newspaper that were the color of nicotine stains. There were advertisements for small-machine repair kits, knife sharpeners, portable sawmills, devices that cut down the amount of oil a furnace burned, or directions to convert automobiles to burn alcohol, and next to them there were catalogs from the university's extension program. Inside, the courses had been circled, Calculus and Mathematical Analysis, First-Year Law, Chemistry, although the one that had been marked up the most was a course in Latin, as though an old language would have been useful, and next to the course description Dean had written some Latin phrases he had seen in the newspapers, *deus ex machina*, *op. cit.*, as though by writing them down he was on his way to understanding them. There was also a note on the "Scientific Method," which said, in Dean's large, neat hand, "Collecting Data, Formulating Theory, Testing Theories." Next to this there was a circular for learning tattooing through the mail.

Ray closed the file up, and put it away, and went back into the kitchen.

A car pulled up in front of the house, the lights illuminating the street, making the objects on it, mailboxes, a fence, the winter-burned grass, emerge from the shadows. In the house, the atmosphere changed immediately, just vanishing the way the golden haze of a headlight on a white wall disappears when the light is turned off. Ray put the coffee cup down.

Dean appeared at the kitchen door. His shirt wasn't tucked into his pants, and he was carrying the tie he had worn earlier. He needed a shave, and his eyes were bloodshot. He came inside and closed the door quietly, not gently but with the air of a man who doesn't want to make any noise for reasons of his own. He took a pint bottle of bourbon out of his jacket pocket and had a drink. Then he put it on the table and stood there for a moment.

"Well, well," he said. "Well, well. What the hell are you doing here?"

"I came home," said Ray.

"Well, well," said Dean. "Is that right?"

Ray nodded.

"Do you want some coffee?" said Ray.

"Sure," said Dean. "I'd like some coffee. I guess I can have a cup of coffee here. It's my house, isn't it?"

"I'll make a fresh pot," said Ray.

He went to the cupboard and took down the can of Hills Bros. coffee and measured some into the top of the percolator, feeling, as he did so, that the objects in the kitchen, the neat array of the cans on the shelf, weren't as comforting as they had been just a few moments before. Now they seemed dull and ordinary. He put the coffeepot on the stove and turned on the gas, but even though the pilot light was lighted, the gas didn't go on.

Dean took a box of matches from the cupboard and lighted one, put it under the pot, and the fire came on with a whoosh.

"Thanks," said Ray.

They sat for a while, on opposite sides of the table. The water in the coffeepot began to make an unpleasant roiling.

"Well?" said Dean. "Explain yourself."

"I've got some unfinished business here," said Ray.

"Oh?" said Dean.

Ray nodded, then he looked across the table at Dean's reddish eyes.

"Why don't you have something to eat? There's a dinner in the oven. Then we can talk."

"I ate downtown," said Dean.

Dean turned around and looked at the stove, the oven door of which he opened. He stared for a moment at the tuna casserole, and then looked back at Ray.

"The coffee will be ready soon," said Ray.

"Here," said Dean, offering the pint. "Maybe you should have a little. It loosens your tongue."

"All right," said Ray. "Why not."

Ray began to pour some into his coffee cup, but Dean reached over and stopped him and said, "Naw, not like that. You and I always took it right out of the bottle. Have you gotten fancy on me?"

"No," said Ray. He took a sip from the bottle and sucked his lower lip for a second, which made his chin pitted exactly like Dean's. "No. I'm not getting fancy."

Dean shrugged.

"You don't convince me," said Dean.

The coffeepot went from that roiling sound to a steady perking, the fluid in the glass knob at the top still about the color of tobacco juice. Dean took another sip and said, "What kind of clothes did they wear back there?"

"Just clothes," said Ray.

"What kind of answer is that?" said Dean. "Give me some details. They didn't wear blue jeans, did they?"

"Yes," said Ray. "They did."

"And what kind of shirts?" said Dean. "Button-down? Knit ties? Tweed jackets?"

Ray nodded.

"Tell me," said Dean. "Did you ever get dressed up? Did you go to New York ever?"

"What's the difference?" said Ray.

"We're just having chitchat," said Dean. "Tell me."

"I went to New York," said Ray. "A friend invited me to go home with him. We had to dress for dinner."

"What did you wear?" said Dean.

"Evening clothes," said Ray. "I rented mine. Black tie."

"I'll bet you looked like a penguin," said Dean.

"I didn't look so bad," said Ray.

"Don't tell me," said Dean. "That's no way to dress. You got to have a black shirt and a white tie, slacks that have a little movement to the fabric. French-toed shoes. Maybe you slick your hair back. Maybe you carry a gun . . . let people get a glimpse of it now and then. You got to live."

"Is that right?" said Ray.

Dean nodded and had a sip from the brown bottle, pitting his chin as he felt the harshness of the bourbon in his mouth and its long, burning descent.

"What else did you wear?" said Dean.

"Let's talk about something else," said Ray.

"I like this," said Dean.

"Screw the clothes," said Ray.

Dean put back his head.

Ray reached across the table, where he picked up the bottle, and took a sip, glad for the sweet rawness of bourbon against the taste of coffee.

"Jesus," said Dean. "You think you can go away and then just walk back in here as though nothing happened. Well, I got news for you, bub. You can't do that."

"Everyone has dreams," said Ray.

"Is that right?"

"Yes," said Ray. "Come into the living room."

"You watch what you say to me," said Dean.

They went into the living room and stood in front of the rolltop desk. Ray reached down and pulled open a drawer and took out the manila file marked OPPORTUNITIES. Then he opened the top of it, flicking the manila panel through a line of shadow. On top of the pile inside was the catalog from the university extension program.

"You've been snooping through my papers," said Dean. "Stay out of them. I'll fix you good if I catch you at it again."

Dean closed the file and looked out the window at the street. It was silent, the streetlamp shining, the shadows of the leaves of the trees lying on the sidewalk in a lacy pattern that suggested black lingerie. Ray looked too. There was a sheen on the asphalt and on the parked cars, and there were shadows between the houses. In the shadows there was a frankness, a bald, almost disinterested quality, as though the street had about it an air of everything that had already happened and was inescapable anyway.

Dean turned back now, and with his face slack with amazement, he said, "How could I have been so stupid? It was that little high-school piece of ginch, wasn't it?"

"What?" said Ray. "What did you call her?"

"Sure," said Dean. "That's it. Well, well. So you were sliding over there too. Isn't that right?"

Ray stepped a little closer.

"Give me a chance, bub," said Dean, making a fist. "I'd love to. . . . Come on, tell me I'm wrong about the girl."

Ray shook his head.

"No," said Ray. "I won't tell you you're wrong."

"I should have known it all along," said Dean. "It's just that. Well, hell, you can't let a piece of ass—"

"What did you say?" said Ray.

"You heard me," said Dean.

"Oh, God," said Ray. "Why don't you stop acting like a . . ."

"Like a what?" said Dean.

"Never mind," said Ray. "Let's just leave it that it's better not to talk."

"No," said Dean. "Come on. You were going to say something."

He stepped closer, and as he did, Ray realized that his father wasn't as tall as he used to be. For a while they had been the same height, but now, as the years had passed, Dean had actually lost a little height. Dean stood up a little straighter.

"Well, come on," said Dean.

"Let's let it go," said Ray.

"Naw," said Dean. "You mean to say you came three thousand miles to stand here like a coward?"

Ray shook his head. Dean reached out and slapped him, not hard, just making a snap, first one way and then the other. The sounds weren't loud, about like the noise a rubber band makes when it breaks: the snaps hung in the living room. Ray stood there, looking at Dean.

"Come on," said Dean. "Say it."

"You want to hear it?" said Ray.

"If you dare," said Dean.

"Stop acting like a small-time crook," said Ray.

Dean stood there, his hand raised, palm flat. For a moment they stayed that way, opposite one another. Then Dean made a fist and cocked his arm back, shaking his head a little.

Dean looked down at the open folder, and for a moment he flipped the pages in it, the old advertisements, the clippings from the paper, the catalogs from the extension service, and as he did so there was the smell of musty old paper.

"I just wanted things to be ordinary," said Ray.

"So what?" said Dean, flipping the file cover. "I wanted things too." Then he looked up at Ray, dropping his hand as he did so. "You know something, Ray? There's a beauty to what I do, and you can't see it. Sometimes I'm really free." He shoved the folder back into the desk, and then he said, without looking up, "Get out. I don't want you here anymore."

Ray turned away and went into the kitchen, where the coffee was on the stove, percolating hard, a long rope of steam rising from the spout. Ray turned off the heat, watching the flames wick out.

"I'll go now," said Ray.

"Stay on the couch," said Dean. "I won't put you out on the street. Go tomorrow."

"All right," said Ray. "Thanks. I'll be going then, down to L.A."

"You think you're going to be able to find her down there?"

"I don't know," said Ray. He shrugged.

"L.A.," said Dean. "I'd like to see you in L.A. That's a tough place, you know that? Yeah, I'd like to see you in L.A."

Ray sat down at the table and Dean did too, the two of them opposite one another. Dean started crying now, saying, "Ah, shit. Ah, fuck it. I didn't want you to see me like this."

Ray got up and went to the other side of the table and put his arm around Dean, amazed at the size and strength of the shoulders and the power of his sobbing.

"I'm sorry," said Ray.

Dean looked up now, though, his eyelashes wet, the moisture diamond colored.

"I guess I just had too much to drink," said Dean. "I guess that's it."

Ray held him a moment longer and then went back to the other side of the table, where he picked up the pint bourbon bottle and had a sip, pulling in his lower lip and making his chin pitted.

"Let's talk about something else for a little bit," said Ray. "I'll be going soon."

THE END OF THE
WORLD

Along Ventura Boulevard in Los Angeles there are a lot of motels, but none of them seemed right. Ray kept saying he'd stop at the next one, and then one after that, but by that time he was in the Cahuenga Pass and looking toward Chinatown. He went out on Santa Monica, seeing the green and yellow sign of the Golden Palm, which he pulled into, glancing at the oil pressure gauge of the Mercury and listening to the sound of the engine, reassured that he hadn't done anything to it on the way down from Bakersfield. He'd driven pretty fast.

The motel was almost filled with members of a church who had come to Los Angeles for the end of the world. Some of them had come from as far away as Chicago and Twin Forks, Tennessee, although a lot of them had come from northern California and the Pacific Northwest.

Ray went into the office and rented a room, and as he filled out the card, the manager, a man named Barstow, said, "Don't let these people bother you."

"Who?" said Ray.

"The other guests," said Barstow. "They came here to watch the world blow up. But I put more chlorine in the pool, so it's all right. You can go swimming as much as you like. You won't catch anything from them."

Ray's room was next to the office, through the wall of which he could hear Barstow talking to himself. After a while Barstow started drinking and listening to the radio, Mantovani mostly, the sound of which was broken by Barstow's opening his small icebox and getting out an ice tray. He drank vodka and fruit juice, as a kind of health food, and when he was done he had a can of Metrecal, which he thought was a way of subtracting the calories he had just consumed. Then he took two Valium to go to sleep.

Ray sat on the bed with his suitcase next to him. Inside there were some shirts and socks, underwear, some books from the East (*Problems in Modern Engineering*, *Thermodynamics for the Practical Man*, and *Classical Scores for the Trombone*). Ray looked at these things, which he had packed along with a box of black-powder caps, a windup alarm clock with brass bells on it, a box of Tampax (which were used as fuses for a bottle filled with gasoline and soda), a bottle of acid, some potassium chlorate, a bag of sugar, and a matchbook. The books and the other things all seemed to be evidence of what he knew, his patrimony included here too. Then he closed the suitcase and put it on the stand at the end of the bed, taking some consolation in the fact that this was what he had. Outside, there were the lights of Chinatown, but it was only about eight o'clock.

The New Church of God had been founded by a man who had been a stockbroker and a financial adviser to a South American dictator, and who from time to time had visions of such piercing beauty as to leave him crying for hours. One of the visions that had convinced the founder of the church that the end was near was of a trout pond in the Sierras. In the vision he caught enormous, red-sided rainbows on midges, just little mayflies about the size of a pinhead. The founder of the church hadn't shown up in L.A. for the end of the world, but this didn't bother the members of the church who had made the trip.

Ray walked across the parking lot to the pool, where the church members were sitting. They were of all ages, male and female, and they spoke quietly among themselves, and the light from the pool was a light blue, which made their faces appear as though lighted by fox fire. They seemed pale and a little ethereal.

One of them was a tall man with gray hair and long thin arms who wore a sport shirt, a pair of jeans, and a string tie. His name was Fuller Wright and he had been a snake chunker in southern Ohio, a man who demonstrated his faith by handling rattlesnakes, although he had made his money in a car dealership in Chillicothe. It seemed obvious to him that the world was going to end, since for a while now he had been sleeping with his children's baby-sitter, who had been blackmailing him, not only for money but for the deed to a house and five acres he had been renting to her. He had heard the prediction about the end of the world the morning his wife had discovered the baby-sitter in her bed with just a sheet over her and drinking a glass of cold white wine, although the thing that had made the wife decide to file for divorce was the loss of the house and five acres. She had cut the baby-sitter with a paring knife, and the baby-sitter went around town, even in the supermarket, showing her wound (removing the skin-toned tape she had received in the emergency ward) and talking about the entire thing as though she had had an accident in the parking lot. She described some of Fuller's intimate habits, saying, "When he wanted to do that, I just didn't know what to *say*." Fuller got into one of the demonstrator cars from his dealership and started driving west, going out along the flat stretches of Interstate 80, thinking about the rattlesnakes as he had held them by the tail (the snakes arching their backs and standing almost straight out from his hand) and cursing the baby-sitter, whose name was Sally McGhee, and his wife, and thinking, too, that both of them would get theirs when the world ended. He had caught up with the caravan of church members' cars in Lincoln, Nebraska, and then they had all gone west, their lights on, like a funeral procession. They had stopped together in the same motels, driving all night and sleeping during the day, arriving at most places just as the previous guests were leaving in the morning.

Fuller said he had been able to feel the approach of the end of the world in the bodies of the snakes he had handled. The serpents had been unsteady and one had struck at him. There were other signs too, especially in Los Angeles, a shooting star, a carhop whom someone had seen in tears, a particularly high tide, a cinnamon-colored moon, reports in the newspaper that another young woman had disappeared. There had been some remains in an out-of-the-way cove north of Santa Monica, up toward Trancas, or Ventura. The newspapers didn't seem to agree about precisely where they had been found, although there were some hints, too, of a ceremony: there was a reddish powder thrown around, ciphers left in the sand. There were other things, too: a volcano up north in Washington had begun to smoke, and the birds were restless at night. Most of the people around the pool looked scared, and although they were in the position of people who knew a secret that was about to prove them all right, the moral superiority of such a moment wasn't enough.

Fuller looked up at Ray and said, "What are you doing here?"

"I'm waiting," said Ray.

"Amen, brother," said Fuller. "It'll all be over at six o'clock tomorrow."

"Have you made your peace?" said a woman of about forty-five. She was wearing a faded blue dress that seemed to match her eyes. Her hair was the color of steel wool.

"No," said Ray, glancing toward Chinatown, "not quite yet."

"Well, you better," said one, a woman at the side of the pool who sat in a chaise lounge. "Before tomorrow morning."

"Amen, sister," said a man who had bad teeth.

"Wouldn't you like to make your peace?" said a young woman with long blond hair. Her hair was very straight and shiny and it looked as if she had ironed it to make it that way.

"Yeah," said Ray. "Maybe I'll get a chance after midnight."

"Oh?" said Fuller. "You think it could be that soon?"

Ray shrugged. "Maybe," he said.

He looked toward Chinatown, the glow of the lights golden in the mist of the evening.

"I just don't want anyone lying to me," said Ray.

"Amen," said Fuller. "The time of lying has come to an end."

"That's right," said the woman in the chaise lounge. "Thank God."

"They say it will be fire this time," said Fuller.

Ray nodded.

"Just a blinding flash of blinding white love," said Fuller. "Something like an atomic bomb. That's the way it's going to be."

"How do you know what an atomic bomb is like?" asked the woman in the chaise.

"I don't know," said Fuller. "Who can have seen an atomic bomb and lived to tell about it?"

"It's like false dawn. Not so much gray as white," said Ray.

"Amen," said Fuller. "That's what it's going to be. Are you coming out with us tomorrow morning?"

"Maybe," said Ray. "I've got some business tonight."

At the side of the group, next to the woman in the faded blue dress, there was a boy, about eleven. He had blond, sun-bleached hair, and he wore high-top sneakers, faded blue jeans, and a striped T-shirt. His teeth weren't straight and he had freckles. He had been listening and now he started crying. His mother said, "Hush, Everett, hush."

The boy went on crying.

"I don't want to die," he said.

"Think about love," said the woman in the chaise. "Divine love. That warm, beautiful light will bathe you forever."

"I don't want to die," said Everett.

"This is God's way of helping," said Fuller.

Everett went on crying, although he kept his head down in the shadows that were around the pale, bluish light from the swimming pool.

"May I buy your boy a Coke?" said Ray. "Maybe he's thirsty."

"Well, thank you," said the woman in the blue dress.

Ray turned and started walking toward the Coke machine, but the boy hung back. Ray stood there, smelling the extra chlorine that Barstow had put in the pool. The boy was ashamed now, and he was quiet, his head down. Ray went over to him and said, "Come on. Let's get a Coke."

They walked across the parking lot of the motel, the asphalt of it glittering a little and appearing a little like dark water. Above the office there was the neon sign, the green palms and the yellow trunks, which flickered unsteadily over the new Coke machine, which was about eight feet tall, red and white.

"Have you got a handkerchief?" asked Ray.

"No," said Everett.

"Take mine," said Ray. "It's clean." He opened it up and held it out, seeing in the corner the *D.G.* of his father's monogram. Everett took it.

"I always carry one in case I start crying," said Ray.

"I don't want to cry," said Everett.

Ray shrugged. They stood in the light of the neon sign and of the Coke machine while Ray reached into his pocket for some change. He passed over the quarters and said, "You put it in."

Everett put the money in and pressed a button, the Coke coming out with a hard *kerchunk*.

"Nothing's going to happen," said Ray.

"How do you know?" said Everett. "Tell me. Say it again."

"It's a secret," said Ray. "Don't blab over there. You'll get in trouble."

"Tell me again," said Everett. "Are you sure?"

"Yes," said Ray.

"Then why are they talking over there like that? Flashes of light. You know."

"Listen," said Ray. "Just leave it that nothing's going to happen tomorrow. Be quiet about it or you'll get in trouble. All right?"

"I don't want to die," said Everett.

"I told you about that," said Ray. "If there's going to be any dying, it's not going to be here."

"Then where?" said Everett.

"Maybe Chinatown," said Ray. "Drink your Coke."

"You want your handkerchief?"

"No," said Ray. "You keep it. I don't plan to do any crying tonight."

"What are you mad about?" asked Everett.

"I lost my girlfriend," said Ray. "I just let her wander off. Can you believe it?"

"Why did you do that?"

"I got some bad advice," said Ray. "You know, sometimes you try to do the right thing, or to do the smart thing, and you know what? You find yourself in deeper than before. Come on. Be quiet about tomorrow."

"Are you sure?" said Everett.

"What do you want?" said Ray. "A written guarantee?"

"I haven't got any paper," said Everett.

"Come on. Let's go back," said Ray.

"Are you going to come tomorrow?" asked Everett.

"Why should I?" said Ray. "I've got something to do."

"I want to see your face, just in case you're wrong. Well?" said Everett.

"All right," said Ray. "Fine."

"You aren't lying to me, are you?" said Everett.

"What did I tell you?" said Ray. "If we're going to get along, you've got to realize I'm not saying any blab that comes into my head. I'll be there."

"Do you think I can go to Disneyland?" said Everett. "If nothing happens?"

"I don't think your parents are going to be in the mood to go to Disneyland tomorrow," said Ray.

They walked across the asphalt. Ray and Everett looked like dark figures, one small, the other tall, with the shape of the green neon palm behind them.

"Don't you see, Everett?" said the woman on the chaise. "All your troubles are going to be over. Don't you see? No more suffering."

"Amen," said the man with the bad teeth.

"He's coming tomorrow," said Everett, pointing at Ray.

"Are you?" said Fuller. "Well, you're welcome to spend the time with us."

"So, you've made your peace after all?" said the woman in the faded dress.

"Not quite yet," said Ray. "I've got business."

"What kind of business?" asked Fuller.

"It won't take long," said Ray.

Some of the church members looked at the sky, a pale, rust-colored dome that seemed to cover the entire city. It was a color that came from the endless red lights in the city, or maybe was just a muddy accumulation of all the lights, the effect of it suggesting claustrophobia or maybe just a subterranean place.

"You won't let me down, will you?" said Everett.

"No," said Ray.

"I got to find an all-night supermarket," said Fuller. "I'm hungry for some fruit. Maybe some grapes or melon or something."

"There's one right out on Santa Monica," said Ray.

"That's good," said Fuller. "Is it safe to leave your car there in the parking lot? I hear stories about how in L.A. you can have your car stripped in two minutes flat. Isn't anything left but a carcass."

~

After midnight, in Chinatown, it was foggy. On the street, in the distance, there were the dim outlines of people. At first they appeared to be nothing more than half-imagined shapes, but then they emerged from the mist, their faces cold. Ray stood in front of the grocery store. The door in the back room was open, and light from it fell across the floor. The yellow slash cut into the darkness, and there seemed to be in it a kind of certainty.

Ray put his hand to the window, and while he touched it, a man came from the back room. He wore a pair of dark pants and a white shirt with a bow tie.

"What you want?" the man said.

Ray looked again at the dark interior of the store.

"No one here," said the man.

"I used to talk to someone there," said Ray. "Back there." He pointed to the back room.

"Not here anymore. You want to see him, go around the corner. Up there. See?" the man said, pointing to the opening of a small street or alley. "There. Gambling place. You find him there."

The man stepped out into the street and pointed.

"Up there," he said. "See? That alley. You go there."

In the alley there were some young men, and each of them wore jeans, running shoes, and a jacket made out of shiny material. They stood quietly, three of them all together, the purple light from the streetlamp falling over their hair, their shiny jackets, and into their eyes. The walls of the buildings were wet with dew, and on them there was a muted reflection of yellows and reds, like a Chinese lantern mirrored on the surface of water. The black shadows of the rails and steps of the fire escape slid over Ray as he walked into the alley. The three silent men, their dark hair gleaming, turned to watch him go, but they did so briefly, with a glance that was at the same time ill-meaning and indifferent.

Ray passed some zinc-colored trash cans, the tops of which had been dented and which were filled with rainwater. The kitchens of restaurants faced the alley, and there was the smell of fried rice, broccoli and garlic, velvet chicken and black mushrooms, sweet and sour soup, roasting duck, the dry, clean odor of pancakes for moo shu pork.

Above an anonymous doorway, as though it were the back entrance to a warehouse or an import-export business, there was a bulb in a tin cone that hung from an S-shaped piece of tubing. Under it there were more young men, all dressed in new running shoes, jeans, and black jackets. One of them turned to Ray and said, "For Chinese people only."

"I want to talk to someone," said Ray.

"Chinese people only," said the man.

"Listen," said Ray. "You tell Mei Yaochen that Ray Gollancz is here to see him."

The men in the alley turned to look at him.

"Tell him," said Ray.

"Wait here," said one of the young men.

The young man pushed the door open, and in the well-lighted room beyond there were some tables at which Chinese men played a fast-paced card game. They didn't bother with chips, making their bets in cash, which changed hands quickly. Beyond the gamblers, along three sides of the room, there was a raised gallery with a chrome rail. On two sides of the room the gallery was narrow, and there were only small tables behind it, but at the back the gallery was deeper, and there, at a round table, sat Mr. Mei and another man, both of whom were wearing silk suits from Hong Kong or Singapore. Then the door swung shut.

The young men in the alley didn't say anything while Ray waited, although when the door opened again, and someone inside beckoned, one of them said, "All right. Come over here. We're going to frisk you."

Ray stood against the wall while a young man patted him down.

"Is he expecting trouble?" said Ray.

"No," said the man who had patted him down. "Go in."

There was an island of cigarette smoke hanging above the players, and through it each light appeared in a yellow nimbus. In the corner, Mr. Mei smoked a cigarette, flicking the ashes neatly into a glass ashtray, and in front of him there was a package of Kent cigarettes, the paper of it having thin black lines under the cellophane. Mr. Mei glanced at Ray and then looked away, back to the face of the man he was speaking to.

After a while a waiter said, "All right. You go over now."

Mr. Mei's hair seemed grayer than before, but it was perfectly trimmed and combed. His eyes were a little bland, or so they seemed, behind the academic glasses. A waiter put down a clean ashtray and took the old one away and silently disappeared.

"Well?" said Mr. Mei.

"May I sit down?" said Ray.

Mr. Mei lighted a cigarette and tossed the match into an ashtray and then looked at Ray through the thread of smoke that rose from it.

"Usually when people sit down here with me, they do so for business," he said.

"I understand," said Ray. "I have something to ask you."

Mr. Mei looked around the room. Then he said, "All right. Sit down."

Ray sat down.

"Would you like a drink?" said Mr. Mei.

"No, thanks," said Ray.

"No?" said Mr. Mei. "Usually when someone comes to do business, he has a drink. Tea. Whiskey."

"Whiskey," said Ray.

Mr. Mei spoke to a waiter, who brought two glasses with a little whiskey in the bottom, the color of it brownish, the film of it clinging to the side of the glass where it had swirled around.

"Did you come to talk about your father?" asked Mr. Mei.

"No," said Ray.

"Are you sure?" said Mr. Mei. "Because if you want to talk about your father, you're wasting your time. I don't owe you anything, young man. Not a cent. Absolutely nothing. Dean should have put money aside for an attorney."

"He's got a lawyer," said Ray.

"A cheap one, I'll bet," said Mr. Mei. "From Bakersfield."

"It's the best we could do," said Ray.

"Your father knew better than to hang around. Can you tell me what the hell he was doing?"

Ray shrugged. "I don't know," he said.

Ray put his hands on the table, comforted by the clean, starched cotton under his fingers.

"So," said Mr. Mei. "It's been a long time. How have you been?"

"All right," Ray said.

"Good," said Mr. Mei.

They both drank. In the room there was the flick flick flick of cards being put out on the table and the slight tinkling of ice in glasses. Mr. Mei leaned forward and said, "Sometimes you can feel luck. Have you ever noticed? Like an eddy."

"I haven't noticed," said Ray.

"Well, you can feel it. You can feel it change. It's like a cold wind that blows into a room."

At the tables there was a man who had lost his last dollar: He got up from his stool, his eyes bright, his hand holding a glass with liquor in it. Then he put it down, and with a profound fatalism, he turned away from the table.

"So," said Mr. Mei. "What do you want?"

"A little information," said Ray. "Just between old business partners."

Mr. Mei blinked. "What information?"

"Have you seen the young woman who was with me when I came to see you?" asked Ray.

"Oh," said Mr. Mei. "Her."

"Well?" said Ray.

Mr. Mei took a sip of his drink, which he rolled around in his mouth, considering. He glanced at the tables where the card games were being played quickly, the money changing hands with a kind of legerdemain. Then Mr. Mei turned back to Ray and said, "Young man, I'm going to give you a word of advice. Don't come to me asking for help. Or for information. Come here to tell me what you can do for me."

"You know what I can do," said Ray.

Mr. Mei nodded. "Yes," he said. "I know. I've never inspected a building myself. But I've seen pictures in the paper."

"Well?" said Ray. "Do you think there's something Dean knows that I don't?"

"No," said Mr. Mei. He went on staring at Ray, and then he looked away, saying, "You know, Dean's not working anymore. It'll probably be a while before he's back in business. What can you do about that?"

"You mean to help you?" said Ray.

"Yes," said Mr. Mei. "Everything doesn't just stop because Dean hangs around a fire. For instance, there are some condominiums in Las Vegas. I don't know what it is with developers these days. Everything they build just sits around. Then there's the bank to worry about."

"Is that right?" said Ray.

Mr. Mei nodded.

Ray looked into the room and, for a moment, there were flecks before his eyes, little gold bits that looked as though someone had thrown a handful of glitter into the room, each point, in the throb of his headache, bringing a sense of sharpness, and in the piercing flecks there seemed to be some reminder, some infinitely repeated hint of the distant, but no less unreal, possibilities of malice.

"I'll get rid of the condominiums," said Ray.

"Are you sure?" said Mr. Mei. "We have to have an understanding between you and me. We'll have an arrangement, then. I'll depend upon you. Like I depended on Dean."

Ray sighed.

"I was glad to be away from it," he said. "I liked being in the East. I was learning something."

"What can I say?" said Mr. Mei. "This pays good money."

"Does it?" said Ray.

"Yes," said Mr. Mei. "The job in Vegas pays twenty-five hundred."

"All right," said Ray.

Mr. Mei spoke to the waiter, who returned in a moment with an envelope that had a comforting weight when Mr. Mei pushed it over.

"You can trust money," said Mr. Mei. "It's the one thing that never cheats."

Mr. Mei's glasses flashed as he glanced around the room.

Then he took a small gold pencil from his pocket and a notebook and he wrote a name and a telephone number on it, ripped off the page, and pushed it across the table as though it were a check.

"This man will drive you up there. To Vegas," said Mr. Mei. "I'll call him for you. He'll be around to pick you up tomorrow."

The handwriting on the slip of paper was neat, angular, appearing almost like a diminutive drawing of a row of small houses in a village, but even in the angular quality of the writing there was a hint of an ideogram, of the graceful slash and lines of Eastern script. The beauty of the handwriting, the order of it, the gold pen, the blue ink slowly drying, all brought, for the briefest instant, something like hope, but almost as quickly as it had come, it was replaced by the atmosphere of gambling, of the cards coming down on the felt tables with a steady flick flick flick.

"Where are you staying?" said Mr. Mei.

"The Golden Palm," said Ray.

"That place out on Santa Monica?" said Mr. Mei. "That fleabag? It's filled with lunatics who think the world is going to end."

"It was the best I could do," said Ray.

"Next time, get in touch with me," said Mr. Mei. "I'll find you a place to stay."

"Sure," said Ray. "Next time. In Vegas, I'll need a car."

"We'll get you a car to use up there."

Ray sat with his drink.

"Okay," said Ray.

"And that other matter," said Mr. Mei. "She's in Vegas, too. Iris. Was that the name? You can get her address from the man who will show you the condominiums. All right?"

Ray nodded. "Okay," he said. "All right."

Mr. Mei watched him carefully now.

"Tell me," said Mr. Mei. "Can I still trust Dean? Will he keep his mouth shut?"

Mr. Mei's hands rested on the table, the nails manicured, the tips looking like clear new moons, and the shirt he wore was fresh, carefully ironed, the collar of his jacket fitting neatly against it. Ray glanced at the hands and the suit, wondering precisely what it was he was being asked.

"Yes," said Ray. "Dean never talked much."

Mr. Mei rubbed the lower part of his face, as though concentrating on the smoothness of his skin.

"What did you and Dean do for fun?" asked Mr. Mei. "You can tell a lot about people by what they do for a good time."

"Sometimes Dean played the trombone," said Ray.

"He never talked about music to me," said Mr. Mei.

Ray whistled, the sound of it barely above a whisper. He went through part of "Sweet Georgia Brown" and then stopped.

"Sometimes we sing in my house," said Mr. Mei. "My wife and I."

"What do you sing?" said Ray.

" 'Green Grow the Rushes, Oh,' " said Mr. Mei. "We used to watch Mitch Miller. We'd follow the little ball, remember? My wife likes 'Clementine.' "

Ray nodded. Then he stood up, taking the money.

"Good night," said Ray.

"It was good to see you again, Ray," said Mr. Mei. "You know, I'm depending on you now."

Mr. Mei remained motionless in the corner, not quite nodding to himself, not quite smiling either, just ruminating, his eyes set on some spot in the center of the room. Ray walked under the cloud of smoke and out the door, passing the young men who stood in the alley, and as he walked into the cool air, which came with a bracing chill, he wondered if you could really feel luck after all. He decided not, and then walked up the alley.

Ray walked for a while, feeling the weight of the money in his pocket. The mist was cool and it collected in his hair and on his jacket, the beads of it showing the colors of the lights, silver and gold, yellow and orange. At the restaurant where he and Dean ate, Ray turned in and sat down. There were no customers in the place, although one waiter sat in the back, head down, and around him there were the long tables, the chairs with a sheen to them, the greenish walls, the small lights in holders at the sides of which were cone-shaped shadows. When the waiter came over he said to Ray, "Long time no see. Where you been? Wasn't it a number four you used to have?"

"That's right," said Ray. "Sweet and sour soup. A number four."

"One number four," said the waiter. "Sweet sour soup. All right. Say hello to your father for me, okay?"

The world was going to end at dawn, or a little after, but before that the people in the Golden Palm were up. In the half-light of four o'clock they sat around the pool, some of them drinking coffee they had brewed in coffeepots they had plugged into the sockets of the rooms, and as Barstow, the manager of the place, had smelled the odor of the coffee, he got out of bed and turned on the light and looked at the list of emergency telephone numbers so as to have the one for the Los Angeles Fire Department handy. The wiring in the Golden Palm hadn't been done by an electrician with a license. Barstow sat there, looking at the telephone number and making plans to go, as soon as the hardware store was open, to buy a sign, printed in Day-Glo orange, that said, NO COOKING IN ROOMS.

The surface of the pool looked as glassy as a pond in the hours before dawn. The still water was gray, and around it there sat men and women and children, all of them seemingly mesmerized by the image that lay before them, the mirrorlike reflection of the sky, at the edge of which were the dark outlines of the people who huddled there. Between them there were black, irregular shapes, which revealed themselves to be, after a moment's consideration, lawn and pool furniture. The faces of the men and women weren't blank so much as drawn, or numb, all of them considering the possibility of the day. Fuller put his head in his hands, thinking about the uncanny sensation there had been in his fingers when he had last handled rattlesnakes. Never had he been more certain about the prediction than when he remembered that sensation, which now seemed to meld together with the atmosphere of the people, each dark and humped up and some even with blankets over their shoulders, who sat around the quiet water.

Fuller knocked on Ray's door and said, "It's time. You still coming?"

Ray sat up, instantly awake.

"Yes," he said. "I'll be there."

The people were still sitting around the pool when Ray came out, their faces having a color that Ray recognized as being like all that is left after a fire, the remains ashy and even tired looking, as though the fire had taken something like effort on the part of the things that had burned. The city was quiet aside from an occasional car that went by on Santa Monica, its headlights yellow and its tires black and shiny. None of the people around the pool, or even those who sat in collapsible lawn chairs in front of the rooms they had slept in the night before, turned to look at the cars that passed. The only other sound was the occasional soft crying of one of the children, including Everett, whose belief that things were going to be all right had simply evaporated when he saw the faces of the people who were preparing to die.

Then, without a word, they stood up and got into their cars, which they then lined up, one behind the other (funeral style), all with their lights on, although it seemed as though they were on not because it was dark so much as to bind everyone into a group. Fuller sat and looked at the pool, nodding to himself, and then he said to Ray, "Give some people a ride out there, will you? It will make everything more comfortable."

Ray started the Mercury and then Everett and his sister, Belle, a girl of six who wore a new pink skirt, climbed into the back. Everett's mother, whose name was Franconia (a name her mother had picked off a map of New Hampshire), and her husband, Tyler, got into the front seat with Ray. Franconia still wore the same faded blue dress she had worn the day before, although her hair had now been brushed out as she had worn it as a girl. There was a ribbon in it, too, a blue one. Tyler wore a clean blue shirt and a black bow tie.

Ray pulled into line behind the others. The Mercury sounded very loud in the morning. In the rearview mirror Ray saw the boy's face, which was now as numb as the others. The girl was biting her nails.

"Hey, Everett," said Ray. "Have you ever seen a real Moon tachometer?"

"No," said Everett.

"You know," said Ray, "this thing is bored and stroked. It's got a cam."

Everett looked at Ray through the mirror and said, "You see my dad's tie?"

"Yes," said Ray.

"He inherited that from my grandfather. It was one of three things he got."

"Well," said Ray, "it's a nice tie."

"My mother bought that blue ribbon special for today," said Everett.

"Hush, Everett," said Franconia, putting a hand to the ribbon she wore.

"I used to have a Pontiac," said Tyler to Ray. "It would go a hundred on the road outside of St. Albans. That's in West Virginia."

"You shouldn't have driven that fast," said Franconia.

"We were courting," said Tyler.

He shrugged now.

"Everett," said Ray. "Look at the tachometer."

"I think you lied to me," said Everett.

"Hush," said Franconia.

Belle started crying, although she didn't make much noise. It was a steady, repetitive noise that sounded like a squeak in a spring of the Mercury.

"There were a lot of things I wanted to do," said Franconia. "I wanted to have a real silk dress. High-heel shoes. I wanted to drink champagne."

"I'm sorry," said Tyler.

"Have you ever had champagne?" asked Franconia.

"Yes," said Ray. "You can feel it in your nose a little. A little tingle. And on your tongue, too."

"I wanted to have a bathtub, too," said Franconia. "A big long one. We have nothing but a shower at home, and once a woman gave me some bubble bath. I cried to beat the band."

"You used the tubs in the motels," said Tyler.

"They were real nice," said Franconia.

"Stop that sniveling," said Tyler, turning back to look at Belle.

"Hush," said Franconia. "Everyone hush now." Then she turned to Ray. "I always wanted to go to New York. You know? I'd get all dressed up in my silk dress and walk down one of those avenues. No one would know I lived in a town outside of St. Albans."

"There's nothing wrong with St. Albans," said Tyler. "This is no time to be vain."

Franconia stared directly ahead. In the back seat Everett said, "I don't want to die."

"It's just a change," said Tyler. "Like a mayfly. It's a nymph for a while and then it is borne up on wings."

"You lied," said Everett to Ray. "You lied."

Ray shifted down and watched the tachometer, and then he reached over and tapped it, glancing up in the mirror at Everett's face.

"No," said Ray. "We'll be there soon."

They went through the Cahuenga Pass and then turned into the hills. They climbed for a long time on back roads, the cars in one long accumulation of dark shapes bound together by those cones of light. At the top they came to a field, at the edge of which there were eucalyptus trees and below which there was the outline of the Hollywood Reservoir. It was irregularly shaped, the water making bays in the canyons between the ridges of the hills. At this hour, when there was no wind, the water was still, too, and four or five of the brightest stars were reflected in it. They were butter colored. The men and women left the cars at the roadside and walked under the eucalyptus trees, the medicinal odor of which seemed at this moment to suggest the essence of the earth. One of the children sniffed the air and started to cry. They went out through the tall grass, their shapes halting, dark, and ill-defined, the accumulation of them making a mass in the middle of the field. They stared at the water below. Ray stood at the rear of the crowd, smelling the eucalyptus trees and wishing he had something to drink.

The sunrise came with a slow, constant seeping of light into the sky, the blue-black giving way to gray, which in turn gave away to yellow, pink, and misty blue. No one spoke. They all faced the east, waiting for that first flash, that golden radiance that would appear as ignition. They seemed to be holding their breath when the earthquake began.

At first there was an almost inaudible squeaking, almost a hiss, which probably came from the roots of the trees holding fast in the ground. The trembling began with the same cadence and with almost the same sensation as when someone's knees shake after a bad scare. The soil seemed a little loose, or unsteady, as though the trembling ground were the physical manifestation of fear. There was a louder noise now, a hush, which came from leaves moving in the breezeless air.

The people in the field were absolutely still, although one or two said, "Ah, ah, ah," and another said, "Praise God. Oh, praise God." Then Fuller began to sing, "Rock of Ages, close to thee . . ." No one else joined in. Everett turned around and glanced at Ray, who felt the earth tremble a little and then a little less.

They went on waiting. The sky became paler, almost white, and then the first golden ray struck the tops of the trees: for a moment the treetops appeared as though they had been splashed with some reddish gold powder. There was no sound now, and the people went on staring into the light, which was at the edge of the field where the cars were parked, all of the machines, in the glare, looking like a line of animals—buffalos, say—that were grazing in a silent procession.

As the sun rose, a figure emerged from the black shapes of the cars, and as it came, the sun was at its back. In the beginning it was almost impossible to say what it was, and the only way of knowing it was there at all was because its undulant movement in front of the sun made a few rays seem to flicker. The grass was still in shadow, but the tops of the blades, which were wet, shimmered with a million needlelike flames. The figure approached, revealing itself to be a man, tallish, with long arms: he came across the grass, his head in a nimbus of light. The people turned now, each face expectant, if still frightened. The man emerged, walking fast. Then he came to an abrupt halt and looked around, finally saying, in not much more than a whisper, "Psssst. Hey, I'm looking for Ray Gollancz. Is he here? Is that him there? Well, it's time to go to Vegas. Come on. We want to get through the desert before it gets hot. My name's Milton Schlage."

Ray stepped forward. The sun had risen now, and the people in the field weren't waiting for something anymore so much as just waiting, trying to avoid facing that moment when they would turn and walk back to their cars. Everett stood in the grass, the stems of it trampled down where the people had nervously assembled, shifting their weight, trying to abandon themselves to that moment when they would disappear. He stared down below at the reservoir, which looked, with the sunlight making countless points, like blue paper covered with sequins. Ray waved to him, and then Everett turned with the others, who had now begun the long walk up the grassy hill.

"The guy at the motel told me you were up here," said Milton Schlage. "That's how I found you." They started walking. "There was a little earthquake," said Schlage. "Did you feel it? I always think it's going to be the big one."

SOLEDAD AND THE
ROAD TO VEGAS

The morning light came through the door in a long wedge in which there were bits of dust, just bright flecks, that turned once and disappeared into the gray-brown dimness of the room at the Golden Palm. Ray began to pack, picking out the shirts he had put in the drawer of the bureau, which had been lined with freezer paper. In the corners, it was held down by red thumbtacks. There was an odor in the drawer, an accumulation of scents, of perfume and soap and dust, powder and mildew, all of which seemed to be the essence of the anonymous. Ray half turned toward his bag, in which he had already put the box of Tampax, the black-powder caps, a box of latex prophylactics, the acid, the potassium chlorate, and the bag of sugar. The bed in the room had a polyester cover, and the pillows were filled with artificial fluff. The paintings on the wall had probably been made in a factory by a machine. These things and that scent made the shirt in his hand, which had been worn over the years until it was smooth and soft, seem to be a reminder of ordinary life. Ray ran his finger over the material, insisting on his own presence, on his own speck of perception. Then he went over and dropped it into the bag.

He turned back to the anonymous room again. Then Ray went into the bathroom, where he folded the towels and put them neatly on the rack. He fluffed up the pillows, too, and straightened out the bedspread. As he did so, Ray thought, Maybe I won't get in any deeper.

"What are you doing that for?" said Milton Schlage. He stood in the doorway, that golden light behind him. "We're already going to have to drive through the desert in the hottest part of the afternoon. Let's go."

Milton Schlage was tall and had reddish brown hair and blue eyes. His features were regular and there was about him an athletic quality. His skin was freckled and his teeth were white, but there was in his expression something that made him seem as though he were peering out of a mug shot. He had the palpable air of being one jump ahead of people who were looking for him.

"Where you from?"

"Bakersfield," said Ray.

"Jesus, what a town," said Schlage. "Nothing but hicks up there."

"I guess so," said Ray.

"That's the most important thing about a town," said Schlage. "It's got to have sophistication."

"Uh huh," said Ray.

Outside, in the parking lot, was the car that Schlage was driving, a newish Volkswagen bus, bright red, the chrome showing as long streaks. Schlage looked at the car, at the sky, and then turned back, saying, "You don't look like a firebug."

"What?" said Ray. "What did you say?"

"You heard me," said Schlage. "What do you use to burn down a building? Gas?"

Ray went on staring at him. Then he zipped up his bag and looked around the room.

"Where did you meet Mei Yaochen?" asked Schlage.

"My father did business with him," said Ray.

"Is that right?" said Schlage. "So it's a family business. Like people in a circus. Those people who work on the trapeze. They all have the same names. 'The Daring Capallinis' . . . "

"Yeah," said Ray. "It's like a circus."

"A lot of those guys get hurt," said Schlage. "They work without a net and then they take a fall."

Ray parked his car behind the motel. There was a tree there, and Ray put the Mercury under it, and Schlage said, "It's your funeral. If you leave it there the birds are going to shit on it."

"I'll take my chances," said Ray.

He got into the Volkswagen, sitting up front, next to Schlage. The Hollywood Freeway was made of concrete that had once been whitish, but now in the center of each lane there was a long, sooty stain that the cars endlessly followed. There were houses on the sides of the road, the trees around them shuddering in the wind of the traffic.

They passed City Hall, the tower clean and looking bright in the center of the city, the buildings there newish, the entire sprawl, with the concrete ramps curving into one another, the glass in the windows, the clutter of signs, the mist from a fountain in a park, all having the air of dread. It was impossible to say why this was the case, although it was there, distinct, unshakable. Ray supposed it came from the city's smugness.

"I hate to leave L.A.," said Schlage.

"Why's that?" said Ray.

"There's no place like L.A. Everything's for sale here. A lot of people forget that's what made America great."

A car pulled in front of them, and Schlage swore in Spanish. It was a long, elaborate curse, and Ray said, "Where did you learn to speak Spanish?"

"Soledad," said Schlage. "You been in?"

"No," said Ray.

"I didn't think so," said Schlage. "You don't look like it, but you can never tell. It isn't so bad inside. You get used to it."

Schlage ran one hand back and forth over the top of the plastic-covered steering wheel. "I always liked driving. I never wanted to go inside, you know, right into a damn bank or liquor store . . . the car was always the best place to be."

They passed buildings that seemed pale or gray, and there were endless houses and storefronts along avenues that had a supermarket every mile or so. The people in their cars had a sleepy quality, although from time to time one weaved in and out of traffic, not doing this out of bad manners so much as desperation.

"I remember one time I had stolen a 'Vette. The cops were after me on the Hollywood Freeway, right there at Gower. I was really cooking. You could see the needle in the damn gas gauge move."

"Did they catch you?" asked Ray. "Is that why you went to Soledad?"

"What's it to you?" he said.

"Nothing," said Ray.

"Naw," said Schlage. "Not for the damn car."

"What for?" said Ray.

"This and that," said Schlage. "This and that."

On the shelf underneath the dashboard there was a switchblade knife, the handle of it whitish plastic, and the ends of it had small, silver pieces of metal. There was a silver button, too, that made the blade switch out. Ray looked at it, and Schlage said, "You like that? It's a souvenir from Mexico."

"You were down there?" said Ray.

"Sure," said Schlage. "I have a little business down there."

"For Mei?" said Ray.

"Ah," said Schlage. "Who's asking questions now?"

"Why are you going to Vegas?" asked Ray.

"I'm delivering something," said Schlage.

"What's in the car?"

"This and that," said Schlage. "This and that."

Outside of San Bernardino they stopped for gas. It was a new place, with long, curving standards and clean cement. A young woman came out and put the gas in the car. Schlage smiled at her and she smiled back.

"I'd like to drive for a while," said Ray.

"Sure," said Schlage. "Don't get stopped, though. I really don't think we should get stopped."

"Have you got the registration?" said Ray.

"Sure," said Schlage. "Everything nice and clean."

Schlage had put his bag, a brown duffel, between the two seats. It was stained and had marks, circular, odd-shaped ones, where it had mildewed. The thing sat on the floor, scuffed and travel worn and looking like something carried by an itinerant executioner. It wasn't zipped up, and inside there was a short-barreled shotgun, a pump gun, with a pistol grip. Ray glanced down at it and then looked up the road, thinking about precisely how many hours there were between here and Las Vegas. Schlage zipped up the bag.

"You got to have some protection," said Schlage. "You know there are pirates working this section of road. Especially between here and Vegas. They get word you're carrying something and they try to stop you." Schlage shrugged. "Pirates are the worst. They've got tattoos and no teeth."

They came into a drier landscape, not quite the desert yet, but getting there, and on both sides of the blacktop that went through a flat plain there were plants, dusty and brownish, which in the distance, just before the hills, merged into a smear. There were some birds flying close to the car, dark, largish ones that propelled themselves with a languid beating of their wings.

Schlage reached down and picked up the knife, opening and closing it, delighting each time in the slight *swick* as it flicked out of the handle. Ray looked away from him and concentrated on the ribbon of asphalt, and then he looked over at Schlage. Schlage opened and closed the knife.

"Put it away for a while, will you?" said Ray.

Schlage folded it up and held it in his hand.

"Hey," said Schlage. "What was the funniest thing you ever saw?"

"I don't know," Ray said.

"Well," said Schlage, "I've seen some funny things. Like a guy I knew in prison who was always someone's punk inside, but then I saw him outside, all tough guy, you know, with his girlfriend. He saw me looking at him and went pale. You woulda laughed if you'd seen him."

A truck passed, the airy rush of it making the car shiver, and then the aluminum box of it disappeared into the silver on the road up ahead. Ray tried to concentrate on something funny.

Schlage was quiet for a while. Then he started laughing.

"What's so funny?" said Ray.

"I was just thinking," said Schlage.

"About what?" said Ray.

"Well," said Schlage, "sometimes you just got to wait for the right moment, you know what I mean? A good idea has its own life. Like I've been thinking of starting a business. I'll drill a deep well. And I'll get good, pure, clean water. And I'll buy a generator, too. And you know what? Some summer there'll be a blackout. So, guess what?"

"What?" said Ray.

"What are people going to do for their water?" said Schlage. "I'll tell you what. They'll have to come to Milton Schlage, that's what. How about three dollars a gallon?"

"Maybe that's a little high," said Ray.

"Where else are they going to get it?" said Schlage. His laughter came again as a "heh heh heh," steady, repetitive. "But you know what's really the best part? You make everyone bring his own container. Don't you see? It won't cost a cent for the bottles or jugs or anything. That's the beauty of it. The bastards will have to bring their own."

He snapped open the knife.

"Say," he said. "What do you say we hit one of these little groceries?"

"What for?" said Ray.

"A little excitement," said Schlage.

The desert began after Barstow, and at the edge of it there was a dust storm. The soil in which the scrubby brush grew was reddish, dusty, almost the color of bricks. In the afternoon the wind began to blow hard and the dust looked like a tall fogbank of some reddish substance that drifted across the flat land. The hills, the greenish brush, and the road were obscured by it.

The white lines on the road were visible for about a hundred yards, and then they became vague and finally disappeared altogether in that red, windblown prospect. At first the dust made a sifting noise, but when the wind rose, it sounded as if the car were having its paint removed. The dust came into the car, too, through every minute crack, and Ray and Schlage tasted it and felt grit between their teeth.

"It'll stop in a minute," said Ray.

In years past, this part of the desert was almost always dry, but now the weather seemed to be changing. There were theories about how the building of so many houses in southern California had changed the climate, but whatever the reason, there were thunderstorms out here from time to time. Ray watched the dust on the glass, which suddenly turned dark as rain hit it. The large raindrops, the color and size of clear marbles, broke on the windshield, splashed there with a bright, silver explosion that then immediately mixed with the dust to form a red mud. The dust washed off the car and dripped away like some rust-colored fluid. On the roof, the rain made a sizzling sound, like someone frying a steak in a cast-iron pan. Against the clouds in the distance there seemed to be an infinite number of tinsel strands, all sloping a little to one side, as the drops of water fell.

So it was raining when they picked up the girl. She was standing at the side of the road, in the rain, wearing a T-shirt and a pair of blue jeans, her small-hipped figure leaning against her pack. She had long, reddish blond hair, blue eyes, and freckles. She probably wasn't twenty-one.

The girl had her thumb out, and her eyes searched out Ray behind the wheel, her expression not pleading exactly, but there was about it a plain statement of the facts. She was wet and wanted a ride. The rain fell hard enough to make a white-silver mist on the blacktop, and the mist came up to about the girl's shoulders.

"What do you say we have a good time?" said Schlage.

Ray looked across the seat.

"Pull over," said Schlage.

The girl went on staring at Ray, her eyes having something of an accusation in them, as though it were clear what she thought about somebody who drove by and left her standing there in the rain. She reached up and wiped her forehead, doing so with the back of her hand. She shifted her weight from one hip to the other, the movement revealing an impatience, a disbelief that she had managed to end up in circumstances like these. Her thumb made a quick jerk east as she went on looking at Ray.

He pulled over. The rain seemed very loud as they stopped. Then Schlage rolled down the window and said, "Hey, get in! Get in! You're getting wet!"

The girl was bent at the waist, as though this would somehow keep her from getting any wetter. Her hair was dark now, a copper-blond color, and it was plastered against her cheeks and onto her shirt, the shape of the strands there like scraggly roots. The T-shirt was wet too, and her skin and the bumps of her backbone showed through the cotton.

"Oh," she said, laughing, coming out of the spray in a rush, dragging her pack with her. Schlage opened the sliding door for her, and she got in, panting a little with the effort, laughing again and saying, "I'm wet. I'm soaked."

"This rain," said Schlage. "I've never seen it like this."

"You're going to Vegas?" she said.

"You better believe it," said Schlage. "This is the Vegas Express."

The girl sat on the back seat, bringing with her the scent of the rain on the hot asphalt and the odor of suntan lotion. Then she said, "It's like standing in a shower out there." She sat there breathing hard, her shirt clinging to her shoulders and breasts. Then she let out a large breath and shook her head.

Ray looked at her through the mirror. It was still raining, and Ray pulled back onto the road, the sound of the engine rising and falling as he went through the gears. The girl opened her pack and took out a towel and dried her hair. She did it with two hands, rubbing hard, her head bent and her hair falling forward and exposing the nape of her neck, which was white, slender, and covered with whorls of copper-colored down. Schlage turned and stared at her as she worked.

"Oh," she said, "Oh."

She had opened her legs a little, and as she rubbed her scalp she had her head between her knees. The rain made a pulsing hiss on the roof and windshield, and there was still the odor of dust in the car.

The girl looked up for a moment, into Schlage's eyes, and then she smiled sweetly.

The distance between the front seats and the one in the back was big enough to make talking difficult. The two front seats were separated by the space that held Schlage's duffel, and the girl pulled her pack up close to the space, just behind Ray and Schlage, and sat on it.

"Are you going all the way to Las Vegas?" she asked.

"Yeah," said Schlage. "That's where we're going."

"What are you going to do there?" she said.

"He's going to look at some condominiums," said Schlage.

"Oh?" said the girl. "Are you in the real estate business?"

"No," said Ray.

She went back to drying her hair, turning her head to one side as she worked. She found a comb in her bag and began working the tangles she'd made with the towel, making small cries when she pulled on a snag. Then she took a dry T-shirt from the pack and turned toward the rear of the bus, stripping off the one she wore. Her back was freckled over the shoulders and then tanned down to the top of her pants. No shadow. Her skin was still a little damp. Then she pulled on the dry T-shirt, tugging it over her head and then lifting her hair through the neck.

The girl turned and looked out one of the windows at the side of the bus. The rain was stopping, and in the distance there was a distinct rainbow, the colors bright and cheerful.

"Look," she said.

Schlage turned and looked out the window. Ray glanced at it once and kept driving. From time to time he looked in the mirror and saw her sitting on her pack and facing the side window, her eyes set on the landscape. She bit her lip and closed her eyes.

"Hey," said Schlage. "Hey. What's wrong?"

"I'm just pissed off," she said.

"I never lose my temper," said Schlage. "It gives me bad dreams."

"Yeah?" said the girl. She looked at Ray through the rearview mirror. "What about you?"

In the mirror Ray looked at her eyes, the freckles on her face, her lips that were pink and full. Then he went back to facing the road.

"Is that something you know about?" said the girl.

"You could say that," said Ray.

"Well, I'm pissed off," said the girl. "I was out here with my boyfriend, but we stopped getting along somewhere west of Salt Lake City. Maybe even back in Cheyenne."

"Uh huh," said Schlage.

"We had an argument. You know what he said? That I had to stick with him because I had no place to go. Well, you should have seen his face when I packed my bag. He's an architecture student. A big deal, you know? We were going to get to the beach. Maybe go dancing. But all we've been doing is looking at buildings and washing our clothes in laundromats. And camp."

"Yeah," said Schlage. "You got to have excitement."

"That's what I told my boyfriend," said the girl. "And you know what he said? 'Isn't this exciting enough?' We were in a laundromat when he said it. I mean, what was I doing there?"

She shook her head.

"My name's Marylee. People call me Lee," she said.

"Yeah," said Schlage. "Some guys . . . they just can't get loose." He turned to Lee and said, "Glad to meet you. My name's Mike Kennedy."

"Are you related to the Kennedys?" asked Lee.

"Me?" said Schlage. "Hell, no. They're all a bunch of drug addicts. Ups, downs, sideways. Bombitas. Any controlled substance."

Lee giggled a little.

"Yeah," she said. "I guess that's right." She had long fingers, the nails broken and a little dirty. "What's your name?" she said to Ray.

"His name?" said Schlage. "Ah, his name is Jimmy—"

"It's Ray. Just Ray Gollancz."

"Mike said it was something else," said Lee.

"Just call me Ray."

Schlage looked over and said, "I'm getting in . . . you know, the mood."

"For what?" said Ray.

"To have a good time," said Schlage.

"Me too," said Lee.

"That's good," said Schlage. "Yeah, why don't you stop at the next store we come to. Maybe I'd like a couple of beers. I'm thirsty."

Sweat stood out on Ray's forehead and upper lip.

"I've got a headache," said Ray. "Maybe I can find some aspirin in one of these stores."

The road was still dark with the rainwater, but the water was drying fast. In the distance there were some hills, low, scrubby things with the clouds above them. The hills looked hot and without water.

Schlage began to sing, glancing once toward Lee. He sang, "Bye-bye unhappiness, bye-bye loneliness . . . I ain't a-gonna die-ay. . . ."

"That's the Everly Brothers," said Lee. "Golden Oldies. You ever listen to Jerry Lee Lewis?"

"Does a bear do it in the woods?" said Schlage. "Sure."

"When we go to the store," said Lee, "I'd like to see if they have any chips. Down on the Mexican border I bought a pack of fried plantain. Really, out of this world. I may never go back to potato chips."

"Pull over at the next place, Ray," said Schlage. "I'm thirsty. Lee here is hungry."

Ray didn't say anything.

"Say, Lee," said Schlage. "You want to help me stick a place up?"

"What?" said Lee. She leaned forward, her bluish eyes a little larger now, her face mildly distraught, although she was still smiling.

"You want to help me stick up the next place we come to?"

Lee waited, fingering her wet hair, looking at Schlage. He was wearing a pair of white jeans and a pink shirt, and his auburn hair was brushed straight back. He smiled when he looked at her, and although his grin was a little lopsided, it had a certain cracked attractiveness to it. She just waited, bending forward, looking at him.

"Oh," she said. "You're joking. I get it."

Schlage laughed, his head back. Lee laughed too. Ray thought about taking aspirin, of maybe chewing one, just to taste the salty bite of it. The road steamed in the bright afternoon sun.

"You coming in with me?" asked Schlage.

"Sure," said Lee. "I want to look for those chips. You wouldn't believe how good they are. Right between a Frito and a potato chip."

"The next place, Ray," said Schlage, looking down at his bag, in which there was that short-barreled shotgun with a pistol grip.

"This isn't a good idea," said Ray.

"Good ideas are what you got to have when you got no balls," said Schlage.

"You heard me," said Ray.

Schlage turned to Lee. "You see what I've been riding with for all these miles?" he said.

"Maybe he just doesn't think it's a funny joke about the store," said Lee.

"Who says I'm joking?" said Schlage, smiling, his eyes having a look of pleasure in them.

"Oh," said Lee. "The next thing you're going to tell me is you're a convict or something—"

Schlage laughed. "You hear that, Ray?" he said.

Ray looked into the mirror again and found that Lee was watching him closely.

"He is," said Ray. "Armed robbery. Or was there something else?"

"Watch what you say," said Schlage.

"Well?" said Ray.

"There might have been," said Schlage.

"What was it?" said Ray.

"So you're joking too," Lee said to Ray. "I knew it."

"Yeah, sure," said Schlage. "Ray's a funny guy. He's good to have around, like at . . . you know, a barbecue."

"I'll tell you one thing," said Lee. "You don't ever really get to know someone until you're traveling with them. All my boyfriend wanted was to eat freeze-dried goulash and to have lots of buildings to look at." Lee put a finger and a thumb around each eye so as to look like someone wearing glasses and she pretended she was peering at one building and then another, her face very serious now, ponderous. She was very funny, her eyes wide open behind the glasses, her lips grim, her nose sniffing a little. "He was always talking about beauty, but you know, if it hit him in the face, he wouldn't have known it. Yeah, you get to know someone when you're traveling."

She said this a little coldly as she looked out the window, where the scrubby landscape rolled by. "I had hoped it was going to work out."

"Yeah, well," said Schlage. "Let's have a few beers and forget it."

Lee went on staring out the window.

"Sure," she said. "Let's."

"That's the ticket," said Schlage. He looked back.

"You're funny," said Lee.

Ray looked down at the small duffel bag that Schlage had between the seats.

"You think so?" said Schlage. "Well, yeah. I'm pretty funny."

He didn't laugh, though, as he faced the oncoming road.

"Can you do any tricks?" said Lee. "With cards? Or any magic?"

"Me?" said Schlage. "Are you kidding?"

"What about table tapping?" said Lee. "Or having a séance? Some friends of mine in San Francisco communicate with other worlds—"

"No shit," said Schlage. "Always seemed to me that there was plenty of trouble right here. Don't you think, Ray?"

"I guess so," said Ray.

"What about you?" said Schlage to Lee. "Do you talk to other worlds?"

"No," she said. "But I can read palms. It's amazing what you can tell."

Schlage held out his palm, turning in the seat to do so. Lee was sitting on her pack, just behind the two of them. His palm was clean and pinkish, a little sweaty. Lee took Schlage's hand in both of hers, cradling it something like the way she would a sick bird. She made the hand into a fist and looked at it from the side, then opened it again and went over the lines, measuring them, tracing them with a finger.

"You're going to have two children," said Lee. "Two wives. A broken heart."

"That's all right," said Schlage. "I already know about the heart. What about a small grocery store? Is one of those in my future?"

"I don't see anything about that," said Lee. "Ray?"

"Maybe later," said Ray.

"Oh, come on," said Lee. "Give me your hand."

Ray held his hand out, palm up.

"Oh," said Lee. "Look."

"What's that?" said Schlage.

"He's got a short Lifeline," said Lee.

There was still the scent of suntan lotion on her skin.

"What else?" he said.

"Listen," she said. "This is just for fun. It doesn't mean anything."

Ray stared at the upcoming road. Then he said, "I guess that's right."

Lee's fingers were cool as she traced the lines of his palm: the movement left a slight tickling from the whorls on her fingertip. Her breath smelled like oranges as she leaned forward.

"What else do you see?" Ray said.

"That's it," she said.

"Sure?" he said. "What about this line?"

"I don't know," she said. "I don't know that much."

She put his hand down. Ray went back to concentrating on the road, glancing at her from time to time. She caught him at it once and smiled a little before she looked away.

"I just need some aspirin," said Ray.

"Up there, Ray," said Schlage. "There's a place. Stop."

At the edge of the perfectly straight road there was a store. Beyond it there was some scrubby growth, and in front of it the parking lot was just dirt, a brownish color that still had puddles from the rain. There were no other cars in the parking lot, although every now and then one came from the east, going fast and passing with a shove of trembling air. The store was small and isolated. It was a brownish, mud-colored place with two windows, an opened door, and a Coca-Cola sign.

The last of the clouds drifted in wisps and gray shreds, and in front of them there was a rainbow, the thing wide and curved, the colors of it seeming garish over the road and beyond the dirt-colored store. Lee looked at it and said, "There. See that? Isn't that something? I wish I had my camera out."

"You want something to drink, Ray?" said Schlage. "I'll get you a Coke."

Ray looked at Schlage and said, "I just need some aspirin."

"Sure, sure," said Schlage. "Aspirin."

He smiled at Lee, who stood outside on the dirt apron around the store's gasoline pumps.

"Just aspirin," said Ray. "Nothing else."

"Come on," said Schlage. "I'll show you how it's done."

"You heard what I said," said Ray.

Schlage swung his duffel bag out of the space between the seats and faced the store. The bag looked shabby in the sunshine, the splotches on it distinct and having a sheen, too, like the elbows of an old suit. He slammed the door and said through the window, "Keep the engine running."

Lee giggled.

"That's funny," said Lee. "Like from a gangster movie."

She went over to the gasoline pumps and looked at the rainbow beyond the store. Ray looked at it too, holding the steering wheel and seeing the scrubby land that stretched to the horizon. Schlage ran his hands through his longish hair, sweeping it back from his forehead.

Ray switched off the engine and stepped out into the sunshine.

"I'm coming in," said Ray.

"I thought you were going to keep the engine running," said Schlage.

It was hot, and the mist from the road brought with it a sandy odor. Schlage stood there, one hand on his hip, his head back.

"All right," he said. "Come in. The more the merrier."

"Where's your gun?" said Lee, her face in a smile. "Hey, Mike, how are you going to do it without a gun?"

"I got it in here," said Schlage.

"Really?" said Lee.

"Sure," said Schlage. "When I take it out, you do what I tell you."

"Are you still kidding?" said Lee.

"Come on," said Schlage. "Let's find those chips."

"My mother never let me play with toy guns," said Lee. "We didn't have any violent toys."

"No shit," said Schlage. "What kind of mother is that?"

"She did her best," she said, "but you know, I'd like to see a shotgun. Maybe shoot it just once."

"Just once," said Schlage. "There's no such thing as just once."

They walked up to the store. The puddles in the front of the place were like brown mirrors, although they trembled when a truck went by. There were some black birds wheeling in the air behind the store, big vultures that funneled down on some dead thing, a dog probably. Schlage went in first, then Lee, who pushed her hair over her shoulder before stepping into the place, and finally Ray, who stopped at the threshold.

It was a small store with a few bare bulbs for light. There was a counter, and beyond it there was an enormous and new cooler, the light from its fluorescent bulbs coming through the glass door with a cool purple glow. On the inside of the glass there were long lines of moisture that ran into the frosty mist at the bottom of the door. Ray wanted to put his head against the cool glass.

Schlage went up to the counter, which was a board with a piece of green linoleum glued to it. The owner of the store, a heavy man in a short-sleeved shirt and dark pants who was wearing bifocals, sat behind the counter with a copy of the *Los Angeles Times* spread out before him. The man was Mexican, his eyes large, dark, and steady too, as though his Indian ancestors had passed along not only the color of their eyes, but also their weariness and alertness.

"Hiya," said Schlage.

"Good afternoon," said the man, looking up from his paper. "The rain stopped, didn't it?"

"Yeah," said Schlage.

Behind Schlage there was a rack for chips, and Lee stood in front of it, looking from one small bag to another, humming now, swaying from side to side a little and then singing, "Bye-bye happiness, hello loneliness, bye-bye, my love, good-bye . . ." She turned around and said, "Hey. I knew there was something wrong. You had it wrong in the car. It's 'Hello loneliness.' "

Schlage came over and stood next to the rack of chips and brushed back his hair with both hands.

"Listen," he said. "The guy isn't a half-wit. That makes it easier."
Lee went on humming, looking through the chips.

"See," said Schlage, "if I grab him, he knows what it's all about."
Lee picked up one bag and then another.

"You never stop, do you?" she said. "What did you say to the man behind the counter?"

"Nothing," said Schlage. "Jesus, there were a lot of his kind in Soledad. I never got along with them."

"Soledad?" she said.

"You never heard of Soledad?" he said. "Where you been?"
Schlage looked at her.

Then he said, "We'll talk about it later. When I tell you, you take one of those paper bags on the counter and put what money he's got into them. All right?"

"Hey!" said Lee. "Look. Here they are. Plantain chips like I was telling you about. I promise you, if you have one of these, or even just a half of one, you're doomed, you know? You have to sit down and eat the whole thing."

"Is that right?" said Schlage. "Listen . . ."

Ray was still looking at the glass door of the cooler, but now he turned his eyes away from it and walked over to the rack of chips. There he put his hand on Schlage's shoulder and gently turned him around.

"I'm warning you. Don't touch me. Ever," said Schlage. He looked at the owner of the store and started singing, "That'll be the day, oo-oo. Oh, that'll be the day when I die. . . ."

Lee stood up with three packages of chips in her hands. They were small bags, each one bright yellow and red and green, and on the front there was a bunch of plantains. Inside were the chips, sliced on a bias so they were oblong. They were crispy and brown and in the middle there was a neat star of seeds.

"One for each of us," said Lee. She turned to the owner of the store and said, "How come you're selling these? I've only seen them on the border. Or in Mexico."

"My wife's family comes from Guadalajara," said the owner. "I buy them down there. People from Mexico shop here sometimes."

"My treat," said Lee to Ray. "What are you going to get to drink?"

"A lemonade," said Ray.

"I guess I better have some beer," said Schlage.

The owner of the store brought out six bottles of beer in a cardboard carrier and put them on the counter next to a bottle of lemonade. He kept looking at Schlage and at the bag Schlage carried. Lee brushed her hair out of her eyes. Ray leaned against the counter, feeling the greasy although cool surface of it against the palms of his hands.

"Do you ever have any trouble out here?" said Ray to the store owner. "The store's pretty isolated, isn't it?"

"Yes," said the owner, "but I have a pistol here. Under here."

The owner's hand was under the counter, beneath the spread-out copy of the *Los Angeles Times*. Behind him there was a greenish wall, which had been painted with shiny paint, and it looked almost damp in the reflection of the bare overhead bulbs.

"What?" said Schlage. "What did you say?"

The owner just looked at Schlage and then turned back to Ray.

"Will there be anything else?" said the owner.

"Aspirin," said Ray.

The owner reached over to the small glass case he had next to the cash register, in which there were a couple of tubes of toothpaste, some mouthwash, a few packages of Kleenex, and some candy and gum. The aspirin were in a small plastic bottle. He picked them up with his left hand.

"Are you threatening me?" said Schlage to the owner.

"No," said the owner.

Lee looked at Schlage and the owner, and then she just stopped, waiting, her eyes a little bigger than before.

"Hey," she said. "You were joking, weren't you?"

Schlage looked at the owner, and the only sound was the compressor of the cooler, which came on with a steady, insistent throbbing. There were some flies in the room, and they flew around, the minute legs of one touching Ray's skin as it landed on his arm: Ray wondered what there was about the touch of the fly that put his teeth on edge so much. Maybe it was the fact that you could chase it away, but it kept coming back. He was thinking this when he heard the slow, deliberate unzipping of Schlage's duffel.

Lee opened one of the bags and took out a chip, her fingers trembling a little as they brought it up. The first one slipped away and dropped on the floor and then she picked out another. Outside there was the airy rush of wind as a car went by, traveling fast. It must have been going at ninety, maybe even a hundred miles an hour.

"Why don't we step outside," said Ray to Schlage. "I got something to say to you. In private."

"I'm not done," said Schlage.

"Here," said Lee, holding out the chip. "Just try one."

Schlage ignored it, but then he opened his mouth, still looking at the man behind the counter. Lee put the chip in.

"Jesus," he said. "Jesus Christ."

"What's wrong?" said Ray.

"Nothing," said Schlage. "That's the best thing I've ever eaten."

"See," said Lee. "I told you."

She looked down and saw, through the unzipped opening of the duffel bag, the blue barrel of a shotgun.

"Here," she said. "Have another."

Schlage smiled and reached over for the bag. He forked a chip out of it with two fingers and put it into his mouth.

"Ray, try one of these. You won't believe it," he said.

"That's all right," Ray said, and turned to the owner. "How much?"

The owner added up the things they had bought and Ray paid for them, taking a bill from his wallet and sliding it across the greasy linoleum. The owner paused, looking at Ray, and then he opened the cash register with one hand and made change, pushing the coins and a bill across the counter with only one hand.

Ray picked up the aspirin and the lemonade and Schlage reached over for the beer. Then they all walked back into the muddy parking lot, where the shadows of those black birds wheeled from the back of the store toward the road. Ray went around to the driver's side of the car, feeling the heat on the chrome handle. He waited, looking at the birds, at their shapes endlessly moving around, all of them going to the same, invisible spot.

Lee was on the other side of the car, eating the chips too, waiting for Schlage, and when he came around she said, "Hey, you were serious in there, weren't you?"

"Maybe," said Schlage. "I hadn't decided."

Lee looked up and swept a hand through her hair, untangling it, letting it fall over her shoulder. Her blue eyes were a little wide, and then she blushed.

"Yeah," she said. "That's what I thought."

Ray looked at her as she stood in the sun, her face not so much serious as intrigued. She shifted her weight and brushed her hair back again, and Ray stepped a little closer. She tossed her hair over her shoulder as she looked at him, the gesture at once youthful and defiant, and in the silky movement, in the quick, pink licking of her tongue over her lips, in her steady glance, there was the delicacy of some forgotten thing, like a pressed four-leaf clover found in a book and put there by someone who believed in luck or in pressing flowers: it was as though something in her sweet-smelling sweat or in the smoothness of her neck or shoulders brought with it the seduction of forgetting—if only for a little while, anyway—how one really was. Ray looked up the road, at the end of which the mountains looked like a train of pack animals, camels, say, that were walking from north to south.

"You better get another ride," said Ray.

"Why's that?" she said.

"It'll be better that way," said Ray.

"Goddamn it, Ray," said Schlage. "What the hell . . . ?"

Lee looked at Schlage, and then up the road, where there was the silvery movement of the heat, above which, with an unsteady reflection, there flew more black birds. Behind them there was the bus, which sat in front of the store.

"Maybe I want to go along," said Lee.

"Even if we've got some trouble?" said Ray.

"At least it isn't dull, is it?" said Schlage.

"No," said Lee.

"Well?" said Schlage to Lee. "What's the matter? I thought you wanted to have a good time."

"I don't know what I think," she said. She licked her lips.

"This is a lot better than hanging around looking at some buildings, isn't it?"

Lee giggled.

"Yeah," she said.

Schlage opened the back door of the bus.

"The Good Time Express is leaving from right here," he said.

Lee got in. Schlage climbed into the front and opened a beer and then passed it back to her. She drank with small sips, puckering her lips against the mouth of the bottle. Ray shook a couple of aspirin out of the bottle into his hand and swallowed them with the lemonade, the sweetness and the bitter aspirin putting his teeth on edge.

"Yeah," said Schlage to Lee. "That's the way to live."

"Listen," said Ray, "I think you should get another ride."

"I don't know," she said. "I've never done anything like this before."

"Don't you see?" said Schlage. "She likes it here."

"I'm just going to go along for a while," she said.

"A while," said Ray. "How long is that?"

"I don't know," she said. She licked her lips again, tasting the salt of the chips. Ray put the car in gear and started driving toward the constantly distant silver on the road. "Yeah," said Lee. "This beats architects all hollow."

"Sure, sure," said Schlage. "I'll tell you one thing. These are the best fucking chips I ever ate."

The aspirin seemed to help, although there was still an echo of Ray's headache, a distant, steady throb that seemed to be driven by the heat of the road and its glassy shimmer. For a moment Ray found himself wanting to go into a church, where he could sit in the cool shadows for a few minutes.

Lee sat on the back seat, her legs crossed Indian style, her head bent forward. She had a map spread out over her thighs, and from time to time when she looked out the window, she would put one hand to her hair and push it over her shoulder, revealing the freckles over her nose and her cheeks. The blue jeans were tight against the flat place between her legs. Her eyes were clear and blue, her lips seeming so full as to be swollen. One of her fingers traced a line on the map, following it with a calm absorption, tracing a road into the Sierra Nevada. Then she shrugged and looked away, resigned now that she'd never get into the mountains. At least not this trip.

In the evening the landscape became pinkish, and the air was the temperature of skin. The sand and brush turned a little darker pink, more rose colored as the sun set, and the wind blew with a soft caress. In the distance there were mountains, which seemed purple, and above them and to the west there was some dry fluff of clouds, edged with a color like the tip of a cigarette. It was only the edges of the clouds that had any color, really, and as the sun went down, and as the clouds were seen only as silhouettes, they looked like a piece of newsprint that was smoldering along the edge. Finally, over the land and the low, gray-green plants, the sky turned purple, and in the east one star appeared with a harsh twinkling.

Lee curled up on the back seat and slept, and Schlage sat up front, drinking the beer that was now warm, not saying much, not blinking, just staring at the road ahead, although once he turned to Ray and said, "Aren't you thinking about it?"

≈

They were getting closer to Vegas. Lee woke up and said she was thirsty, so they stopped at a place at the side of the road. It was a diner, made of aluminum, and it had lights around it that attracted insects, the lights looking a little purple, almost the color of the last of the sunset that had just vanished from the sky. They went in and sat down in a booth with a machine that took quarters for the jukebox. The names of the songs were on boards under a piece of clear plastic. Lee ordered some juice after asking if it was organic. Ray and Schlage had Coke.

"What's Soledad?" asked Lee.

"Soledad?" said Schlage.

"Yeah," said Lee. "Remember you said we'd talk about it later?"

"You hear that, Ray?" said Schlage. "She doesn't know what Soledad is."

Ray was hoping the Coke would help his headache.

"Why should she know?" said Ray.

"It's a prison, isn't it?" said Lee.

Behind Lee's head there was a swirl of insects, which were the color of cotton candy. They moved in a constant, streaking motion, the eruption of them seeming to perfectly describe the motion of chaos.

"Bingo," Schlage said. "You guessed it."

"Yeah," she said. "That's what I thought. You know, you look a little like Richard Widmark."

"Do I?" said Schlage.

"Don't you think so, Ray?" said Lee.

Ray looked across the table.

"I guess so," said Ray.

"Well, I want to tell you, Richard Widmark wouldn't have lasted long at Soledad," said Schlage. "For crying out loud."

Lee's T-shirt had been washed at a laundromat and had been put into her pack when it was warm, and now it was a little wrinkled. She drank her juice, her larynx bobbing as she swallowed: the delicacy of it, the quick throb made Ray stare, as though in that detail there were evidence of her vulnerability.

Lee went into the bathroom and Ray and Schlage walked out to the car. The sky was a dark blue in which the stars appeared as though by magic, the brightness of them looking like pinpricks in a piece of blue paper that is being held up to the light. It must have been the season for meteors, because now two of them raked across the sky, leaving a path that momentarily looked like scratched glass. Schlage stretched and said to Ray, "Won't be long now. Some of them like it rough, you know."

They drove toward the lights of Las Vegas, which showed as a fuzzy glow on the horizon.

"Hey, Lee," said Schlage. "Do you want a little company?"

"Sure," said Lee. "There's plenty of room back here."

Schlage picked up the knife, the whiteness of it glowing in his hand. In the bus, with only the darkness of the desert sky outside, the knife handle had the color of the Milky Way. Schlage pushed the button and the blade made a diminutive *swik,* the sound cutting through the dark and the blade showing as just a silver line, which, as Schlage moved it around, appeared and vanished.

"There's that moment," said Schlage. "It's like you're standing on a high diving board. You're scared, but you still know you're going to jump."

"What are you talking about up there?" said Lee. "I can't hear."

"Diving," said Schlage. "You like to dive?"

"What do you mean?" said Lee.

"Stay up here," said Ray. "What are you thinking about, anyway?"

The blade of the knife moved in the darkness, and for a brief second it was almost disorienting. The silver metal hung there, suspended, and it looked like moonlight reflected on black water. Ray glanced at Schlage, who sang, "Bye-bye unhappiness, bye-bye loneliness . . ."

"You still haven't got it right," said Ray.

"The song?" said Schlage. "I know how it goes." He was quiet for a moment and then said, "She's been sitting back there mile after mile."

Ray looked ahead where the white lines appeared out of the depths of the road, the accumulation of them looking like some kind of enormous perforations, the neat pattern, one always following the other, coming as a relief, or as just a small thing that was predictable.

"Don't do anything stupid," said Ray.

"What?" said Schlage.

"We'll be in Vegas soon," said Ray. "You can have fun in Vegas."

"You don't get it, do you?" said Schlage. "This is a real chance."

"What did you say?" said Lee.

Ray concentrated now, looking in the rearview mirror and at the shimmer of passing headlights on Lee's hair, her eyes bright with it too. He saw her bag, his own bag, a map, and he tried to push them into a pattern that made sense, but the things seemed to be floating in a clear, distilled fluid that had a whiff of folly.

"Keep your eyes straight ahead," said Schlage.

Every now and then a car or a truck went by, the blast of wind making the bus shudder. The bus tilted over and then back again, not quite rocking but seeming unstable, almost buoyant for a second.

"Hey," said Lee. "What are you whispering about?"

The road seemed unsteady and Ray slowed down, and for a moment he felt something like dizziness, and he had, almost as a physical sensation, the awareness of the possibility of panic, over the abyss of which he seemed barely suspended. For a moment the lightest touch, the slightest wind, the most inconsequential impulse was capable, or so it seemed, of pushing him the wrong way. He waited, breathing quickly, feeling from time to time the light tickle of sweat along his side. There was, at the back of his mind, as he seemed to sway between impulses, the certainty that whatever happened was irreversible, and so the lightest touch, the most inconsequential sight (those lines on the road, for instance), seemed to carry an enormous weight.

"Just sit still until Vegas," said Ray.

He looked across at Schlage.

"There's nothing wrong with taking it easy," said Ray. "So take it easy."

"Well, well," said Schlage. "Are you threatening me?"

"Yes," said Ray.

Schlage stared at him in the dark.

"Oh, no," said Schlage. "You don't want to do that. I promise you, that's a mistake."

Ray looked down now at Schlage's bag, where there was the blue gleam of metal.

"Architects, nonviolent toys," said Schlage. "Shit. What's a nonviolent toy?"

"A beanbag," said Ray.

A bus went by, the airy wake of it making the VW shudder. The passing bus was a secondhand one that a company in Los Angeles had bought to run gambling junkets to Vegas for retired people: it left behind a smear of lights, windows in which there were the orange glow of cigarettes and ghostlike streaks of white hair that showed through the glass.

Lee came forward now, pulling her pack up so she could sit on it.

"I guess we're almost there," she said.

"That's right," said Schlage.

Ray drove a little faster, keeping his eyes on the lights in the distance.

"Slow down," said Schlage. "You want to get stopped?"

"I want to get to town," said Ray.

"I'm not in any hurry," said Lee.

"There are some lights up there," said Ray. "Gas stations and car dealerships."

"There's still time," said Schlage. "Slow down."

"Time for what?" said Lee.

Lee looked into Schlage's lap, where the blade of the knife had a sheen like an icicle seen by moonlight. For a moment she stared at it, trying to determine what it was.

"Don't you want to have a good time, Lee?" said Schlage.

"No," said Lee.

"Sure you do," said Schlage.

She sat back, still watching Schlage, and then she said, breathing quickly, "What's going on?"

The glow of the city was brighter now, almost banana colored against the desert sky. Ray drove through the strip, past the car dealerships, a McDonald's and a Burger King, a Wendy's and a Pizza Hut, used-car lots, all of which Lee looked at with a kind of horror, as though she had finally gotten a glimpse of the anonymous promise of these places.

"You didn't answer me," said Lee. "What's going on?"

"Nothing," said Ray.

"I don't know," said Schlage. "I'm not happy. This could be real nice."

"Nothing has to happen," said Ray.

"Mmmmmmm," said Schlage. "It could be real nice."

They came up to a stoplight.

"I don't know where the bus station is," said Ray.

"What do you want that for?" said Schlage.

"That's where we're going to leave Lee," said Ray.

"Is it?" said Schlage.

Schlage stared ahead, into the still car lots and the restaurants, in which there were people waiting in line.

"Turn right," said Schlage.

Ray flipped on the turn signal and the car was filled with a steady *tock tock tock* while they waited at the stoplight. The street on the right was a long, dark avenue, and as Ray stared at it, he said, "Is this the way? It doesn't look like it."

"Turn right," said Schlage.

In the rearview mirror Ray saw Lee bite her lip, and then she reached out for the door, which she began to rattle, trying to open it.

"Sit down," said Schlage. And then he said, "Turn here," or "Turn there," still holding the knife. They went along streets that were filled with golden light, and the people in the street, while casually dressed, seemed to be on their way to work. The bus station had an enormous gray dog in front, the skin of it silver, bright as heat on the road.

Lee got out, jerking her bag with her. She walked quickly, saying over her shoulder, "I'm going in there. It's light inside. Maybe I can get a cup of coffee. Just a fucking cup of coffee."

She started to cry now.

Schlage said, "Bye-bye, sweetheart. See you some other time." He kissed his hand, making a loud smack, and blew in her direction.

Ray got out of the car and stood in the yellow light of the bus station's marquee. The place had the smell of stale popcorn and hot dogs, and as a bus pulled out of the alley next to it, there was a long trail of exhaust that, when the bus stopped at the corner, curled around it like a boa. Ray and Lee walked up to the front door of the terminal, through which people came and went as though they were at an amusement park.

"Listen," said Ray. "I've got to get out of here. I've got an appointment."

"Oh?" she said. "Do you have to see your condominiums to-night?"

"Maybe," said Ray. "Could be tonight."

She closed her eyes and shook her head.

"Wait a minute," she said. "Can't you just wait?" She looked back toward the Volkswagen, where Schlage waited. "Look." She held out a hand. "I'm still shaking."

"I'm sorry," he said. "But I've got to get back to the car."

"You're not like him," said Lee. "I can tell."

"I've made my mistakes," said Ray.

Lee glanced toward the car again, although her eyes didn't linger there.

"Listen," said Ray. "He might leave me here. Then what would I do?" Ray stood in the light, looking at her. "Go inside," he said.

"Just stay a minute," she said.

Ray shook his head.

"Please," she said.

"I've got to go."

She stared at him for a moment and then said, "Okay, okay. I get the message. Go on. Why don't you go see your condominiums if they're so important."

"What did you say?" said Ray, stepping closer. "What do you think I'm going to do with them? Did he say anything?" Ray pointed at the car where Schlage sat.

"No," she said. "I don't know anything about the old condominiums. Jesus, you act like you were going to burn them down or something."

Ray stared at her.

"I've got to get back to the car," he said.

"Okay," she said. "Fine. Sorry I asked."

Then she turned away, into the bright light, her gait small hipped and quick as she carried her pack in front of her like a sack of groceries. Ray waited until she was absorbed by the swirl of people inside, then turned away, thinking, I'll get Iris's address soon. Maybe even tonight.

On the hoods and on the windshields of the cars in the street there were reflections from the streetlights, which looked like an endless series of diminutive suns. The drivers and passengers of the cars seemed frightened mostly, as though each had something hidden, although some were pointing out someone on the street, a whore or a drunk man who had obviously lost everything. Ray watched them with the sensation of being at a threshold, a place where he simply stepped forward, not so much unconcerned about the consequences as not able to do much about them.

Ray got into the car and looked at Schlage, who was now sitting behind the wheel.

"Pssst, hey," said Ray. "Have you got any money on you?"

"Sure," said Schlage.

"How much?" said Ray.

"Three, four hundred," said Schlage.

"Get out a couple of twenties," said Ray. "Read off the serial numbers. You want to bet I can't read them back to you?"

"How much you want to bet?" said Schlage.

"Couple of hundred," said Ray.

"Make it the serial numbers on four bills," said Schlage.

"Fine," said Ray. Then he took the money from Schlage and said, "You want to try it again?"

"That's all right," said Schlage, looking suspiciously across the seat.

They went out to the north side of town. As Schlage drove, Ray thought about those mornings when he had gotten up early with his father to watch the light from the atomic bombs that were set off at Yucca Flats, the luminescence coming as a pulse, not yellow so much as a sudden, white, and unstoppable flash. Ray always thought that on those mornings he had seen in the light a hint of the world behind the ordinary appearances, a pure, brilliant illumination of the powers that one so rarely saw: in that flash everything had been mixed together, beauty and malevolence, innocence and corruption, youth and age. Ray had said to his father, "Don't you think that's what it was like in the first instant of time?"

They drove out to the edge of the desert.

"Say," said Schlage. "You don't think I was serious about that girl, do you? Hey, that was just a joke. I didn't mean anything."

"Whatever you say," said Ray.

Schlage stopped at a service station that had a large garage and a couple of buildings behind it, which, in the dark, Ray guessed were places that could be rented. There was the smell of the desert on the night air and a residual scent of sand. Inside the garage there was a man who was wearing a pair of overalls, rimless glasses, and who hadn't shaved for a couple of days. His eyes were blue and he was wiping his hands. Schlage said to Ray, "Get out," and when they were both inside, Schlage said to the man who was wiping his hands, "Here's the firebug. I got to drop something off downtown."

THERMOPYLAE

LILY, LOLLIPOP,

AND GINGER BEE

The man who was wiping his hands looked at Ray for a moment, not stopping his hand cleaning altogether, but just doing it more slowly. The man's name was Jackson Burgess, and he was six feet tall, or a little more, had graying hair, blue eyes, and a tattoo on the back of his right hand that said, JESUS LOVES ME. He was forty-eight years old. Years before, when he had lived in Los Angeles, he had had a towing service that picked up wrecked cars on the Hollywood Freeway. He was a good mechanic and a good welder, too. Before he had his own business he had worked for the Yellow Cab Company in Los Angeles, picking up a car on the freeway that looked like a yellow accordion and that, in twenty-four hours, he had back on the street, although sometimes the paint was a little wet.

He had made good money on the freeway. It was a job other people didn't really want, since it was easy to get killed when using a tow truck to pick up a car that had broken down or had been left, after an accident, at the side of the road. People drove fast, not to mention that many of them were drunk or high: the Los Angeles Police Department put up roadblocks one afternoon and found that 30 percent of everyone was taking something.

There were times when Burgess had ideas of perfection. Once, he had seen a picture of a greyhound in a magazine, and he had stopped, holding the photograph at arm's length, not so much amazed by it as somehow mesmerized.

He was married to a woman from Arkansas, a tall, thin blond woman who liked to crochet doilies and watch the late show on television, and who took a delight in the ferociousness of the wrecks on the Hollywood Freeway, which, in their twisted metal and cracked glass, in their smashed seats and the engines that were forced into the passenger compartment, proved to her that she was somehow correct in thinking that Los Angeles was a place where only fools lived if they had the chance of being somewhere else. She was interested in making money, enough of it to move to northern California, where she wanted to open a trailer park. She looked up from her crocheting and said, "What are you looking at?"

"Here," said Burgess. "Look for yourself."

He held out the magazine.

"It's a dog," she said. "So what?"

"That's all you can say?" said Burgess. "That is the most beautiful animal I have ever seen."

"I don't know," said his wife, Dahlia. "Kind of skinny looking, if you ask me."

Burgess took the magazine back and carefully cut out the photograph, which he put into a frame he bought at a stationery store on Sunset, walking in in his greasy overalls and his short-billed cap and dark boots, picking the frame up and taking it to the counter, where he put it down and said, "How much?" He reached into his pocket and brought up a fist full of crumpled bills. And when he had paid and had brought it home, he put the photograph in, carefully pressing the small wires at the back of the frame over a piece of cardboard he had put in too.

For a while he was content with just the photograph, which he had in his garage on Western Avenue. The dog itself was seen running, legs out, ears blown back in the wind of its own locomotion, its paws out, and in its side there were cleanly defined and geometric sections of muscle. They were triangular, like the shape of a blade of a mortar trowel. Burgess came back to the garage after having picked up the pieces of a car in which there were still the stains and unmistakable eddy of someone having died in it, and when he stood in the silent garage, where he remembered the shapes of the torn metal and the bright debris of the broken glass, he looked up at the dog, which then appeared to him as the antithesis of the disasters that Burgess seemed to spend his days in the midst of.

In the beginning, the wrecks had been exciting, or evidence of a ferociousness Burgess was able to avoid himself, although the proximity to it had made Burgess think, when he was reaching under what was left of a Chevrolet or a Buick, a Ford or a Pontiac, that he was standing right at the brink of it. It had left him alert, and had even given him the sense of somehow being in the know, since the cars (and how they ended up this way) were something he felt he alone understood. But as the time passed, as the weeks he spent on the freeway turned into months, and the months into years, the sight of the crashed cars, the crumpled truck boxes, the stains from transmission fluid, from radiator water, green and unearthly with antifreeze, not to mention the dark, blackish residue of blood, all left Burgess with a sense of discomfort, a quality of being ill at ease (as though he were a spectator whose opinion mattered not at all). The image of the dog now became more important than ever; its order and beauty and its possibility of victory, if not satisfaction, had a soothing quality, and as Burgess stood in the silent garage, hearing only the distant, eerie sound of the cars on the freeway, he felt all the anxious turmoil of hope.

There were magazines dedicated to greyhounds, and Burgess subscribed, and there were dog tracks, too, that he went to, not caring about the grubby atmosphere of gambling or the seedy air of something that was a surrogate for the complicated elegance of a horse racetrack, or at least a good one, like Santa Anita. In fact, this even made it better, since Burgess saw the grubbiness as a way of making the dogs more clear, more graceful, and so obviously the opposite of the wrecks he saw on the Hollywood Freeway.

"They're just dogs," said Dahlia when she had come to the track with him.

Burgess shrugged and looked at his wife, unable to say precisely what it was that made him resist this. He went back to his racing form and began to pick out a bet for the next race, but after that he was happier when he asked if Dahlia wanted to go to the dog track and she said she had a headache.

He began to read about the history of the breed. It was the existence of these dogs, so sleek and fast, that seemed mysterious (as though there were something they contained, some part of grace or celestial speed that could almost be felt, or understood, or better, even participated in, through breeding, by a human being). When he hitched up to the wrecks, from which there rose ghostlike whiffs of steam, he thought about lineage and the endless possibilities the mixing of genes suggested, and as the cars went by at seventy miles an hour, Burgess thought of the names, King's Mystery, Greek Artist, Hope's Handle, Summer Song, all of which seemed to pierce the noise and wind of the freeway and the sense that yet something else had gone wrong and that he was powerless to do anything about it.

He bought two dogs, a male and a female, Charlotte's Jimmy and Moon Spot, and he did so after keeping records, scoring the dogs at the track not only on the basis of their speed or stamina, but also on a system that ranked the efficiency of their breeding against the variables that went into it. He had studied line breeding, hybrid vigor, had made charts and boxes, had gone to the library and had read what there was about genetics, his research taking him into considerations of DNA, the double strands of which he saw as twisting around each other like stairs around a pole in a lighthouse or fire station, and the order of them, even the elements themselves (guanine and cytosine, good names, Burgess thought, for dogs: Sweet Cytosine, or Cytosine Streamer), all contributed to that same anxious hope, which gave Burgess the illusion that in the midst of twisted metal and the flashing lights of the tow truck he had a glimpse into the heart of the natural world, a glimpse that suggested order and beauty and the presence of something else, not an object, not even an array of elements, but a sublime peacefulness that is at the center of all real power. In the evening, after his reading, after going over the lists of names of dogs and the possibilities of combining the qualities of one dog with those of another, he had a sensation of actually seeing the DNA, which in his imagination was so enlarged as to be the size of galaxies, the dark surfaces of which were speckled with bits of red, green, and yellow light, something like Los Angeles seen at night.

This, of course, was before he actually bought the dogs.

He brought them back to his house, which was on a side street off of Western, in a pickup truck that had been rear-ended on the Hollywood Freeway and that Burgess had put together with a cutting torch and green paint, debating for a moment, even before he bought the dogs, whether or not to paint on the door, in white letters and with an image of two running greyhounds, BURGESS FARMS, QUALITY BREEDING.

He had the dogs in two square carriers, which had wire doors through which the dogs looked, their eyes bright, dark, their feet making a scratching sound on the plastic floor. One dog was black and brown mixed together, and the other was a white dog with pale brown patches. Burgess pulled into the driveway, which went by the house and to the beginning of the backyard, and then he got out, standing at the rear of the truck in the Los Angeles twilight, in which the city, as though by magic, was vanishing into a gray-blue gloom pierced by golden lights. He looked at the dogs, and in the depths of their eyes, through the black marblelike sheen, he saw some beguiling evidence, and for a moment Burgess was convinced that he was looking not only into the dogs' eyes but also through time and the endless combinations that had gone into the dogs' breeding, the bright opaqueness of the eyes seeming to be an accumulation of time and possibility, the sheen of them like oil that has been underground for aeons and has finally bubbled up to the surface. Burgess spent a few moments in the twilight, with the trees and the houses vanishing (or being absorbed) into the obscurity of early evening.

He had built two pens. He had rented a posthole digger and bought some pressure-treated four-by-four posts, and he had dug holes in his backyard and mixed concrete to put around the bottom of each four-by-four post. And between them, with a delicious sense of making preparations, not to mention acting on an idea of beauty, he had put up a fence, a wooden one with latticework he'd bought at the lumberyard, the kind of thing that is seen in a country house rose garden and that, because of its prettiness, had seemed more appropriate than gray wire. He had built two gates, and bought four bowls, one for each dog for food and fresh water. He had made two doghouses, too, with aluminum doors made with a raised lip so that a dog could open them. The doors had been advertised in one of his greyhound magazines, and he had spent an evening looking at them, thinking what a good idea they were.

Dahlia had watched from the window. She didn't say anything about the fact that she had always wanted to have a grape arbor. One of her dreams was to sit outside in the heat of an August afternoon, drinking a lemonade in the beautiful, new-leaf light that would come through the vines, and that would fall, too, over the clumps of grapes, green ones with a little delicate dust on them. She thought, for a moment, of how the breeze, scented with grapes, would touch her skin, making it cool and bringing a slight, delicious tang. Maybe she could even sit there late at night, when it was hot, nude in the dark. She'd like to make an ice-cold martini and drink that, feeling the cold bite of it and the breeze on her skin.

Burgess came into the house after building the pens, and she had said, "Are you going up to the market?"

"Yes," he said. "I thought I'd get some big bags of dog food."

"Could you get me some grapes," she said. "Some nice green ones?"

"I haven't noticed you ever liking grapes," he said.

She shrugged.

"I don't know," she said. "I've just been thinking I'd like some."

"Okay," he said. "What do you think of the kennel?"

"I guess the dogs will like it," she said.

Now, Burgess unloaded the dogs, running his hands over their sleek coats and feeling as he did so the geometric musculature, the smooth, hard flesh that had about it the suggestion of having been made for one purpose, which was to run. Burgess opened the carriers and led each dog to its pen, where he let it go, saying, "Sure, go on. Get comfortable. That's fine."

In the evening, after a day with those wrecks and ambulances and flashing lights, Burgess came and sat on a bench he had bought, a concrete one for a formal garden, and while the dogs ate, crunching their food, Burgess watched, taking comfort in the sound, in their constant voraciousness, which seemed to be a symptom of the power he had suspected and even felt close to when he had read about the mixing genes, between which the spark of life, with such directness and order, was almost visible as it jumped between two strands of DNA that were entwined around each other in the oldest caress in the world.

Sometimes, when he sat there, he thought of the breeding of the dogs, of the accomplishments of their ancestors, not only in speed over various distances (and with various conditions of the track), or in money earned, but of how, over generations, the dogs had picked up easily, or so it seemed, the qualities that Burgess was convinced went into making not only a fast dog, but the fastest of all. Now, as he rested, glad to be away from the stink of the freeway (which more and more seemed to have about it a vile stench and a whiff of something deadly), he thought of a dog in a race, breaking away from the box, its speed revealing (to those who understood these things) the power and beauty out of which every living thing has come. He sat there until the sun went down, listening to the dogs rustle, to their scratching and occasional whimpering, which seemed, in the half-light, to carry with it a promise.

Burgess then went inside, where Dahlia sat, listening to the Harmonicats on the record player. They were playing "Clementine," "Roll Out the Barrel," and "Dipsy Doodle Polka," and when Burgess began to turn it down, she said, "How are the dogs?"

"Fine, fine," said Burgess. "Do you mind if I turn this down?"

"No," said Dahlia. "I don't know why you want to. You used to like this music."

"Did I?" said Burgess.

"Before the dogs," said Dahlia.

"Things change, I guess," said Burgess.

"Why?" she said. "I don't want anything to change."

Burgess turned off the music, and then the two of them sat in the silence for a while. Burgess got back up and turned it on again, although much lower.

"What's happening?" said Dahlia. "Will you tell me?"

"Nothing's happening," said Burgess.

"Do you love me?" she said.

"What do you think?" he said.

"Well, I don't know," she said. "You seem distant. It's hard to know."

Burgess looked out the window where the dogs were, their coats, when they moved behind the latticework fence, showing as a compelling shimmer, like moonlight on water. Then he turned back to Dahlia and said, "I'm going up to the market. Do you want anything?"

"Grapes," said Dahlia. "I'd like some grapes."

The female came into heat. Burgess had been waiting for some time, and now, when the signs were there, he opened the door of the male's pen and let him in, closing it after him and hearing the metallic click of two objects that were made to fit together. He sat down on the concrete bench and thought things over. Inside the house he saw the golden light from the kitchen, and Dahlia as she went about cooking, the steam rising around her from the stove, her eyes glancing, from time to time, into the backyard.

At night, as they lay in bed with the window open, they heard the rustling of the dogs outside, and Dahlia said, "I was thinking. Maybe we should get out of town now. Maybe we could go up north. We could find a little place up there."

"I don't know," said Burgess. "Somehow, I don't want to get up there as much as I used to."

"I still want to. There are lots of things I wanted," said Dahlia. "I always wanted a child."

"I don't know why we didn't have one," said Burgess. "It wasn't because we didn't try."

"Maybe I should go to a doctor?" said Dahlia.

"If you think it would help," said Burgess.

"I don't know," said Dahlia. "Just listen to those dogs. I bet the neighbors will call to complain."

Burgess lay on his back, staring at the ceiling.

"Sometimes I miss not smoking," she said. "You know that?"

"Yes," he said. "I know what you mean."

"Come on," she said.

"What?" he said.

"You know," she said. "Tell me you love me. Tell me you really love me. Maybe that will help with a baby."

"Do you think so?" he said.

"Maybe," she said. "Anything's possible, isn't it?"

In the morning, Burgess stood out by the pens, looking at the dogs, the two of them moving around with an anxious, alert gait, as though they each knew that they were carrying pieces of a perfect puzzle that, with a nervous excitement, they knew they were going to fit together with an almost perfect success.

At work Burgess was called downtown to the interchange, where the cars were piled up, the broken glass and chrome glittering in the morning light, the interiors of them exposed, the engine compartments dark and oily and disordered, the cables and wires and gas lines twisted, the radiators, or what was left with them, making a slow, long hiss or sigh. As he bent down to hitch onto one of the wrecks (which had two rear wheels that still turned), he heard someone saying the accident had taken place because a man had been driving at seventy miles an hour with a book propped up in the steering wheel and a cup of coffee on the dashboard. The man had read a line, glanced up, had a sip of coffee, and then read another line until he plowed into the back of a new Bronco. Burgess listened to the story and thought of the dogs, who were always more alert than the people who ended up in these piles of twisted metal. Or perhaps it was just comforting to think of creatures who did one thing at a time.

The female, Moon Spot, became pregnant. Burgess was convinced she had conceived, not because the glance in the animal's eyes was complacent or anything like that at all: it was more a mixture of courage and a kind of impatience. Soon, though, it was obvious to anyone that she was pregnant, and Burgess said to Dahlia, "Do you think she'll be comfortable in the pen?"

"Yes," said Dahlia. "She'll be fine."

Burgess kneeled next to the latticework fence and put his fingers through it, stretching them toward the dog.

"Only thirty days more," said Burgess. "We'll have a pup that . . . well, I'll say this. This dog is going to have speed. That I can guarantee."

Then he went through the list of dogs that had gone into the breeding of the two that Burgess had bought, Hard Mountain out of Green Wishes, Lollipop out of High Sierra, Blue Bird out of Perfect Water, Rubber Willy out of Lacy Lady, Ginger Bee out of Thermopylae Lily, the qualities of each coalescing into an aura of possibility that settled into the pen where Moon Spot now passed back and forth, glancing up at Burgess and Dahlia, the animal already feeling a little hungrier than she usually was.

"I went to the doctor," said Dahlia.

"Oh," said Burgess. "What did he say?"

"Not much," she said. "He thinks I've got a scar. Maybe there's still a chance though."

Burgess looked out beyond the pen, to where the sky was turning that blue-gray. In the distance, from Western Avenue, there was a red-burnished glow of light.

"Okay," he said.

"That's all you have to say?" she said.

"What more is there to say?" he said.

"I don't know," she said.

She shrugged.

"I don't get it," she said. "I just want to be normal. That's all. I can't stand the feeling of being separated from things, just ordinary things you can depend upon, like having kids."

Burgess stood up now and took her hand and they started walking back to the house, away from the pens.

"It'll be all right," he said.

"Tell me again," she said.

"*Everything* will be all right," he said. "You want to go out for dinner?"

"No," she said. "I'm not up to it. Did you have a hard day? Were there any bad wrecks?"

"Yes," he said.

"Tell me about them," she said.

⚡

So now they watched the dog get larger, which seemed to happen slowly, the creature not gaining a lot of weight until the end. Burgess weighed her, bringing her in and putting her on the scale in the bathroom, over which he had built a wooden platform for her to stand on, and as he recorded the weight, the growth became a matter of contention between Burgess and his wife. She saw the animal, as it grew, as proof of how things weren't working out for her as she had wanted, each pound, each change in shape appearing to her as some irrefutable evidence, and as she looked at Moon Spot with a growing resentment (not for the dog itself, but for what it represented), Burgess felt just the reverse, seeing the dog's growth as proof of his knowledge and understanding, not to mention something like faith. He carried the dog back to its pen, feeling the extra bulge in its stomach and believing that soon the issue would be settled once and for all.

The pup was born, and Burgess brought it into the house, its umbilical cord brown and dry like a piece of beef jerky, its head compact and its brow wrinkled, looking then like a face of wisdom.

"All right," said Dahlia, as she got up to make herself a drink, a cold, sharp martini that made the glass she drank it out of mist up. "So what? Let's forget about things. That's the best thing."

"There's no need to be jealous of a goddamned dog," said Burgess.

"I'm not jealous," she said. "I'm a little sad, that's all."

"Life goes on," said Burgess. "Things work out."

He held the puppy up as proof.

It grew quickly, and now on his days off Burgess took it down to the beach, where he let the thing run, the dog going along the long, flat, and shiny stretches of sand (where the waves washed up and left a gray sheen that, for a quick moment, was almost like a mirror). The dog, whose name was Iron Mike, went straight away, sometimes getting caught by a wave, and for a moment, in the splash that rose around the animal in a white shape like an enormous flower, there seemed to be a reminder of that unseen world of perfect patterns, held in those strands that Burgess had so often imagined and that had just been waiting to be combined in the right way.

In the afternoon of the first day the dog was going to race, Burgess loaded him into the carrier he had in the back of the truck. The dog was a light grayish color, about the color of a bullet, and there was in the high-backed, loping gait a frank, unruffled patience, as though the animal were already convinced of its own speed, so much so that it wasn't excited by it as much as soothed. The dog had developed this slowly, becoming quieter, more steady, obviously drawing strength from some discovery.

At the track a handler put the dog into the box. Dahlia and Burgess stood by the fence, and from the box seats behind them cigarette smoke came in a gray, slowly roiling cloud. On the slight breeze there was the smell of popcorn, cooking hamburgers, and beer. It was evening and the lights of the place were very bright, which suited Burgess since he was comforted by the appearance of things that were lighted like animals in a photo finish. Dahlia looked out at the track with a kind of sourness, as though this place were somehow a reflection on her own incapacity. Burgess hadn't had a cigarette in years, but before the race he had bought a package of Marlboros, one of which he smoked now, the sudden and unfamiliar drag of it, filled with nicotine, making Burgess see things as being even a little brighter than they were.

The race began with a mechanical rabbit on a long arm making a circular approach. It came from a distance behind the boxes where the dogs were, and the track that the metal arm ran on made a harsh, steady rumbling. Burgess tried to think what it was precisely that the sound reminded him of, a distant train traveling fast, perhaps, or someone driving at high speed across a metal bridge. The rabbit passed the boxes, and the doors opened with a clang that was obscured by the crowd, which made a sound as though by one, amazed human being.

The dog came out in a high-shouldered gait that was, in the beginning, almost impossible to see, since, no matter how much Burgess told himself that no dog could run fast enough to be perceived as a blur, nevertheless this was how, in a kind of gray stream, the dog appeared. It seemed that it was a length or maybe a length and a half ahead after they had gone only a few steps, and the other dogs, while running with a speed that had seemed wonderful, now appeared, in comparison, somehow sluggish and even lazy.

A man who was down the rail from Burgess looked out at the pack and at that gray, bullet-colored streak in front of it and said, "I have never seen anything like that. Am I dreaming? It's got to be some drug."

"It's not drugs," said Burgess, who put his hand down to the rail carefully, his fingers shaking there. He looked at the tracks that the dog made as it moved away from the pack, a straight line in the loamy soil, the footprints implying the presence of the dog better, in a way, than the dog itself did, as though the animal and its speed could be grasped only in the imagination, in the evidence of it rather than in the flesh. The dog's head rose and fell, and it drove forward with a muscled leveraging that implied a force so smooth as to give Burgess a tactile sense of it. It was impossible to say whether the other dogs in the race lagged behind because they just didn't have the speed or because they had given up. They approached the first turn, and the accumulation of dogs, each wearing a number on a red, green, or yellow band, made a muddle in which no one back or head could be distinguished for long, the entire mass sweeping along with all the disorder of a swarm of some kind. Out ahead there was that gray, bounding streak, and as the crowd watched it, there was no sound at all, no cheering, no common sigh of amazement or surprise. The crowd watched, some with a paper cup of beer or Coke suspended midway between a tabletop and an open mouth. Burgess gripped the rail now, leaning forward, keeping an eye on the gray, mistlike motion, which now began to lean into the first turn.

It wasn't really even in the turn when its feet went out from under it. The dog didn't appear to realize that while the track curved to the left, its speed was carrying it straight, and, as the dog was airborne for a moment, its legs went right on running in that same powerful gait, although there was a little more quickness to it: one leg touched the ground, and with the speed and the movement, the dog rushed forward, although now it was in disorder, its legs straight out in a pattern that could come only from the centrifugal force of the dog's own furious spinning. It hung in the air, its shape awkward and misshapen, still turning until it slammed into the Cyclone fence at the beginning of the turn. Even from the distance there lingered, over the barking of the dogs, a wiry hum from the fence. The pack went by, and from the mass of backs and shoulders and heads in muzzles, one dog and then another came to the front of that constant, seesawing motion, all of them passing the fence, which went on buzzing with the impact.

The dog got up and started to run again, limping a little and even seeming dizzy. It went along behind the pack and crossed the finish line last, where it was gathered up by a handler. He brought the dog back to Burgess, who was now waiting at the dogs' entrance to the track, and said, "Here. Tough luck. He sure looked good for a minute, though."

"Yeah," said Burgess. "I guess that's right."

On the way home, with the dog in the carrier in the back, Burgess and Dahlia said almost nothing. It was a long drive and Burgess drove slowly, once even going about ten miles an hour as he thought things over, at which point Dahlia said, "How much did you have on him?"

"A thousand dollars," said Burgess.

"Not a thousand," said Dahlia. "Was there some of it to place and show?"

"No," said Burgess. "It was all to win."

Burgess put the dog in the pen and fed him, although now, while Burgess sat on the concrete bench, the sound of the dog's crunching as it ate had a different quality than before. He remembered the hum of the fence at the track. At first the sound had only been irritating, like the buzz of a mosquito, although as Burgess thought about it some more the sound began to change, with each passing moment, into something else. Burgess looked at the red glow over the city and listened to the distant sounds of police and fire sirens.

On the freeway now, when he went to work on a wreck, he heard in the slight twang of a piece of chrome that hung from the side of a car, or in the vibration of a hood that was sprung open, or in the creak of a door that no longer closed, that same hum. He kept his head down when he heard it, the sound penetrating his skull with the same insistence as a dentist's drill. In the evening he sat by the dogs' pens, and when he looked into their eyes he saw in the black, shiny globes not the depths of time or breeding but the opaqueness of delusion, of his own inability to understand or to control the things around himself. He felt betrayed.

The smashed cars didn't seem so horrible anymore. The twisted metal and the broken glass had their own intensity, which Burgess confronted with something like appreciation or just an abiding interest. There was an evening in Anaheim when, in the fog, three hundred cars had crashed together and Burgess had pulled a lot of them to a parking lot, hearing, in the crashing, almost musical noise of the smashed loose ends of the cars he towed, that mocking hum of the fence.

Burgess hadn't been sleeping well, and he had gotten a prescription for Seconal, which had made him sleep in a warm, blank darkness. Now he got the prescription renewed once and then again, sitting in the backyard afterward and looking at the dogs. He knew, from his reading, that dogs had enormous livers. This is why they could eat almost anything and not get sick, but it also meant that they were hard to poison. Dahlia watched from the house as he opened the capsules and mixed the powder into the dishes, which were filled with food, and then he took them over to the pens, saying as he did so, "Here."

Dahlia came out now and said, "Please."

"No," said Burgess. "I get these crazy ideas about things. I should know better. I'm forty years old and I shouldn't get these ideas."

"I like it when you have crazy ideas," said Dahlia.

"Not me," said Burgess. "I'm through with stuff like this."

"Please," said Dahlia. "It feels like you're giving up."

"No," said Burgess. "I'm not giving up. I want something you can trust. I want loyalty."

"What are you going to do?" she said.

"I'm going to make some money," he said. "Some real money."

"We're doing all right," said Dahlia.

Burgess shrugged now, and said, "The first thing will be to get rid of these pens. What was that you wanted? You once were going to tell me you wanted something out here."

"A grape arbor," she said.

"Okay," he said. "I'll build you a grape arbor."

"That would be nice," said Dahlia. "That would be real pretty."

Now, when a new car had been wrecked on the freeway, Burgess bought it, paying the owner a hundred or two hundred dollars, doing this not because the cars were worth anything but because the papers were, and soon word got around among car thieves that if you wanted papers for a new Mercedes-Benz or Jaguar or BMW, there was a place you could get them. It wasn't long before Burgess was buying not only the wrecked cars to get their papers, but also stolen cars to stand in, so to speak, for the cars that he was going to junk. Then he transported the stolen cars (with papers that seemed to describe them perfectly) to Phoenix, and from there they went to Mexico or South America, the cars simply vanishing into the heat of the desert on the other side of the border and leaving behind, as a lingering reminder that they had existed at all, a pile of money, usually cash.

Mei Yaochen needed transportation, on a regular basis, of packages to Las Vegas, and since Burgess had started a drive-away service in addition to moving stolen cars to Mexico, he worked out a deal with Mr. Mei, too. So, Burgess sent cars to Vegas as well, doing so until it made more sense for him to move the entire business up there (since there were plenty of wrecks in Vegas, and a lot of them were foreign imports from Germany and England), and when he told Dahlia that they were going to move to Las Vegas, she was sitting under the grape arbor, the lime-colored and moist light washing over her skin. The arbor hadn't been built by Burgess. He had paid a man to do it, an ex-convict who was waiting around for a car to drive to Phoenix.

"I always thought we were going to go up north," said Dahlia.

"Not now," said Burgess. "We can do all right in Vegas."

"Can we?" said Dahlia.

"I think so," said Burgess. "Better than we are here. Are you coming with me?"

"I always thought that northern California would be right," she said. "I never liked the desert. Your hair frizzes out. You have to live in front of an air conditioner."

"There's money to be made," he said.

"Oh," she said. "Is that all you think about now?"

"No," he said. "I think maybe you better go up to northern California. You'll be happier there."

"Just like that?" she said.

"I think it will be better," he said, and then walked out of the arbor. "I've put some money in an account for you. It should be enough."

So now, Burgess wiped his hands, watching Ray, who stood just inside, carrying his bag. Then Burgess turned and looked at the doorway through which Schlage had just walked, the sound of the man's footsteps coming on the still desert air. He did so while the word "firebug," which Schlage had used to introduce Ray, died with a slow resonance, like the lingering vibration after someone has dropped a crowbar on a concrete floor. Burgess stared outside, thinking things over, and then he said, gesturing toward the door, toward Schlage, "He shouldn't talk that way. He's going to get in trouble doing it."

The garage was filled with fan belts and tires, tool chests with their drawers open, arranged so as to suggest a model of a pyramid, and on the wall there were gaskets, the holes in them for cylinders neat and perfectly round.

"Come on," said Burgess. "I'll show you where you can stay."

They walked out into the dark, toward the low, motellike building that was there. It was one story, covered with pink stucco, and above each door there was a small, yellow porch light. None of the lights were on, and the interiors, through the windows, seemed to be brooding, as though the darkness itself were the leavings of some secret that was best not known. On the road one car passed, the sound of it diminishing until it couldn't be heard at all, and then there was only a fading glow of the taillights.

"In here," said Burgess.

Inside there was a bed, a chair, a bureau, and there was a bathroom. Ray put his bag down and said, "Thanks. I'll need a car for a couple of days."

Burgess nodded. "Okay," he said. "Out here. I'll show it to you."

They went around to the side of the garage and in the darkness there was a plain Chevrolet, anonymous, with black sidewalls, looking in the dark like a police car. They got into it. Burgess gave directions until they came to a deserted row of almost completed condominiums.

"There," said Burgess. "Are you going to remember how to get back up here?"

"Yes," said Ray.

They turned back now, toward the garage and motel, and as they drove, Ray said, "There was another matter."

"Oh," said Burgess. "That. You want some woman's address."

"That's right," said Ray.

"After you've done your job," said Burgess, "I give it to you."

"Not before?" said Ray.

Burgess shook his head.

They pulled back up at the service station. It was late now, but in the distance there was the glow of the lights. They hardly ever went out in Las Vegas, and they had about them a fierce constancy, as though they represented a kind of belief in escape from ordinary restraints.

Ray got out of the car and started walking to his room.

"Hey," said Burgess. "Are you in love with her?"

"Yes," said Ray.

"Well," said Burgess. "I don't know. Love is one of those crazy ideas. You got to be careful about getting crazy ideas."

BOOK III

THE MEETING

Ray sat in the car for a while before going up to the door of the house. It was a small place, and in front of it there was a split-rail fence, gray as clouds, and in the yard, which was sunbaked earth, there was yellow grass that grew in those places where there was some shade. The house was what was called a "one-story ranch": it had a slightly peaked roof, plywood siding that was grooved so as to suggest planks, and a couple of large windows in the front. Instead of steps, there were two cinder blocks with a piece of two-by-eight across them. There was a dead tree in the yard, one that had been planted in a burlap bag and that was still held up by guy wires.

Beyond the house was the desert, the scrub and subdued colors, pastel grays, browns, and yellows, stretching away into the distance. It was six o'clock in the evening, and as the sun set, the western windows of the house were filled with reflections that looked like orange foil, and the siding was covered with a pinkish cast, a dry, dusty hue that made one think of a powder. The desert had the scent of brush, sage probably, and of the clean earth, which had been burned by the sun.

Ray put his hand on the door handle of the car and began to open it, but then he stopped and went back to considering the house. In the quietness of the late afternoon, it appeared to be somehow dangerous. For a moment, Ray couldn't even say what it was that left him hesitating, but as he stared, concentrating, it appeared to him that the house, as it sat there at the edge of the desert, was dreadful because, for all its ordinariness, it still revealed the vicious thing that lay in wait for those who took chances and who were so young as to think that the only thing they'd get out of danger was a thrill.

There was something else, too, he was able to see about the place, if only because the street was quiet and he had a moment to sit and think, the car being filled only with the sound of his quick breathing and a slight, distant ticking of the engine as it cooled off. The very ordinariness of the place gave him pause, since so many of the things he knew had seemed ordinary and unassuming (the house where he had grown up, for instance) but had, underneath, been anything but ordinary. As he heard the ticking of the engine, he was certain that if he wasn't cautious, the same thing that the place revealed (that essentially cunning thing that waited for you to make a mistake) would blow everything sky-high. All he wanted was to walk in and ask Iris to get in the car with him, but it seemed that nothing so simple and direct would do anything but cause trouble. So he sat there, thinking of a way to be gentle, while his hands shook with rage, if only because he couldn't just go and tell a woman that he loved her.

The keys to the car were on a chain made of small brass balls, and when Ray first turned off the engine they had swung back and forth, making a click where they bumped up against the steering column, that steady *tick tick tick* being a diminutive reminder of the passage of time. There was the odor of kerosene on Ray's hands, and he sat there smelling it, thinking that for two cents, if he had the chance, he'd burn the house to the ground. He thought, I can't just walk in there and ask her to come with me, can I?

He smelled coffee, a fresh batch, and as he got out of the car and walked over the hard-packed earth, he supposed Iris was just getting up. He guessed she worked at night. In the house across the street there was the flicker of a television, which filled the room with erratic pulses of light. The door was hollow and his knock sounded a little too loud and at the same time thin, insubstantial.

Ray turned toward the west to look at the sunset, the filaments of cloud as red as the wire in a toaster, and as he waited, Iris came to the window next to the door and looked out. She just stared, one hand reaching out to the glass. Then she bit her lip and shook her head. Her hair was shorter than it had been before, not permed, a little curly, although it hadn't been combed. Her skin wasn't the way it used to be. She had been vain about it, looking at how clear and peachlike it was, but now she had a little acne, and her skin didn't seem so smooth.

Ray turned around and faced her, the glass between them. One of her cheeks had small red creases from the pillow, and her eyes had in them the same orange-foil color as the windows. He put his hand out, next to hers, the glass warm between them, although the outside of it was dusty and reminded Ray of the desert. He said, "Why don't you open the door?"

She took her hand away and stepped back into the dim room, her shape barely visible as she stood with her arms crossed beneath her breasts, thinking it over. Ray waited on the step made out of a dry board, smelling the kerosene on his hands.

After a moment she opened the door and said, "Hello, Ray."

"Hello," he said. "It's been a long time, hasn't it?"

"Yes," she said. "I guess that's right."

"I never really got a chance to say good-bye," said Ray. "When you left Bakersfield."

"Is that what you came to say?" said Iris. "You wanted to say good-bye properly? Is that it?"

"Something like that," said Ray. "Can I come in? Are you alone?"

She stood in the doorway, one hand on the knob. The room behind her had a hardwood floor without a rug on it, and there was a sheen to it in the otherwise dim room. She shifted her weight and put her hand to her hair, fluffing it out.

"Yes," she said. "I'm alone."

She stepped back, holding the knob of the door, and Ray went in, smelling coffee. The room itself was bare, although not completely empty. There was a new, green velveteen–covered love seat and a chair next to it, a rocker that had a wicker bottom. There was a bookshelf made out of bricks and planks of wood that had some paperbacks in it, and there was a television on a wooden fruit crate with a label that said, SAN MATEO VALLEY PEACHES . . . THE WORLD'S FINEST, and on it there was a picture in an antiquated commercial style, almost like Norman Rockwell's, that showed a young woman with blond hair and red lips eating a peach. She had very clear skin. Beyond the living room there was a kitchen with a yellow Formica counter where there were two stools, a cup of coffee, and the day's paper.

Ray went through the living room, seeing her go before him, her hips in that silk robe, her hair in a haze around her head. The room's dimness (there were no lights in it at dusk) was filled with a reddish cast from the sunset, and the furniture, the white walls, the floor all had a crimson glow that came through the curtainless windows.

In the kitchen she turned and faced him.

"What are you doing in Vegas, Ray?"

"I just thought I'd look you up," he said.

"And what if I don't want to be looked up?" she said. "What if I don't want to be reminded of anything that happened before I got to Vegas?"

Ray glanced around the room and then came back to her, looking directly at her.

"I guess that's going to be a problem, then," said Ray.

"Well," she said, "some things haven't changed, have they? You still haven't got the sense to stop telling the truth."

Ray felt the weight of trying to smile now, almost as though he were picking up something that weighed one more pound than he was capable of lifting. He was afraid it was more of a grimace than a smile. He winked.

"I'm glad to see you," he said.

"Are you, Ray?" she said. "That's real sweet."

She looked at him for a moment, and then she turned away abruptly. She reached into the sink for another cup, which she washed quickly, and filled it, putting it down on the other side of the counter. Between them there was the newspaper, the front page of which showed a large black-and-white photograph of a row of buildings, one constructed against another, about thirty-five of them altogether. They were built on a small rise, and the picture was taken from down below so that they seemed to be enormous. They were on fire, and the flames showed as flowing white streams, although there were places where the flames were too bright, and they looked like white globes, like suns or globular galaxies. There was a lot of smoke, too, dark plumes of it as if from a smokestack, and in it, visible even in the photographs, there were sparks, which came through as small stars, distorted in crosslike shapes. The caption said, EMPTY CONDOMINIUMS BURN. DEVELOPMENT A TOTAL LOSS. HOT FIRE LEAVES NOTHING BUT THE FOUNDATION.

Iris sat down and picked up her coffee, bringing it to her lips, and with it suspended in the air, she looked across it at Ray and said, "I was thinking about you just now."

Ray looked down at the paper.

"Is that your work?" she asked.

"Yes," said Ray. "These condominiums aren't selling at all, you know?"

"Well, well," she said. "Are you moving up here?"

"No," said Ray.

"How much did you get for it?" she asked.

"Twenty-five hundred."

"Have you got it with you?"

He looked down at the picture of the fire again, his hand holding the coffee cup, which was as warm as skin.

"What's it to you?" he said.

"I was just curious," she said.

He nodded, saying, "Yeah, I've got it. Hundreds." He reached into the pocket where he had them, folded over, just to make sure they were still there. Then he reached down and touched the photograph in the newspaper. The glow of the fire made a kind of backlighting, and the outline of the roof, where it hadn't yet fallen in, looked like enormous black steps.

"That's a lie," said Ray, pointing to the caption. "I bet I got the foundation too."

"Did you?" she said, looking at him.

"Yeah," he said. "You know, I remember when Dean used to come home with a pile of money. Sometimes he told my mother to wash it because it smelled of accelerant."

"What's an accelerant?" she said.

"Anything that burns fast," he said. "Lacquer's a good one."

"Are you trying to impress me?" she said.

"In a way," he said.

"Why's that?" she said.

He shrugged, unable to say why, exactly, although already feeling they had begun to struggle somehow, and that he would offer one detail and then another of how he had burned down buildings, not to prove that he had done something wrong so much as to prove that he could be trusted. Ray swallowed and put both hands on the counter, pressing against them.

"You know," said Ray, "no one pays you for smoke damage. Any jackass can do that."

She went on looking at him, realizing what he was doing, nodding.

"Yeah?" she said. "What else?" She spoke with a mixture of curiosity and regret, as though recognizing something: it seemed that now, as before when they had jumped off bridges together or driven a car fast, they were momentarily bound together, and his confession had about it all the terror of that long, windy plunge into the cold river below. She shifted her weight and stood a little closer, her eyes set on his, her entire aspect a little sultry and filled with a dare. "Well?" she said.

"You know, there have been a lot of great torches," he said.

She put a finger to her lip, running it back and forth.

"Like who?"

"Jimmy Avery and Max Hillboro in Chicago," said Ray.

"That's all?" she said.

"No," said Ray. "There were others. Charlie Blue in Atlanta . . ."

She put her hand into her hair and slowly pushed it backward, still looking at him.

"There was Joachim Solarius in the Bronx...," said Ray. "There's a whole language to it. Like a smoking fire is a 'dinge,' and a match is a 'blue tip' or a 'barn burner.'"

She went on looking at him.

"Maybe Dean was a pretty good torch," said Ray.

"Dean," she said. "You know, we never talked about him. Maybe we should."

"Okay," said Ray. "Go on."

"You know why I got involved with him?" she said. "It was dangerous. I liked that . . . it was a thrill. It just got to the point where I wanted to get away, though. It just got to be claustrophobic. I always liked it when things were scary."

"I know," said Ray, already shaking his head, not wanting what was coming since she had begun to push back, good and hard now. Ray closed his eyes, just as he had when they had hit the water in the river, but even so he was hoping they could stop, but he was sure they wouldn't.

"What I do is scary," she said. "Don't you want to hear about it?"

Ray pushed down on his fingers and looked directly at her.

"Yes," he said, feeling, for a moment, the old intimacy that came from speed or fear.

"You can never tell what's going to happen," she said, looking at him. "You're in a room, some anonymous room with some guy . . . maybe he looks all right, maybe you think you can spot which ones are okay, but you can never tell. What are you going to do then? How can you control it? How can you be able to give them just what they want and get out alive?"

"Is that all?" he said.

"No," she said. "You want to hear more?"

"I don't know," he said.

"You mean you'd stop, just like that?" she said. "Are you afraid?"

"Yes," he said. "But go on. I'll go along with you. You know that. What else is there?"

She told him. She said she knew all kinds of things, described the two silk cords she had, one with seven knots in it. She talked for about ten minutes, looking at him. Then he said, the sound escaping him, "All right. All right. Please stop." He sat down on one of the stools by the counter. "Have you anything to put in this coffee? Maybe brandy?"

She went to the cabinet and brought a half-empty bottle of Jim Beam, which he poured into the cup, sipping it and then pouring a little more in. He could still smell the kerosene on his hands, even though he had washed them four or five times. He spent a moment looking around at the house now, tasting the bourbon.

"You like the place?" she asked.

Ray swallowed.

"I don't know," he said.

"It needs a little more furniture. I wanted to get some new curtains and a carpet and a real bookshelf. Maybe some colonial stuff."

"Like a wing chair," he said. "Maybe a sofa with a curved back, you know?"

"Stop it," she said. "Please."

"All right then," he said. "Maybe not a sofa with a curved back."

"Please," she said.

"Okay," he said. "All right."

He put the coffee cup down and then he folded up the paper, pushing it away so they couldn't see the photograph anymore. For a while they sat there, each staring out the window or into the living room. Ray noticed that on the counter and in the trash can there were a lot of the square white boxes that take-out food comes in, some with a spoon or a fork still in them. The moment of intimacy seemed to end, and Ray was left sitting there with the cup, feeling that somehow, in a way he didn't quite understand, the intimacy had turned into anger.

"Look," he said. "I just wanted to see how you were doing."

"Well, I'm doing fine," she said. She ran her hand over the skin of her face and said, "The air-conditioning here is hard on my skin."

"Maybe you could get something for it," he said. "An astringent."

"No," she said, "I think it needs a moisturizer. Everything is dry here."

She turned away, looking into the room where there was that rose-colored light, which was so strong as to make the place look as though it were being seen through a glass of red wine.

"I've got to go to work in a half hour," she said.

"What time are you going to get home?" he asked.

"Late," she said. "Sometimes the sun is already up."

"Where are you working?"

She looked right back at him now.

"Downtown," she said.

"Do you have to go right away?"

"Look," she said. "I was doing just fine here. I didn't ask you to knock on my door, you know that?"

She sipped her coffee and looked over the rim at him, thinking it over. Then she got up from the counter, carrying her coffee with her as she moved into the bedroom, saying, "I've got to get dressed."

Ray sat at the counter, and opposite him was the kitchen window, through which the desert was getting dark. It didn't seem as though light were leaving so much as that the desert was giving something up, retreating into itself in such a way as to make the landscape inscrutable, just dark fuzzy shapes and an erratic skyline. Ray looked down at the folded paper, trying to concentrate now on the constellations that would soon appear, Orion, Andromeda, Taurus, and even as he tried to imagine the points of the stars, he stood up, carrying his coffee cup through the empty living room, his shoes sounding very loud as he walked toward the rectangle of light that came from the bedroom door. The living room was getting darker, and for a moment he felt that he was being absorbed by it, almost not completely there: it was with something like relief that he came into the light.

Iris was sitting at a dressing table, one with a mirror with five or six bulbs, which gave it a theatrical quality. She was wearing a small brassiere and a pair of underwear that looked like a G-string, both champagne colored, and when she was finished with her face (putting something over the shadows of acne on her cheeks), she stood up and picked up a dress off the bed, a bright yellow one, one piece, which she slipped on. The things she wore had a utilitarian quality in that she could get dressed and undressed very quickly. She took a bottle of perfume that had a glass stopper and touched the stopper behind her ears, staring right at herself when she did so.

"I don't look so bad," she said. "What do you think?"

"I . . . ," said Ray, glancing down into the coffee cup. "I think you look real nice."

She glanced at him for a moment, holding a brush now and reaching up to touch her hair. There was the scent of perfume in the room, and Ray wanted to sit down on the floor. Or maybe stretch out on the bed and close his eyes for a while.

"I've got to get to work, all right?" she said.

"Well, sure," said Ray. "If you've got to go."

"It was nice seeing you," she said. "It really was. You look me up again sometime, okay?"

Ray stood in the doorway, feeling the warm coffee cup in his hand. It was more of a mug, really, made of heavy porcelain, the kind of thing that you see in every diner and truck stop in the country, and as Ray felt the weight of it in his hands, it seemed as though the pressure in the room had coalesced into that smooth, heavy, ordinary cup. He stood there weighing the heft of it and then looked at her as she sat in front of the mirror, her side, her breast under the clinging dress, her neck and hair all visible in it. Then he said, "How do you think I got your address?"

"I don't know," she said.

"I burned down a building to get it. I could have gone to jail for it and I still might yet. So maybe I'd like to stay a little longer."

She turned back to her dressing table, picking up a brush or a box or a rubber band, her finger going back and forth through the powder there. The top of the table was covered with a piece of black mirror, and the accumulation of the powder had the shape of the Milky Way.

"Sure. You can stay for a while. Have you got the twenty-five hundred on you?"

"Yes," he said. "I told you."

"All right," she said. "You can wait around for me if you want. Make yourself at home. It's your decision."

She stood up in front of the mirror and looked at herself, and then she picked up a small handbag, checked the contents, snapped it shut, and reached for her car keys, the silver shapes of them making a domestic tinkling.

Then she walked across that hard, shiny, and bare floor, her shoes making a banging as she walked with a swagger, disappearing into the gloom and then opening the front door, through which there was the flicker of the television across the street. Above the erratic blinking of it there was the desert sky, the stars emerging, and just before she closed the door Ray thought, Yes, there it is. Orion.

Ray turned and faced the darkened room. Outside there was the diminishing sound of Iris's car as she drove down the street and turned at the corner toward downtown. Ray imagined the small Japanese car as it went, the shape of it dark, just a silhouette of the windows and the rounded hump of the top. Iris turned the corner and disappeared toward the glow of the city, and as he concentrated, imagining her touching her hair or absently adjusting a strap, or squirming behind the wheel as she considered the evening, he thought of how easy it would be for her just to stop and turn around, to come back into the house and pour herself a cup of coffee, but even as he thought this he shook his head, trying not to make a fool of himself, even if only in his thoughts. All he wanted now was to be precise, which didn't seem like much as he stood there, the silence seeping into the room in the same way that cold comes into a house in winter.

The silence had a clarity, though, and a delicacy, too, which made Ray think of an insect caught in amber, and just as one could see the fine hair on such a creature's legs, or the veins in its clear wings, so Ray was certain that for a moment, anyway, some previously illusive or just unnoticed thing was apparent. Now that Iris was gone and he was alone in the empty room, he remembered the sensation of the two of them together, the lack of which made him feel alien, not just to the things in this room, but altogether. The keenness of it, in the silence of the room, left a bitterness that was so strong as to seem almost salty in his mouth. Then Ray went over and looked out the window so he could see the stars.

He sat on the green love seat next to the bookshelf and turned on the light, glad for the warm splash of it on the floor. The small sounds of his moving, of his breathing, of the rustle of his clothes as he sat down, of the squeak of the springs in the love seat had a strangely irritating reassurance, if only because he sat there desperately looking for the right thing to do but uncertain as to how to go about it.

There was a scent from the newish love seat (of sizing, of something that had come from the manufacturing of it and that seemed to be anonymous). Now he stood and went over to the bookshelf, where there was a row of mysteries, a dictionary that looked new, some maps, an atlas that had been well thumbed. There were some field guides, too, to the flowers and animals of the southwestern desert, although they looked as though they had been opened only once or twice. There was a *TV Guide*, the early-morning movie circled with a Crayola, and next to it there was a large book, called *Xamore's Guide to the Apocalypse; or, The Signs at the End,* and as Ray looked through it, he saw that entries had been underlined, all of them with a yellow pen. Iris had marked a passage that ran, "Before the end, there will be meteors and earthquakes. Drought will be common. Men will fight over water."

Ray stood at the bedroom door, through which he saw that the bed was unmade, that the drawers of her bureau were open, scarves and stockings and underwear hanging out. Next to the bureau, in the corner, there was a basket of dirty clothes. It had been so long since he had seen her that the disorder of the room, even as evidence of distraction, was almost comforting to see. Then he sat down on the bed, feeling the house around him (which seemed so mundane and yet so much a kind of vicious dead end) and wanting, more than anything else, to stop whatever it was, the effect of vanity or arrogance or just stupidity, that had brought the two of them to this particular moment. How wonderful it would be, he thought, if I were just wise.

He gathered up some stockings and put them into a drawer, and as he did, he saw a notebook. The thing was covered with green cloth and the paper was lined and numbered. The effect of it was to suggest an antiquated business of some kind where accounts were kept in a careful script written with a pen that was dipped into an inkwell. Ray held it in his hands and sat down, not wanting to open it but knowing that he would.

On the first page Iris had written, "Things I Want." The first entry said,

Why is it that all the men who fuck me hold my head in exactly the same way? They lean on their elbows and put the tips of their fingers against my skull, holding me as though some operation were going to be done to my brain. I wish this wouldn't ever happen again.

I want to be glamorous. I want people to look at me in the street, as though I were somebody.

I wish my legs were a little longer.

I wish I had some idea of God, a real idea, not some hairy old man in a robe. I mean of some substance that flows through everything and doesn't wish me harm.

Sometimes I have spotting. I wish I didn't have that. The antibiotics I take make my stomach upset, even when I eat something. The coke must have some speed in it, because I get awfully jumpy. Elavil helps.

I wish I were sleeping better.

I wish I knew what went wrong. And what the fuck is happening to me.

I wish I could save some money and then I could go down to L.A. and check into the Beverly Hills Hotel and live on room service.

I wish Ray would come to see me but I don't want to be ashamed in front of him.

I'd like to kill Dean. He was the one who was full of shit, who was always telling me that it was all right to be outside of ordinary life. Right and wrong was for suckers. Yeah? Yeah? He should have known better.

In the back of it there was a pile of newspaper clippings, all of them of buildings that had been burned down, and on top there was a snapshot of Ray.

He put it away and sat down on the bed, his head in his hands, and finally he stretched out, the sheets seeming imbued with a presence he recalled from Iris's house. Then he sat up and started walking around the house again. In the kitchen he did the dishes, wiped down the counters, took out the trash. In the bathroom, which he started to clean too, he looked in the medicine chest, where there were two varieties of antibiotic, both of them in large plastic bottles. He closed the cabinet and sat on the edge of the tub, thinking it would be a good idea to get out for a while: maybe he could win a little money.

≈

Downtown, the desert wind blew, and the people walked through the slanting rays of light from the windows, their faces half in shadows that streaked away from a nose, a chin, from the brim of a hat, slanting across a brow or stretching into the cleavage of a woman who wore a low-cut red blouse. The street was dry and clean, and there was a shadow that ran from the curb to the street, obscuring the gutter. There was a man and a woman sitting in the waiting room of an all-night car rental, the man in a brown coat and a green tie, his face set on the clock on the wall, the woman staring at her hands, both of their faces slashed with those dark shadows.

Up the street there were neon signs in reds, blues, and greens, and there were casino entrances that were like theater marquees, the undersides of which were covered with small lights. The effect of the light and color and the desert air was to make one think that taking a chance here was part of a general hilarity, and with it there was something salacious, as though the lights were bright with the golden essence of pleasure. Through a window Ray saw people at the rows of slot machines, each of them working as though they were paid by the piece.

He went inside. There was a constant metallic racket, and the sound of bells, too, over the harsh tinkling as a slag of coins, gray as a shark, collected in a payout chute or spilled onto the floor, the coins twisting end over end and suggesting a shower as they fell. Ray looked around, recognizing in the room a scent or sound that seemed to be common to a lot of things Ray had been confronting, like the atmosphere around the house where Iris lived. Ray walked over to the dice tables, where the white cubes tumbled and made a padded thump before revealing the number of dots to the men and women who waited, leaning into the pit that was as green as a small pond.

It took about three hours, but Ray finally ran into her. She was sitting at a bar, a long oval one made of dark wood that had a sheen like wet lacquer. In the middle of it there was an island on which there were three cash registers, a pyramid of bottles, rows of glasses. Iris sat in her yellow dress, her legs crossed on a stool, smoking a cigarette. She was talking to a man in a Hawaiian shirt who was forty years old, his hair a little gray, almost a metal color. He was smoking a cigarette too, laughing from time to time. He took a wallet from his hip pocket and showed Iris a photograph of his wife and kids.

In the dim light, and with the green dice tables in the background, Iris appeared taut and youthful, unspoiled, not even tired. The smoke rose from the cigarettes into a cloud overhead, and as she put one palm under her elbow, there was in her gesture an ordinary attractiveness. She picked up the photograph and stared at it for a moment, and then gave it back. As she did so, she saw Ray.

She stared at him, raising a brow, and the two of them waited, not saying a thing: her expression was the same as when she had asked him if he wanted to know about what she did, although now the dare in her eyes was one of warning him, of making it clear that he shouldn't say a word. He stood up to it, squared his shoulders, keeping his eyes on Iris, feeling that there was a kind of invisible rope that ran from his eyes to hers and that, for a moment, it held them together. Then she looked away, took a drag on her cigarette, the smoke coming out in a languid stream until she said to the man she was with, the two words visible as puffs of smoke, "Let's go."

The two of them got up and walked away, her gait not inflammatory or swaggering. She went through the sections of light, in and out of the shadows, her shape, in her yellow skirt, finally being absorbed altogether.

*

Ray won three hundred dollars at the blackjack tables, taking the cards and letting his winnings ride. The dealer was a woman with short blond hair and green eyes who seemed to have an accent. Ray guessed she was French-Canadian, somehow displaced all the way to Las Vegas. She dealt out of a long, boxlike container of cards, the speed of her hands having something so precise about it as to suggest a different skill altogether, brain surgery or the work of a magician. Ray tried to imagine what her apartment looked like. For some reason he liked to think she had a sofa covered with an imitation tiger skin and that in front of it there was an enormous TV. The rug was black shag and on the wall there were . . . he couldn't really think of anything, photographs of Monet's garden, maybe, or a view of Montreal taken from a satellite. Instead, he looked in the direction that Iris had gone, the lines of shadows streaking from a wall onto a green carpet.

He glanced back to the dealer and said, "Can you tell me where there's a pharmacy?"

"Down the street," she said. "Go out the door front and turn right. Are you going to bet?"

"No," said Ray. "I've got something to do."

Outside there was a dry wind like one that blew in California sometimes, a dry, constant rush of air that left everyone close to anger. It was a slow, gradually increasing thing: the wind began with a dry caress and an almost comforting warmth, but as the days passed, as you woke with the scratchy sound of it on the roof and went to sleep with your skin itching, there was only the inescapable sense of its drying heat. It put your teeth on edge, and even the sound of a piece of newspaper scraping in the gutter left you close to panic, if only because there was no way to get away from the wind. In Las Vegas, in the streets downtown, there was that dry hush, and the air was scented with perfume and liquor and with something else, too, that Ray couldn't put his finger on exactly, although it was like the scent in a hot, abandoned room where the sheets on the unmade bed are dirty, the ashtrays full, and glasses on the floor are filled with melted ice and bourbon.

In the pharmacy, Ray stood in front of a shelf on which there were lotions, makeup, brushes and combs, sprays and cans of mousse. There was a hopefulness in the order of the bottles and the array of bright silver and gold bottle caps. Ray studied the lists of ingredients on the bottles, not able to make sense of them, aside from the fact they were organic compounds of some kind. It was as though there were an entire, mysterious language that eluded him when he needed information. He thought of moist, smooth skin, of Iris's face when they had driven in that Mercury they had bought together. The time between then and now seemed to be made definite by the weight of the bottles, and, even though he shook his head at his own delusion, it still seemed that he was able, in some small way, to buy a little of it back. He chose one, took the bottle up to the cash register, and slid it across the counter, saying, "It's dry here, isn't it?"

The cashier shrugged.

"Well, it's the desert, you know. What did you expect?"

At dawn, the desert behind Iris's house was black, like a coal-colored sheet that ran to the horizon, which was dark too, a ragged edge against the first luminous blue of the day. Ray sat at the counter drinking coffee, afraid to go to sleep since he didn't want to be groggy, although every now and then he poured some Jim Beam into his cup when the caffeine got to him so much that he couldn't sit still. He had the brown paper sack with the conditioner in it next to his cup on the counter. The refrigerator made a steady *uh uh uh,* and a fly flew around in the room, the insect buzzing a little and describing a path like a squiggle made by a pen on a piece of paper. Ray thought the light and the sound, too, from the explosions at Yucca Flats must have really been something here. Maybe you could even smell the burned desert.

There was a lot of cash in his wallet. The twenty-eight hundred made a kind of lump in his back pocket, a constant, steady discomfort that reminded him of where the money had come from. It made an ache. He took the wallet out and left it on the counter.

Iris pulled up in front of the house and slammed the door of her car. The sunbaked dirt was hard and her high-heeled shoes made a scraping sound as she came around the car and walked toward the back of the house. She faced the desert with the sun behind her, her hair appearing in a glow, her weight on one hip, one knee a little bent, her small bag over her shoulder: she was at the center of the rising sun, not in silhouette so much as just in the middle of rays and a fuzzy gold luminescence. She turned toward the house, dragging her bag and staggering a little, putting her hand to her head.

She pushed the kitchen door open and came in, her face tired and looking a little puffy. At the sink, she washed her hands and then splashed water on her face, the watery dripping and plash in the stainless-steel basin changing the air in the kitchen from one of quiet expectation to something else.

"Here. I got you something," he said.

He held out the bag from the pharmacy and she stood there, looking at him. She swayed a little, not much, nothing bad or sloppy, but there was an obvious struggle to keep from appearing high or drunk or both. One shoe made a slight tapping on the floor, and then she reached out for the bag, taking the bottle from it, holding it, feeling the heft of it. Then she put it on the counter, and next to it she emptied her handbag, the twenties and fifties and hundreds crumpled there like green and white wastepaper.

"Jesus, Ray," she said. "You don't get it. It's not my skin that's the problem."

Ray shrugged.

"The label said it would do some good," he said. "It moisturizes."

"Well, that's nice, Ray," she said. "That's real sweet." She looked at the lotion again. "I'm going to take a shower. I stink."

She kicked off her shoes and started walking into the living room, but halfway to the bedroom door she stopped and said, "I bet you think I should get out of here, don't you?"

Ray took a breath and thought, Careful. Careful.

"I'm not trying to convince you of anything. I just came to see you," said Ray.

"Oh, come on," she said. "Tell the truth."

"All right," said Ray.

"You know," said Iris, "you don't even have to say it. I can see it in your eyes. Well, buddy, I don't want you accusing me, you know that?"

"I'm not accusing," said Ray.

"Oh no?" she said. "Then don't look at me like that."

"I'm not looking at you like anything," said Ray.

"You want me to admit I'm wrong," she said. "That I got in over my head. Isn't that it?"

"You're saying that," said Ray.

"Well, smart guy," she said. "If I got out of here, where the hell would I go?"

"We could get in the car," said Ray.

"And where would we go?" said Iris.

Ray shrugged.

"We can decide that once we get going," he said.

"Ah, Jesus, Ray," she said. "Don't make me feel ashamed. Okay? I'm glad you came to see me, all right? But let's leave it at that."

Ray looked around the kitchen and the living room.

"You know something?" said Ray.

"What?" said Iris. "What have you got to say?"

"This place pisses me off. It's like it was just waiting for you to make a mistake. It was right here, all ready. Come on, tell me, doesn't it make you angry?" he said, walking over to her.

She looked back at him, ready now to go along with him, just as she had before, almost inviting him to continue, and whereas before they had gone toward a turn at a high rate of speed or had confessed to some of what they had done, now she stood there thinking it over, almost curious, in that last moment before giving in to a previously unacknowledged fury, about what he could do to keep the two of them together for a moment longer. She stood there blinking, not swaying any longer. He stepped closer yet, careful not to touch her, the two of them understanding each other perfectly now, if only because they both knew he would go along, that he'd let himself get just as angry as she would, risking everything.

"Yeah," she said. "It pisses me off."

"What gets to you the most?"

"You'd like to know?" she said.

"Yes," he said. "Tell me."

"The way the men hold my head," she said. "Always the same. You know, they put their fingers here . . ."

She put her fingers up to the back of her head.

"Like that," she said.

Then she took her hands down, the fingers trembling.

"What else?" he said.

"Oh, God," she said. "You think you want to get into this? Well, why not. Maybe this is the last thing we should say to each other. . . ."

She stepped forward, the anger making her feel almost light, as though she might float into the air. Ray stared at her, letting go now too, if only so the two of them would exist, for a moment anyway, in that same, bright state.

"The last thing?" said Ray.

"You come around here," she said. "You stir me up—"

"You think I'm not stirred up?" said Ray. "What gives you the right to think you're the only one who's pissed? You think I want to stand here like this?"

"There's the door," she said. "You can do something about it right now."

"Tell me," said Ray. "If you dare. What else makes you angry?"

"I'm confused," she said. "I'm so fucking confused."

She stared at him now, her arms crossed, as though she could stop the trembling that way. Then she said, "And you, what about you? Do you dare say anything to me?"

"Yes," said Ray. He nodded. "Yes."

"Well?" she said.

"Somehow, if I just walk in here and tell you I love you, it'll cause trouble. How do I feel about that?"

"Oh, God," she said. "It's a little late for that, don't you think?"

"No," he said.

"Oh, shit," she said. "Oh, leave me alone."

Ray swallowed.

"I just want to think," he said. "I don't want to say anything without thinking."

He went into the bathroom and washed his face too, scrubbing hard. He washed his hands and sat on the side of the tub. Then he turned and went back into the kitchen, where Iris was. There was the steady dripping of the kitchen faucet, and the refrigerator started to throb. She looked at the wallet on the counter and said, "Have you still got the twenty-five hundred?"

"Yes," said Ray.

She looked at him, nodded.

"You want to spend it on a good time?" she said.

"No," said Ray.

He took the bills out of the wallet and held them out.

"You want the money? You think I give a shit about money?" he said. "Do you want it? Here. Take it."

He stood there holding it out and she watched his face for a moment, realizing that somehow they had come to that same moment when everything seemed light and insubstantial. Then she turned away and said, "I've got to take a shower. I always take a shower first thing when I get home."

Ray went in and sat on the bed. In the bedroom she took off the yellow dress in one practiced motion. Then she sat in front of the mirror and put her head down in her arms, which she had laid on the dust on the black piece of glass. There was a bruise on her left thigh, on the inside a little, a new one, a dark blue-green. There was one on her upper arm too.

"I missed you," she said. "Is that what you want me to say? All right?"

Then she went into the bathroom, dropping the small underwear and getting into the shower, and as she stood under it, the water hitting her head and shoulders, she looked out the open door at Ray. She just let it hit her, although she went on staring, and then she stepped out, taking a towel, walking toward him. She came in and sat down too, her hair dripping, her skin beaded, the towel wrapped around her. Ray picked up her hand, and they sat there, not like the times when they had driven fast or jumped off a bridge or even approached that store in Chinatown, since now they had finally come to a moment that was worse than any of that: the two of them sitting alone in the house with what they both knew.

Ray reached out to the dressing table and touched one of the side mirrors, which were on hinges, and as it swung around, seeming to move with an almost sidereal deliberateness, they waited, neither of them wanting to see the image it finally reflected, Iris sitting with her hair wet and matted, her skin dark on her cheeks, her eyes wide with a kind of disbelief, her legs stretched out before her, the towel opening and showing the bruises, and next to her there was Ray, tired, staring.

"All right," she said. "Let's get out of here. But if you ever throw any of this up to me, I promise, I'll kill you."

She packed a bag, leaving almost everything. While she did so, Ray stood in the kitchen drinking coffee, and as he held the cup in a saucer, he heard the exaggerated clicking, as though there were a small earthquake. He ripped the photograph of the burning condominiums from the newspaper and folded it up. Then she came out of the bedroom, combing out her wet hair. There was a small bag by the front door, and Ray carried it out to that anonymous Chevrolet, the thing gray as dust. The Chevrolet was next to Iris's small Japanese car, and Ray gestured toward it, saying, "What should we do about this?"

"Nothing," she said, taking the keys for it and throwing them into the front seat. "I was just borrowing it."

Then they drove toward Los Angeles, the shadow of the car stretched out before them and the sun rising in the east. Ray watched the road approach in one long, seamless sweep, the glitter in it turning into a kind of blur as it approached the car, the lines having a steady throb, an appearance in the depths of the distance and then a short, distorted pulse before they disappeared under the hood. He drove fast. Iris said, glancing over at him, "You know, I'd like to see Dean. He was the first chance I took that started to turn sour."

"All right," said Ray. "Let's go home."

In Los Angeles it was not so hot, although it was still warm and the air had a reddish gray cast in which the sun hung like a flat, perfectly round disk. There were no shadows in the afternoon light, and the concrete of the freeways, the dry green of the vegetation around the houses, the streets where no one walked all appeared in dull tones, about like the gray of a bullet. On the bus stops' benches there were signs that said, UTTER MCKINELY, FUNERALS ON CREDIT.

"Yeah," said Ray, "I'd like to talk to Dean too."

"What about?" asked Iris.

"Oh," said Ray. "I've got a better idea of how things are now. Maybe I'd like to tell him about it."

Ray left the Chevrolet in Chinatown, in front of the grocery store. He wrapped the key to the Chevrolet in the photograph he had torn from the paper and pushed it through the brass mail slot. Then the two of them walked up to the Golden Palm, where they got into the Mercury and started the drive north.

BLACKERS

◄►

The drive-in restaurant in Bakersfield sat at the edge of a field that had the first green cast of spring, a hue that was so slight as to seem almost hallucinatory. The Mercury was parked so that Ray and Iris could see the field, Ray leaning against the door, one hand on the steering wheel. The women on roller skates wore small, pillboxlike caps, brown shorts, white blouses trimmed in brown. Beyond them there was the field and the distant hills. The women skated with an undulant motion, their upper body and arms swinging one way and then the other, and when one of them came up to the car, she said, "Hi, Ray, where you been? I heard you were in the East someplace."

"Well, there's no place like home," said Ray.

The woman on roller skates stood and looked at him, thinking this over. Then she bent down a little, her face in the shadow of the car, to look at Iris.

"Well, Iris," she said. "Where have you been?"

"L.A., Vegas," said Iris.

"Uhmmmmm," said the woman, still looking across the seat.

Then she looked back at Ray and said, "Well, maybe now that you're back you'll be able to do something about Dean."

"Maybe," said Ray, looking at the menu, which was on a sign where all the cars could see it.

"Everybody's talking about it," said the woman on roller skates. "It's like the World Series around here. You know, people say, 'Did you hear Rainey's got a gun? A big silver .357.' "

"Stainless steel or chrome," said Ray. "Not silver."

"Yeah, whatever," said the woman. "That Dean. You know, people have been waiting for him to make a bad mistake for years."

Ray turned to look at her.

"Well, gee, Ray, I'm just glad to see you back, that's all," she said.

Ray nodded.

"Thanks," he said. "That's real nice."

Iris and Ray ate their hamburger sandwiches off paper plates. The sandwiches were made on toasted buns with seeds on top, and there was lettuce and a slice of tomato and onion. The paper plates had a slight texture to them, and the french-fried potatoes were almost a yellow color, like butter or corn. They ate slowly, methodically, talking about a stunt someone had pulled years ago. A young man, who later ended up selling life insurance, had put so much soap into a fountain downtown that a wall of soapsuds about two feet high had moved across the sidewalk. They didn't laugh, and then they folded the wax paper neatly and put it on the paper plates. Ray looked out at the flat land with the first green blush on it, unable now, with nothing more than the look in a carhop's eyes, to come to anything definite aside from a yearning, which after a moment Ray recognized as regret that he didn't have a gun, but even this brought a kind of counterweight, a sense of claustrophobia, since he knew having a gun would have been the worst thing in the world. So he waited, feeling that useless desire, trying to breathe slowly and hoping it was the disorientation of traveling, the slight gritty dizziness of it, that made him feel that way.

"You still love Dean, don't you?" said Iris.

"I wish I didn't," said Ray.

"That's not what I asked," said Iris.

"Yeah," said Ray. "I still love him."

"I guess it wouldn't do much good if you told him, would it?" said Iris.

"No," said Ray.

They finished eating. Ray paid, doing so with one of the hundred-dollar bills in his pocket. As the woman made change, tucking the hundred-dollar bill into a wallet she carried in a pouch at her waist, she said, "Say, has your ship come in?"

They drove past Ray's house first, the place gray and still looking like a solid, respectable place that had seen better times. The trees around it, the grass in front, the porch all seeming like something out of a small town where nothing ever went wrong. Ray slowed down, but then kept right on going, up to Iris's house, the weeds growing as before, the new lawn furniture arranged more carefully, the new curtains in the downstairs windows appearing a little dusty now. Iris looked at the place and said, "Let's find a motel. On the south side. That's best."

They slept in one of those rooms that had about it the scent of air-conditioned cigarette smoke and disinfectant. The sheets were starchy and almost like those in a hospital, but Ray and Iris went to sleep almost immediately, hearing the cars outside, the dry rustle of the tires as they passed on the hard-top.

Ray woke with a start. Next to him, turned on her side, Iris slept, breathing with a slight sigh. Her back had a sheen in the dim light of morning, the crease over her spine running down between two dimples and the back of her hips. Ray put his hands behind his head, still feeling a sudden surge of fear or alertness, and then he sat up, contemplating the sound of the cars outside, the brown-gray gloom around him, and thinking about Dean. Ray was certain now that being a father was the one decent thing Dean had ever had. It had been a way of being wise and knowledgeable, or appearing so, and there had been a thrill to it. The problem had been in giving it up, not to mention that Dean went about trying to continue being a father (which meant trying to prove he was right, no matter what) with all the illusions of a small-time crook. Somehow, Dean had begun to believe that being a father was 95 percent resistance.

It was eight o'clock. Ray went out to the phone booth and dialed a number, and when Dean answered, Ray said, "Dad, it's Ray."

"Well, Raymond," said Dean. "Where the hell are you?"

"I'm in town," said Ray.

"How did you make out in L.A.?" asked Dean.

"All right," said Ray. "Iris is with me."

Dean didn't say anything for a while.

"We'd like to see you," said Ray.

"Uh oh," said Dean. "I guess I better get ready for some heavy stuff, huh?"

"We'd like to see you," said Ray. "How about downtown, tonight?"

"Well, okay, Raymond," said Dean. "If you're sure that's what you want."

They met in a restaurant that had cartoons on the wall and booths covered in brown leather. The waitresses wore light brown dresses and the bartender had on a bow tie. It was a dark place, and Iris and Ray sat at a booth, watching the door. Dean and Harriet Rainey came in, the two of them standing in the light of the entrance, Harriet tall and wearing a nice skirt, her hair neatly combed, her figure trim, and Dean with his face lined a little, his shoulders broad, his hair combed back: he looked like a character out of a French gangster movie made in 1949.

"Hi, Ray, Iris," said Dean. "Do you know Harriet?"

"Hello," said Ray, getting up and putting out his hand. Harriet's touch was cool and smooth. Iris said hello, too, and then they sat down.

One of the waitresses came over and asked what Dean and Harriet wanted to drink, and Harriet said, "Oh, I don't know. I'd like something different."

"How about a glass of champagne?" said Dean.

"What are we celebrating?" asked Harriet.

"My son here is going to lecture me about something," said Dean. "Isn't that what you're going to do?"

Iris stared across the table at Dean.

"Well?" said Dean.

"Why don't we get something to drink?" said Ray. He turned to Harriet and said, "Have you ever had a blacker?"

"What's that?" asked Harriet.

"Champagne and stout," said Ray. "It's real smooth and nice."

"That's one of your eastern things, isn't it?" said Dean. "Some goofy thing from England or something, right?" He turned to Harriet and said, "Have a bullshot."

"I don't know," said Harriet. "The champagne thing sounds nice."

"Christ," said Dean. "You don't want that. Have a bullshot. You'll get sick on that other stuff."

"I want to try it," said Harriet.

"Oh, come on," said Dean.

"I want to try it," said Harriet.

"Well, all right," said Dean. "Don't complain later."

The waitress brought a pitcher in which there was some champagne and some stout mixed together, the foam dark and looking as if it had been tinted with molasses.

"All right," said Dean. "What's on your mind?"

Iris went on staring at him, saying nothing.

"I just wanted to talk," said Ray.

"All right," said Dean. "Talk."

"I think you've got trouble," said Ray.

"I know how to handle myself," said Dean. "You hear these rumors, you know, but they don't mean anything. I know how to deal with people. You look them straight in the eye and they back down. You don't even have to say anything to them."

"I think you're wrong," said Ray.

Dean turned to Harriet and said, "See? Here comes the lecture." Then he turned back to Ray. "What am I wrong about?"

"Harriet's husband," said Ray.

"Leave my husband out of this," said Harriet.

"Listen, Ray," said Dean. "I'm going to prove something to you. Then maybe you'll listen to me. There isn't anything to worry about. These people aren't something to give a second thought to."

"You don't have to prove that to me," said Ray. "I'm not asking proof."

"Sure," said Dean. "We'll make it a kind of contest."

"No," said Ray.

"What's the matter?" said Dean. "Come on."

"I told you," said Harriet. "Let's stop talking about my husband. It isn't genteel."

Ray turned to the door, through which he saw a car passing from time to time, the chrome and metal looking like a smear.

"I guess you want me to say how great it was that you got things straightened out in L.A.," said Dean.

"Not L.A.," said Ray, turning back to Dean. "Vegas."

"All the way up there, was it?" said Dean. "Well, fine. I guess you want me to say it was great you were able to find Iris. Isn't that it?"

Ray shrugged.

"I don't know," Ray said. "It wasn't that hard."

"You think it was worth it?" said Dean. "Look at her, Ray. She's a whore."

The word lingered in the air like a bad smell. Ray sat on the outside of the booth, and from there he looked at the bar. Above it there was an overhead fixture, and the light from it fell across the bar and then, in a straight slash, down to the floor. There was a man on a stool, his head bent, the shadow from the fixture cutting across the side of his face and then falling to the floor too. One of the man's hands was next to an amber-colored glass of beer, and in the beer there were long, small chains of bubbles that rose from the bottom. At the sound of the word "whore," the man at the bar turned around, his face obscured in the shadow, which fell across his eyes like a mask.

Ray had been reaching for his glass, in which there was a mixture of champagne and stout, the foam thick enough to cut with a knife, but as Dean spoke, Ray's hand hit the glass, knocking it over. The molasses-colored fluid slipped across the table in a long, foamy tongue, almost like a wave on a sandy beach. It came to the end of the table and went over the edge, first in a thin sheet, like water running off a roof, but then in molasses-colored strings, and finally it just dripped. No one moved toward the spill. They all sat there, listening to that steady *pit pit pit*. Ray looked at the sheen on the table now, trying to remember something, a bit of atmosphere, or something that had seemed difficult to grasp, and as he heard that dripping, it came to him: the air around that house in Las Vegas, that certain, palpable sense of just how vulnerable you can be. Here there was something similar, the sense of things being forever out of control. Ray sat there, watching his hands shake and the long, reddish brown sheen of the stout.

"Why do you have to be so rough?" said Harriet to Dean.

Iris looked across the table, not saying a word, as though she were making a careful inventory of Dean's features.

"When we were driving down here from Nevada," said Ray to Dean, "Iris asked me if I still loved you. And I said I did." Ray looked at Dean too. "But then you do this."

Ray looked down now.

"All right," said Ray. "Show me I'm wrong about Harriet's husband."

"Oh, God," said Harriet. "Come on, Dean. Why so rough?"

"He thinks he knows how the world runs," said Dean. "Sometimes I want to tell him he's only been here twenty minutes." He turned to Ray. "All right. It's a deal. I'll show you just how wrong you are."

"Let's talk about something else," said Harriet.

Ray sat there, looking at his father, who sipped his drink and winked. Iris went on staring at Dean, not blinking, and then she said, looking right at him, "You're playing with fire. Come on, Ray, let's go."

SAN PEDRO

Ray stood in front of his parents' house. For a moment, in the early-evening light, he could imagine he was ten or twelve years old and that he was walking up to it with news of school, with a black eye from a fight, or with a question he had about things he had heard: What, for instance, was a missile crisis? And why were they having one in Cuba? Now, he stood in the yard, looking up, feeling the years stretch away from him with an almost elastic quality, the attachment to them becoming finer and finer, if not getting ready to break.

Marge sat in the kitchen, doing the crossword puzzle in the *Los Angeles Times*, and when Ray walked in she was looking out the window, staring into space, supposedly thinking about a word that would fit neatly into the right boxes. Then she turned toward him and stood up, saying, "Hello, Ray. I'm glad to see you."

Ray had a cup of coffee and they talked about how the town had changed, and about things that Marge liked to do. She had always enjoyed driving up north in the spring to see the poppies, almost the color of new bricks, and the lupines, with small sacks of blue on them, that stretched across the treeless hills. She asked him if he'd drive her up there, and he promised her he would. Ray finished his coffee and kissed her, and when he began to go, she said, "Every family has its own way of doing things. This is ours, I guess. We get angry, drift apart, prove to each other how strong we are by staying away. Or by taking chances. But, Ray, don't you think we still love each other as much as other families?"

Now, Ray and Iris made plans, or something like plans. Ray talked about the East, about the river where he had rowed. One afternoon he had rowed, seeing the wake of the boat, the puddles, and a ring where one white mayfly had emerged, its wings like glassine, its body almost transparent. The fatigue of rowing, the air, the mayfly had all run into one moment that seemed like something he could depend upon. Iris said she'd like to come east too.

On the outside of town there was a broad field that was backed up by some hills, and on the side of it there was a windbreak. It was nice to walk there, especially on windy days, when the tops of the trees waved back and forth in a kind of frenzied resistance. Ray and Iris went out there to get away from the roads and town. In the spring-time the light had a cool, moist quality, and Iris walked in and out of the sunshine, touching her face and saying to Ray, "Look. It's getting a little better, don't you think?"

After they had gone a hundred yards from the road, they turned and saw that Harriet and Dean had stopped at the side of the road and had gotten out to walk, too. Harriet and Dean stood for a moment, looking around, trying to decide whether or not they were up to meeting Ray and Iris, and then they starting walking along the windbreak, pretending, or so it seemed, that they were there alone. They came along, their heads up, both of them smelling the almost bitter scent of new growth. The sky was blue, with high, white clouds. Dean and Harriet had brought a lunch and a blanket, and after a while they stopped and spread the blanket on the ground.

They had some sandwiches wrapped in wax paper, and there were eggs with some salt and pepper in a small sack. Harriet put them out on the blanket, which was covered with the gill-shaped shadows of the leaves overhead. Dean was lifting one of the sandwiches, his face set on Harriet's, when he saw, at the edge of the field, Harriet's husband, George, pull up and get out of his car. It was a newish Cadillac, squarish, heavy looking, and covered with dust. The car was dark blue, and George stood beside it, holding something in his hand.

For a few minutes he just stood at the side of the field. There were no cars on the road behind him, and he stood with the enormous sky above him. Then he started walking through the grass, which in the dappling of the noon sunshine appeared to be covered here and there with silver and gold flecks. From a distance, George's figure appeared small and a little dirty against the car at the side of the road, and his jacket, which was made from sweat-suit material, looked ash colored. He walked with a definite gait, like a man carrying a full bucket of water, although it wasn't a bucket that seemed to weigh so heavily on him but something else, which appeared to flash just like the sun on the leaves of grass.

Even from a distance it was clear the man scarcely noticed his surroundings. He came in and out of the shade of the windbreak, through the splashes of light, one shoulder lower than the other, his gait steady, unhurried, not revealing anything really aside from a furious resolve. There were some puddles in the low places near the trees, and he went through them, getting his shoes and even the cuffs of his trousers wet. There were some birds out, feeding in the field, and they flew up around the man, their squawking harsh, shrill, and as Ray watched there seemed to approach not only a man, but a conglomeration of sorts, a small, ash-colored figure surrounded by wheeling birds and the bright flashes of sun on the grass.

Dean and Harriet waited, Dean taking a bite of his sandwich every now and then, chewing methodically, watching the man come. The hard-boiled eggs were smooth, almost as slick as white glass, and on them there was a blue tint from the sky. Dean reached down for one and patted it into the salt and pepper, looking up from time to time as George approached, his arm straight down, almost as though it were broken. Dean took another bite, and then Harriet turned around and stared too. Dean was certain, unruffled, and there was something else in his aspect, and that was a kind of rectitude, which came from the belief that anything was his so long as he was able to bamboozle someone into thinking he owned it.

So it didn't surprise Dean when, about fifty yards away, George stopped. Dean glanced at the man as he stood there, outraged, ridiculous, his stature reduced not only by the spring sky, but by the shiny, large pistol he carried: the thing looked like humiliation itself. Then Dean went back to eating a hard-boiled egg, shrugging as he did so, as though he wondered what all the trouble was about anyway. And as he looked down, he didn't see Ray and Iris, their figures coming along the windbreak, not running exactly, but not moving slowly, either. There was something about their urgent, continuous approach that had made George hesitate, and then, as he had stood there, exposed under the enormous sky, hearing the cars on the road, he had decided it was best to turn around and start walking back to that blue Cadillac parked in the new grass of spring, since more than anything else he wanted a little privacy with his wife and the man she was sleeping with, or just a moment when he could catch them alone.

Ray and Iris went back out to the road too, and when they passed, Dean looked up, raising a brow as though to say, "See, what did I tell you?"

There were rumors, too, about a scene in a restaurant downtown. There had been some shouting and Harriet had left the place, her blouse torn somehow by her husband. The details were passed around the service stations and grocery stores in town, in the hardware stores and in the teachers' lounge at the high school, in the bars and coffee shops. There was an element of hilarity about the entire business since, after all, what was more amusing, if a little ridiculous, than a betrayed man making scenes about it with his wife in public?

Ray and Iris heard the stories, although there wasn't much more to them than just threats and some loud voices. Ray got a map of the country, and in the motel room where he and Iris stayed he unfolded it on the bed, asking Iris if she wanted to go straight across the country, through Wyoming, Nebraska, Iowa, Illinois? Should they cross the Mississippi at St. Louis? Wasn't there an enormous arch there? Ray took a felt-tip pen and began to trace the route, already thinking of the grass around Cheyenne, the slope of the Rockies as they stretched away toward the eastern plains, and the long pieces of road that disappeared into the horizon. He was telling Iris what the Mississippi looked like from the air, a large, clawlike shape in the dull earth, when Pearl called and said, "Ray, he caught them."

"What?" said Ray.

"Come over here," said Pearl. "Don't you understand? Dad's dead. Come on home now. We need you here."

The funeral took place in a church in town, the place dusty at the same time it was perfumed with the scent of flowers, as if the flowers were there to cover up some unpleasant odor. A wall of the place had some cracks in it, and the lines of them, which were squiggly and convoluted, looked like a diagram of rivers, and as Ray came in and sat down, the wall made him think of a map of paradise, one sold to sinners so that they could find their way to their own lot in heaven as easily as to their half acre in a California housing development. But then he turned to the casket, the lid closed, the thing enormous.

Ray was asked to speak, and he stood, meaning to describe how he and his father had waited together in the backyard, watching the light, the sudden appearance of it like the beginning of time or the end of the world or just a vision of possibility. Instead, after trying to talk, each word seeming thin and impersonal, he reached down and opened the trombone case, not his, but his father's, and after he had lifted the thing up and fitted in the mouthpiece, he played "Met the Devil at the Crossroads," using the slide as his father had taught him. He glanced at his mother, and Pearl, and then at Eno, now an aluminum siding salesman, who returned Ray's look with one of grief and of horror too, since he had enough knowledge about how things really happened to last forever. Ray's mother sat there too, listening to the music and shaking her head, as though it were an argument she didn't want to hear.

241

The minister said, "What's that he's playing? What? 'Met the Devil . . .'?"

Mr. Carson, who had been Dean's neighbor, sat in the back of the church, and when he spoke, his words were meant only for his wife, but since his voice was deep and loud, everyone heard him say, "Well, I guess that's Dean's last piece of ginch, isn't it? There isn't any romance or desperate women where he's going. The poor son of a bitch."

Then they prayed, and everyone went out to the cemetery. Afterward, they went back to the house, where people gathered, many of them bringing food, baked ham and beef stew and salads. There was a bottle, too, and friends of Marge sat around telling stories, some laughing. Iris and Ray stood in a corner, not eating anything, talking to the mourners. The room had the atmosphere of a wedding at which everyone cried, and while the mourners stood around with paper plates filled with pieces of ham and mounds of potato salad, black olives, sticks of celery, and smears of yellow mustard, the phone rang.

Ray answered it and heard Mr. Mei's voice, soft and sibilant, offering a job. Ray said, "Where is it?"

"Orange County," said Mr. Mei.

"Oh," said Ray.

"I'll make it worth your while," said Mr. Mei.

"Will you?" said Ray.

"Sure," said Mr. Mei. "It'll be good money."

Ray looked around the room.

"Listen. I'll come down to see you," said Ray. "I want to tell you something."

"Do you want the job or not?" said Mr. Mei. "Aren't you tempted a little?"

"We'll talk about that," said Ray.

➰

Ray approached the grocery store in Chinatown before noon on a weekday. There were no tourists around and the street was somehow both deserted and businesslike at the same time. The garage door of a trucking company was open and a truck had just driven away, leaving the inside of the place filled with blue smoke that rolled up to the top of the door and slowly escaped into the street. Ray stopped for a moment and watched the blue exhaust, and as it gently folded into itself, Ray was left with a longing for some gentle, delicate thing. Then he started walking again, telling himself he must have been more tired than he realized to be thinking that way.

So he was walking toward the store, keeping his eye on it and the gold leaf of the script on the window, when there came from behind him the sound of an engine starting. Ray went on walking, not looking back, and when the limousine pulled up next to him, the hood of it seemed to slide into view. It pulled over and stopped.

Mr. Mei rolled down the window.

"Pssst, hey," he said. "Get in the car."

Mr. Mei opened the door. A young woman sat in the back seat, dressed in a short gray jacket, a gray skirt, and fishnet stockings. The woman was smoking a cigarette, a long white one. She was wearing red lipstick, and as she squirmed in the seat with a kind of nervousness, she did so also with a sultry impatience. Mr. Mei touched her knee, then ran his fingers along the net stockings, his hand stopping at the triangle of shadow at her skirt's hem. She put the cigarette to her lips and drew hard and then exhaled, blowing out a white plume, and as she did so, she reached down and picked up her skirt, not much, a few inches, so that there appeared a soft, white band of skin at the top of her stockings.

"It's hot," she said. "Why don't you have him turn on the air-conditioning?"

Mr. Mei spoke to the driver in Chinese and then said to Ray, "Get in. Can't you hear me?"

Ray stood in the sunshine, hearing the gentle putter of the car.

"Where are we going?" asked Ray.

"Young man," said Mr. Mei, "I'm not going to tell you again."

Ray got in and sat next to the woman, who glanced at him once and then looked away, as though it weren't safe to look at him more than that.

"Close the door," said Mr. Mei, and then he spoke Chinese to the driver. The car seemed to move in a weighted glide, the smoothness of it reminding Ray of the most restful sleep he had ever had. Mr. Mei's driver was careful about stop signs and signals, never coming to a complete halt but slowly coasting up to them so as never to give anyone a chance of shooting at a target that wasn't moving.

The car went on the freeway for a while and then got off, someplace in Downey, Ray supposed. The driver went around in enormous circles, as though giving Mr. Mei time to think. The landscape was ashen and somehow angular. There were fences on which there were rolls of barbed wire, and beyond them there were factories and towers, structures that looked like mines or refineries, the crosshatching and pipes looking functional and obviously having a purpose. There was open land, too, in which people had dumped old refrigerators or stoves or had piled bald tires or scrap metal, sinks and old ductwork, and next to these there were places that had been burned, the ashes stirring in the breeze like dark leaves. There were cars on the streets, their windows cracked into spiderwebs and their bare brake drums exposed by having had the tires stolen. In the grubby landscape, which appeared muted by the tinted glass, and in the rolls of barbed wire, in the burned-out lots, there was a constant reminder of just how things stood.

"So," said Mr. Mei. "You want to get away?"

"Yes," said Ray.

"I can always tell."

Ray shrugged.

"We had a deal," said Mr. Mei. "Remember? I was going to be able to depend on you. Until Dean got back in business. Maybe even after Dean was finished. And just like that, you want to go."

The car went ahead, smooth as before. Mr. Mei said nothing, his eyes straight ahead: it seemed as though he was just trying to make a decision. He looked tired.

"One of the things I came to tell you was about Dean," said Ray. "Don't call the house anymore. Dean's out of the business for good."

"I guess I'll have to wait to hear from him about that," said Mr. Mei.

"No," said Ray. "He's dead now. Don't call the house anymore." Mr. Mei grunted.

"He wasn't working for me when it happened, was he?" asked Mr. Mei.

"No," said Ray.

"Then I don't owe you a thing."

Ray licked his lips. Mr. Mei waited for a minute and then spoke to his driver, and it seemed to Ray that he could make out the words "San Pedro."

"Are you going down to the harbor?" asked Ray.

"I haven't decided yet," he answered. "Maybe."

"So that's the way it is," said Ray.

Mr. Mei looked out the window.

"Why don't you let me out here?"

"No," said Mr. Mei. Then he spoke again to the driver, saying "San Pedro" again.

"I'd like to get out," said Ray.

"Listen," said Mr. Mei. "Everything's going to be fine. Relax. I even think there's a bottle in the front seat. You want a little drink?"

"No," said Ray.

They rode in silence. Mr. Mei went back to his silent considering. The young woman looked straight ahead, although every now and then she crossed and uncrossed her legs, her stockings making a barely audible sound, and then she squirmed in the seat, as though she were uncomfortable somehow. Mr. Mei looked down at her legs, at the pressure of her kneecap, the shape of her foot in her shoe. He just stared, blinking, and then he said, "I wish you didn't want to get away so much. I'd feel better."

"You don't have to worry about me," said Ray. "I can keep my mouth shut."

Mr. Mei looked across the seat at Ray, blinking every now and then, his glance incurious.

"What would you do if I let you go?"

"Get out of town," said Ray. "Maybe I'd go east."

"Is there anything you can give me?" said Mr. Mei. "Something that would insure me against your ever saying anything?"

"No," said Ray. "Just my word."

Mr. Mei rubbed his face and sighed. They passed an oil field where enormous, antlike pumps went up and down.

Ray said, "Are we going to San Pedro?"

The young woman still stared ahead. Her hands were very beautiful, the fingers long and white, and without veins. She looked at them in her lap, where they seemed calm, peaceful.

"How far is it to San Pedro?" said Ray.

"Not far," said Mr. Mei.

He looked at the young woman's beautiful hands.

"We'll go out in my boat," Mr. Mei said. "A cabin cruiser. Cost five hundred thousand. You know what that is with the kind of money I'm making?"

"No," said Ray.

"Peanuts," said Mr. Mei.

"I like peanuts," said the young woman.

Mr. Mei stared ahead again, thinking. He was about to speak to the driver, to say some final word, to give some order, and as he did, the ocean became visible in the distance, misty, blue, calm, and as Mr. Mei looked at it, the young woman lifted one of her hands, the beautiful fingers rising with a kind of magic toward the side of Mr. Mei's face, where they gently touched the skin. At the shore of the ocean there were some birds, long-legged, delicate, flying north: their wings moved with a steady cadence, not unhurried so much as certain. Mr. Mei hesitated, looking at the ocean. Then he looked at Ray and said, "All right." He spoke Chinese to the driver and the car stopped. "Get out."

Ray stepped out, pushing the door into the hazy light.

The sunshine fell through the misty air, which smelled of the ocean and of oil from a refinery, the mixture of the two almost seeming erotic. Mr. Mei went on staring at him.

"You remember," asked Mr. Mei, "when your father first brought you to me? You did that trick with the numbers on a bill? I read them off and you repeated them?"

"Yes," said Ray.

"What a smart boy, I thought," said Mr. Mei. "I hope I don't have to kill him."

Ray looked at the shiny surface of the car and nodded, and as he looked at the waxed surface, at the hard, almost mirrorlike quality of it, he had a fleeting sensation, almost like remembering a horrible dream, of the implications of infinite silence.

"You know why I keep the car shiny?" said Mr. Mei.

"No," said Ray.

"So you can see if anyone has put a bomb in it. If they touch it, they leave smudges."

Ray looked into Mr. Mei's exhausted face.

"If I were you," said Mr. Mei, "I'd leave the state, just to make it harder for me to change my mind. About things."

The young woman looked away from Ray, as though he simply had ceased to exist. The car began to move in the direction of San Pedro. Ray turned toward the Pacific, where, in the distance, the horizon showed as a barely discernible line, as though a fine wire had been drawn across the place where the sea and sky came together. Then he started walking, thinking about the Rockies and the grass around Cheyenne, the spears of it green and sharp, some blades even pushing through the last of the winter's snow. He thought how excited Iris would be when they got over the mountains.